The Perfect Distance

a novel

The Perfect Distance

a novel

kim ablon whitney

LAUREL-LEAF
BOOKS

Published by Laurel-Leaf
an imprint of Random House Children's Books
a division of Random House, Inc.
New York

This is a work of fiction. Names, characters, places, and incidents
either are the product of the author's imagination or are used
fictitiously. Any resemblance to actual persons, living or dead,
events, or locales is entirely coincidental.

Originally published in hardcover in the United States by
Alfred A. Knopf Books for Young Readers, New York, in 2005.
This edition published by arrangement with Alfred A. Knopf
Books for Young Readers.

www.randomhouse.com/teens
Educators and librarians, for a variety of teaching tools,
visit us at www.randomhouse.com/teachers

RL: 6.2
ISBN: 978-0-553-49467-9
January 2007
Printed in the United States of America
10 9 8 7 6 5 4 3 2 1

For Mom & Dad,

Grandma & Grandpa,

and Ace

Chapter One

"No! No! No! What did I say about making a move at the last minute?"

Rob's voice was so loud, I could hear him all the way up at the barn—over a football field's length away. What I couldn't hear was the response from whoever he was yelling at. I hoped it wasn't Katie.

I led Tobey out of the barn and up to the mounting block. Behind me, my dad gave Gwenn a leg up onto Finch. "Thanks, Juan," she said. Even though I'd heard all the riders call my dad by his first name a million times before, it still sounded strange.

As I swung my leg over the saddle, my stomach started to tie up in knots. It was the first day of boot camp, which was what we dubbed the weeks of training before the three junior national equitation championships—the United States Equestrian Team Finals, the United States Equestrian Federation Medal Finals, and the ASPCA Maclay Finals, or just "the finals," as they were collectively known. This was when Rob got tough—tougher than usual, that is.

Tobey, eager to leave the flies of the stable behind, swished his tail and stomped a front hoof as I tightened the girth. "Hold on," I told him. "We're going." Tobey didn't like the girth too tight at first around his belly, so I always tightened it more once I mounted up. I'd learned this the hard way: one of the first times I'd ridden him, I tightened it all the way and hopped on only to have him buck me right off.

I gathered my reins, and Gwenn and I headed down to the indoor arena. West Hills was set on a hill, with the main barn and two outdoor rings on top and the indoor arena and half-mile galloping track down below. With all the buildings and the manicured grounds, the farm was its own little compound, like a mini–college campus.

"Have a good lesson, girls," Dad called after us.

The door to the arena yawned open, but we didn't go in yet. That was rule number one of riding at West Hills: *Wait until Rob tells you to.* And it applied to most everything.

Rob had left the sliding door open because the September sun was beating down on the metal roof, heating the indoor like a sauna. But since two out of three of the finals took place indoors, we practiced inside no matter how hot it was. Rob stood in the middle as Katie cantered a circle around him.

Rob stood five foot ten, had rusty brown hair, and was a little on the beefy side. He had great posture—he never slouched or slumped. No one knew his age for sure, but we guessed that he was around forty-five. If you saw him on the street, you probably wouldn't think much of him, but in the horse show world he was basically God. He was the riding world's equivalent of tennis's Nick Bollettieri or gymnastics' Bela Karolyi, and parents sent their kids from all over the country and paid a fortune for them to train with him. He was notorious for being tough on his riders, but as much as we griped about him, we all knew it was worth it because he was the best.

"How did that feel?" he asked Katie in a deceptively moderate tone. A tone I knew all too well.

Katie answered softly, "Not so good, I guess." Knowing what was coming next, I cringed for her and for how many times I'd been in her situation.

Suddenly Rob's voice boomed again. "Jesus Christ, Katie, have some conviction! Speak up! It was lousy. You were completely out of control." Rob paused. The worst was hopefully over—once he'd exploded, he usually calmed down. He continued in a saner tone, "The course is all parts that make up a whole. You have to ride it in parts and put the parts together. You got going and didn't stop to take a breath or collect your horse the whole way around. Again. And this time, for God's sake, get it right."

Katie cantered off the circle to start over. Her face muscles were tensed, like she was trying to hold it all together. I watched in silence, thinking: *Please don't mess up*. Because the more upset Rob got now, the tougher he would be on me. But also because Katie was my best friend at the barn and probably my best friend, period. If we hadn't met at the barn, I'm sure we never would have been friends. Other than riding, we really didn't have much in common. But horses had brought us together, and we'd found that even though we were from completely different backgrounds, we got along well.

Stretch's nostrils flared with each stride and he expelled the air in forceful snorts. His neck glistened with sweat, and where the reins rubbed against him was white with foam.

All in all, Katie was a pretty bad rider, but she got away with a fair amount because of Stretch. Stretch had won the finals a record five times and was Rob's best horse. He was pure white and was so easy anyone could ride him. In fact, Stretch would probably jump a course with a monkey on his back. When you jump, you have to tell your horse where to take off from. The correct spot to take off from—not too close to the jump and not too far away—is called the right "distance." If you're good at judging the distances and telling your horse where to take off from, people say you have a "good eye." Katie had what people called "no eye." Luckily for her, Stretch had a good eye of his own, and even when Katie didn't see the perfect distance, a lot of the time Stretch did. He was also known for being able to make a really long distance look good—hence the name Stretch.

Katie's father was a big-time New York City litigator, and he paid six figures a year to lease Stretch. The riders leased a horse from Rob or owned their own, except for me, that is. I rode whatever Rob gave me. For the past three years that had been Tobey.

This time Katie managed the course without any major faults. She kept cantering after the last fence because that was rule number one-A: *You're not done until Rob says you're done.*

"Okay, let him walk," Rob said. "Good enough . . . for today."

Katie barely had to tug on the reins and Stretch dropped back to a walk.

"The one thing I want you to think about is being subtle," Rob told her. "When you see the distance, don't make a big move for it. The judges never want to see that big move. Understand?"

"Yes," Katie said. "Thank you, Rob. Thanks a lot." Rule number two: *Always say please and thank you.* The rules weren't printed up and handed to you when you arrived at

West Hills, but if you had any sense at all, you learned them quickly.

Rob turned to Gwenn and me. "Come on in, girls."

I took a deep breath and tried to ignore the butterflies attacking my stomach. After all, I had lived through boot camp and the finals plenty of times before. But it didn't matter. I could do the finals a hundred times and I'd still be fighting my nerves the whole way through. And at seventeen, this was my last chance.

Gwenn had headed into the ring. I realized I hadn't budged.

"Francie?" Rob said. "Would you like to grace us with your presence?"

Here goes everything, I thought, and pressed Tobey forward into the ring.

Chapter Two

As I walked Tobey into the indoor, Katie and Tara were on their way out. Katie's face was sweaty, and she was still breathing hard. Tara, on the other hand, was perched tall in the saddle, not slouching at all. Apparently her lesson had gone a lot better than Katie's, which was no big surprise since Tara was the best rider in the barn.

Katie stopped Stretch for a second to talk to me. "Watch out," she warned. "Rob's in the worst mood."

"Not if you ride well," Tara snapped as she passed us. Besides being the best rider, she also happened to have the biggest attitude.

Katie rolled her eyes at Tara and said to me, "See you back up at the barn."

The stale, damp air of the indoor hit me as I picked up the trot. Soon I urged Tobey into a canter. After a few minutes Tara came back into the arena on a different horse—probably her third or fourth ride of the day. Unlike the rest of us, Tara didn't go to school. She had dropped out at sixteen so she could practice nonstop. This time she was riding her equitation horse, Riley, a bright blood bay with four white socks and a thick white blaze. Riley didn't have as proven a record as Stretch, but he was beautiful and talented. I was certain Rob had cut Tara's parents a deal on his lease fee since they didn't have a lot of money. With Tara, Rob didn't care so much about making money; he cared about winning. The way it worked was that the riders like Tara won, and then the riders like Katie and Gwenn, whose parents had the money, wanted to train with Rob.

Tara rode up next to the observation room, a small room on the long side of the arena with a big window that looked into the ring. Tara's mother was in there, like she was for every one of Tara's lessons because Tara's riding was her life. Gwenn's mother was in there too, not because Gwenn's riding was her life but because *Gwenn* was her life, and she was scared to let her thirteen-year-old daughter travel all the way from Florida to Massachusetts on her own. Like most parents on the circuit, Gwenn's mother would probably get tired of schlepping from show to show. Then Gwenn would be on her own, like so many of the other girls were.

Tara's mother stepped out of the observation room and handed her a purple Gatorade. When Tara finished gulping, Rob called us into the middle of the ring. He explained the course once and only once and then told Gwenn to go first. Making Gwenn go first was a test. This was her first boot camp, and Rob always liked to see how mentally tough new riders were—if they could handle the pressure.

Gwenn moved Finch forward but then looked back at Rob and said, "The vertical to the oxer in five strides?" Asking Rob to repeat information wasn't against the rules, but it still wasn't a good idea.

Rob squinted at her. "Do you need Tara to go first and show you how it's done?"

She bit her lip and didn't answer right away. It was obvious she was in awe of everything around her. Of how Rob taught and how we all listened. Of how much he demanded of us and of how good everyone else but her seemed right now. Of how she was finally here riding at West Hills after dreaming of it for so long and how she was wondering if she had made a big mistake by coming. She shook her head and turned Finch away from the group, departed into a canter. She made it over only two jumps before she fell apart. She jumped the first part of the bending line that she had asked Rob about, but then she didn't aim Finch at the second part. A bending line is two or sometimes even three fences that are set on a curve. It isn't that hard; you just have to be sure to tell your horse where to go with your eyes, legs, and hands. But Gwenn got flustered, aimed Finch at the standard at the side of the jump that held up the poles, and he slid to a stop. You couldn't blame him—he had no idea what she wanted from him. "Go back and try the whole line again," Rob told her.

This time Gwenn didn't aim any better. Instead of stopping, Finch just cantered right by the second jump.

"Gwenn!" Rob called out to her. "Don't forget to steer, okay? Again!"

She nodded and cantered to the line again. Once more Finch cantered right past the jump. I braced myself for Rob to explode.

"Did you come all this way to canter in circles?" Rob yelled at her.

She didn't answer.

"What's that? I can't hear you!"

"No," Gwenn managed.

"I sure hope not," Rob said, his voice still loud. "Because I can't stand when people waste my time. Are you here to waste my time?"

Gwenn shook her head. A few tears had rolled down her face. We'd all been there before—that point where you're deciding if you're going to burst into sobs and quit or somehow buck up and keep going. I just hoped Rob hadn't seen the tears. Rule number three: *No matter what, no crying.* But it was already too late.

"Stop!" he called out to her.

She brought Finch down to a walk.

"Are you crying?" Rob demanded.

Gwenn nodded meekly.

"There's no crying here at West Hills," he said. "Absolutely no crying. Got it?"

"Yeah," Gwenn mumbled.

Poor Gwenn. I wanted to whisper to her about rule number four: *No saying "yeah" or "uh-huh" or anything but "yes" to Rob.* Two rules broken in a matter of minutes.

"Excuse me?" Rob snapped.

Gwenn looked confused.

"What did you say?" he barked at her.

Gwenn's lower lip trembled.

"It's 'yes, Rob,' or 'I understand.'"

"Yes, Rob," Gwenn managed, and I knew right then that she'd be okay. It wouldn't be pretty, but she'd tough it out.

"Again, from the beginning," Rob told her. "When you're in the air over the first fence, you need to be looking at the second jump. Not at the standard. At the middle of the jump."

Gwenn tried the line again. I prayed for her to get over it this time.

"Look where you're going," Rob called to her. "Look at the jump. The middle of the jump. Don't be afraid of it. It won't bite you."

Gwenn kept her eye on the jump, and this time Finch sailed over. He had a funny look on his face: a look like, "That's all you wanted me to do—well, why didn't you just say so?" Gwenn continued around the rest of the course.

When she finished, Rob said, "You just have to look where you're going, okay? You can't be afraid of the jumps."

He walked up to her and patted her knee. "Don't worry, we'll fix you. That's what you're here for, right?" It was moments like this, when Rob seemed actually human, that we all lived for.

She nodded. "Thank you," she said. She managed a smile and came to stand next to me in the middle of the ring. A new thread of nerves wormed its way through me again and I straightened in the saddle, wondering if Rob would call me next. But he looked at Tara, who was back for her second lesson of the day. "You're up. Show us how it's done."

Whatever I felt about Tara, there was no denying she was good. Of course, it didn't hurt that she was five-eight and thin as a rail, so she looked beautiful in the saddle to begin with. At only five-three, I would have killed to have her height. But it was more than how Tara looked; it was how she rode. She was so perfectly in sync with Riley. The two of them together honestly took your breath away. I knew it, the rest of the girls knew it, Rob knew it, and worst of all, Tara knew it.

She rode the course flawlessly. Rob nodded along, and when she sailed over the last jump, he had a cat-that-ate-the-canary smirk on his face. "That girl's gonna do it," he gushed. "She's gonna be one of the few to win more than one final. She's *that* good."

He didn't look at Gwenn or me as he spoke, but Tara couldn't hear him. There was no one else in the ring for him to be talking to except us. Maybe Rob figured he'd inspire us to work harder, or maybe he just couldn't keep inside how happy he was that Tara was going to win for him. Either way, all it made me think was that I'd never be as good as Tara.

"That's enough. Perfect," Rob said as Tara guided Riley back into the center of the arena. "You gonna do that for me at the regionals next week?"

The main goal at the Maclay Regionals wasn't necessarily winning but making the top twelve. Only the top riders from the eight different regions of the country qualified to ride in the Maclay Finals at Madison Square Garden in New York City at the beginning of November.

Tara looked him straight in the eye. "Count on it," she said.

Rob grinned. "That's my girl." Then he turned to me. "Okay, Francie, let's see what you can do."

I trotted to the end of the ring and picked up the canter, my stomach immediately twisting again. Sometimes I got even more nervous for lessons than for shows because lessons were when Rob paid the most attention to me. At the shows he usually had his assistant, Susie, help me. Lessons were my chance to prove that I deserved his attention. My course started well. My main problem was that I leaned with my upper body for the distances instead of using my legs to tell Tobey to jump. I used to lean at the jumps more. I'd gotten better and didn't do it nearly as much now.

Today I was fine until the last fence, an oxer. A vertical is a jump with one rail, but an oxer has two rails with a few feet between them that you have to clear. I leaned with my upper body, and Tobey bumped in an extra little stride. This was called a variety of things—leaning up the neck, chipping, chocolate chipping. But whatever you called it, it was bad.

I kept cantering, hoping Rob would scream at me. Even that was better than silence. Finally he said quietly, "Walk." Then he added, this time so quiet I knew I was doomed, "Come here."

I walked into the center of the ring, faced him, and braced myself. I wanted to look away but couldn't because of rule number five: *When Rob talks to you, you look straight at him.* Otherwise he would snap, "Look at me when I'm talking to you." So I forced myself to stare back at him, at his chin, at anything but his eyes.

Rob exhaled audibly. "I don't know what to say, Francie. You're having a perfectly good course and then you go and blow it. Time and time again I've told you not to lean up the neck." His voice wasn't loud. He wasn't screaming. In fact, there was no intensity to what he was saying; it was more like disgust. All of a sudden I wished he *were* screaming at me. I felt tears pressing at the back of my eyes and I worked as hard as I could to stop them. I was no newbie like Gwenn. I knew all about the rules. I'd lived each and every one of them. If I cried, Rob would kill me. "We're one week away from the regionals," he continued. "This is your last year, need I remind you? When are you going to stop leaning up the neck?"

Rob couldn't have asked a stupider question. If I could, I would have told him so, but I couldn't, per rule number six: *Never talk back.* It was the stupidest question because he asked it like I could decide when I wanted to stop leaning up the neck. When all I wanted *in the world* was not to lean up the neck. When all I wanted *in the world* was to put in the perfect trip and to hear him tell me what he'd told Tara.

Rob glared at me for a second longer and then shook his head. "Think about it, Francie. Stay here and think about it."

He turned and strode out of the arena. "We're done here, girls," he called, but he didn't mean me. Gwenn looked at me and then followed Rob. Tara didn't even glance back.

Then it was just Tobey and me. It wasn't his fault. Some riders blamed their horse, but usually the horse wasn't to blame. I couldn't blame Tobey, because he was only trying to do what I told him. I was just telling him the wrong thing. I had no one else to blame but myself.

So I did what Rob told me to do. I thought about it.

I thought about the first year I had gone along with Dad to New York City to help groom and watch the Maclay Finals— the granddaddy of the equitation, the Super Bowl for riders under the age of eighteen. I remembered how one of Rob's girls choked. When she exited the arena, head down, he turned his back to her. Then Hillary Winston rode. Rob watched her trip, fists clenched. When she landed off the last fence, Rob clapped and whooped. His face was a huge smile, not only his mouth, but his eyes and cheeks too.

Goose bumps had flooded over me that day as they did every time I watched someone win one of the finals, but most especially the Maclay. To hear the announcer's voice over the clapping and cheering as the rider led the victory gallop. Ever since that day, all I thought about was hearing the announcer say, *"And winning the ASPCA Maclay Finals, Francie Martinez."*

Outside the ring that day, Hillary dismounted and Rob threw his arm around her. They both smiled, and a reporter snapped their photo. Like some riders who had won the finals, Hillary rode professionally now in grand prix classes. Other riders went on to compete as amateurs or stopped riding altogether to go to college, to have a career in what riders liked to call "the real world," or to get married and start a family. But I wanted to be like Hillary and ride in grand prix classes. And if I wanted to be a grand prix rider, I had to show the world I could ride, starting by winning one of the finals.

Driving home in the trailer cab that night from the Garden, I'd asked Dad if he thought I could train with Rob, become one of the equitation riders at West Hills. I'd been riding for as long as I could remember, but just with Dad calling out to me, "Heels down," or, "Eyes up." I'd practiced on my own on horses that needed to be exercised, or sometimes Susie would give me a lesson. But Rob had never taught me before. Dad said he didn't think it was such a good idea, but over the next few weeks I begged and begged him, promising to work off my lessons and to keep up my grades in school. Finally he said he'd talk to Rob.

Now here I was in my last year of doing the equitation. I wasn't as beautiful on a horse as Tara and I didn't have as much money as Katie, but I was a good rider. I'd mucked stalls, scrubbed water buckets, cleaned tack, and swept aisles to work off my training. I'd worked too hard to let it just slip by. This year I wanted to be the one Rob put his arm around—and not like I wanted to be his girlfriend or anything like that, although over the years there had been girls who wanted that too. No, this year I wanted to win.

Chapter Three

After the lesson I was sweeping the aisle outside Rob's office when I heard him and Susie talking.

"How'd they go?" Susie asked.

Sometimes Susie got to watch our lessons, but a lot of the time she was busy teaching the other riders at West Hills. Besides us, the equitation kids, there were young riders who one day might ride in the big equitation classes and adult riders who competed in amateur classes. Rob taught the other riders sometimes too, but around finals time, he concentrated all his attention on us. Besides the grand prix classes, the equitation was one of the biggest divisions at the horse shows and the most prestigious to win.

"Tara was good," Rob told Susie.

"Just Tara? What about Francie?"

I stopped sweeping to make sure I heard Rob's answer. Of course I hadn't been very good—I'd been downright awful—but I still hoped he'd say something halfway nice about me.

"Just Tara," he said.

I started sweeping again, brushing the bristles hard against the cement floor. I had the broom handle in a death grip.

"It's not like it has been," Rob continued. "Remember all those years we had so many girls who could win? How many do we have now? And we've got to win this year. You stop winning, people stop sending their kids to train with you."

"You won a few years ago, Rob," Susie said. "You act like it's been decades."

"People have short-term memory when it comes to these things. But we'll work with what we've got. We'll pull it out. Only one winner, so you only need one shot, right?"

Of course Rob meant Tara. He didn't think I could win. I stared at the little pile of wood shavings and dirt I'd accumulated, hoping I could force his words—*just Tara*—out of my head.

"Are the girls still out in the barn?" Rob asked.

"I think so," Susie said.

"Good."

"Rob," Susie cautioned. "They don't need any more pressure."

"Don't worry. Just a little pep talk."

"I've never known you to be one for pep talks."

Susie came out of Rob's office and stopped when she saw me. "Rob wants to see you all. Can you go get the other girls?"

I leaned the broom up against the wall. "Sure." Just what I didn't need—another lecture from Rob about how I was always messing up.

"I heard you didn't ride that well today," Susie said gently. Besides being Rob's assistant, she was also his girlfriend. She was really pretty in an all-American way: blond hair and blue eyes. She was very nice too. She was the complete opposite of Rob, and sometimes I wondered what she saw in him.

"That's the understatement of the century," I said.

Susie smiled. "It's nerves. The day before I was fifth at the Maclay Finals, I had the worst ride of my life."

"Really?" I said, cheering up just the tiniest bit.

Susie nodded. "I swear. You can ask Rob. He got so mad he wouldn't talk to me until I was about to go in the ring."

I tried to picture Rob being mad at Susie or, for that matter, Susie messing up, but it was hard to do. Susie was such a great rider.

Susie grabbed the broom from where I'd left it. "Go get the rest of the girls. I'll finish this."

"Thanks," I said. Even if she was making it all up, it was helping me feel better.

I found Gwenn sitting on the bench outside the barn with her mother. Tara was in the tack room on her cell phone, no doubt talking to her boyfriend, Brad. Katie was feeding Stretch carrots. She reached out to pat his neck, but he shook his head. Katie smiled because it was so Stretch. He never liked to be bothered, not even for praise. It was like he knew how good he was and didn't need anyone else telling him. He also was a huge pig when it came to food. He gobbled the carrots and nudged Katie's shoulder, demanding more.

"Rob wants to see us," I told Katie.

"I guess ripping your head off wasn't enough, huh?" she said.

"Who told you?"

"Who do you think?" Katie said. "Maybe if we all rode as well as Little Miss Anorexic, we'd never get yelled at."

"Maybe."

"Where's Susie?" Katie asked. "We've got to talk to her. Obviously she's not making Rob very happy, if you know what I mean."

"Stop it." Katie always liked to joke about Rob and Susie's sex life, something I tried not to think much about.

"Oh, Francie," Katie groaned. "Don't be such a prude, I swear."

"You swear what?" Tara said, coming up behind us.

"I swear I don't know why Brad hasn't dumped your skinny butt already," Katie said to Tara.

As much as Katie teased me sometimes, it was always in a good-natured way and she never did it in front of Tara. But with Tara, I always had the feeling Katie wanted blood. "Last time I checked, you don't have a boyfriend or a skinny butt," Tara snapped back, and that shut Katie up for the moment.

Rob was sitting in the leather chair behind his desk when we came in. He didn't look at us. Instead he stared up at the collage of photos on the wall above the couch. They were all jumping shots of his students over the years: Hank winning the regionals, Susie winning the USET, Leslie winning the Medal, Hillary winning the Maclay.

We sat down on the couch and waited for Rob to speak. After a few minutes he asked, still without looking at us, "Do you know what it means to be up there?"

"They've all won one of the finals, right?" Tara blurted out.

"Yes, but do you know what it *means*?" Rob said.

This time Tara didn't bite.

"Five years down the road, do you think anyone will remember that last year you were fifth at the Maclay, Tara?" Tara opened her mouth again, but Rob rolled right on. He motioned to the photos again. "But you all know who these riders are. Why? Because they won. No one ever forgets the winners." Rob paused and then asked, "Do you girls understand what I'm saying here?" He might have called us all in, but he was only looking at Tara. I wanted to scream at him to pay attention to all of us, but instead I just slumped back on the couch.

"Yes," she answered, all confidence.

"I just want to make sure you understand what's on the line here." After staring at Tara for a few seconds longer, Rob said, "All right. You're excused."

As we headed for the door, Tara looked back at him. "I won't let you down," she said. "I'm going to win."

Rob grinned. "That's my girl."

Tara's words made me want to puke or, even better, maybe to smack her.

Back in the barn Gwenn's mother was waiting for her. Tara strutted off to get on her next horse. Rob always asked Tara to ride extra horses for him—horses whose owners couldn't ride that day or horses that Rob had in the barn to sell. It was kind of a chicken-and-egg thing. The more horses she rode, the better she got, and the better she got, the more horses he had her ride. At the shows people even asked her to "catch-ride" their horses, which meant competing a horse she'd never ridden before because she was so good that she could make almost any horse a winner. Katie got to ride other horses too, but that was because her father owned them. Besides leasing Stretch, Katie had two hunters and a jumper. I would have loved to ride other horses, but Rob hardly ever asked me to because I was supposed to be working and because Tara was better.

Once Tara was out of earshot, Katie mocked, "I won't let

you down, Rob. I'm going to win." She shook her head. "Can you believe her? Have you ever met anyone so high on themselves?"

"Welcome to Tara's world," I said.

We walked into the main aisle of the barn, where Camillo, one of the grooms, was finishing tacking up Tara's next horse. All of the grooms at West Hills were Mexicans who'd come over looking for work that they couldn't find at home. They were willing to work long hours for little pay. Dad had lived in a really poor town in southern Mexico, and after saving for a long time, he'd made enough to pay the coyotes to smuggle him over the river into Texas. First he'd picked fruit, but the farmers worked you to the bone and treated you like a slave. Dad heard from a friend about work with horses, and since he'd had some experience with farm animals back home, he went to see about it. He worked at a few different stables before coming to West Hills. And that's where he met my mother and had me.

All the riders at West Hills had grooms so they didn't have to do what was considered the dirty work—washing and brushing the horses, wrapping legs, cleaning tack. But I was queen of the dirty work, since it was how I worked off my lessons. I mucked stalls in the morning before school, and in the afternoons I picked out the stalls again, cleaned tack, helped feed and sweep up, and did whatever else needed doing.

Katie checked her watch, a Rolex her father had given her for making the finals a few years before. "I have my tutor in a half hour. I better get going."

Katie went to a fancy all-girls private school in New York City and had a tutor when she had to miss school to ride. During the finals she lived in the gardener's house that Rob had converted to living quarters. A lot of the riders stayed on or near the farm during the finals so they could practice intensely and at other times during the year too when they didn't need to be home, catching up in school. Riders like Gwenn, who came with their parents, often stayed in a local hotel. Tara stayed with her mom in a camper parked by the barn.

"See you tomorrow," I said, heading off to help Dad feed and hay up.

A few hours later Dad and I had finished at the barn and we headed home. Home was a five-room cottage down the dirt road through the woods but still on the West Hills property. It was close enough to walk, but Dad usually drove in case he had to run out to pick up anything for the horses during the day. Not far from the cottage stood the one-story housing that Rob had put up for the grooms, where we used to live when I was younger. After Rob had given him permission, Dad had built our cottage himself in the little free time he'd had. Nothing special architecturally, it was well built, and Dad kept it up, painting it every few years and tending to the yard. Dad loved to garden, so beautiful flower boxes filled with mums lined the front walkway, and he grew the most delicious tomatoes, peppers, and carrots in a vegetable garden out back.

Bandit wagged his tail from where he lay next to the kitchen table but didn't get up. We'd found Bandit a few years back at a horse show, skeletal and flea-infested. He was the best kind of mutt—the kind that didn't look like any one type of dog but like a million pieces of different breeds. He had a collie's long nose, a spaniel's shiny eyes, a hound's floppy ears, a Lab's stocky legs, and a cattle dog's wiry fur. He loved being at the barn, chasing the collection of half-wild cats and begging for scraps of doughnuts and sandwiches. But as he'd aged—we weren't sure exactly how old he was—he stayed home more and more, especially on hot days.

I headed to the shower while Dad started whipping up one of his specialties, his four-alarm enchiladas chipotle. Besides having a green thumb, Dad was also a really good cook. When I came back into the kitchen after showering, dinner was almost ready and Camillo was sitting at the table. Camillo was only a few years older than me, and Dad often invited him to eat with us. He said it was because Camillo was lonely and missed his family back in Mexico. I also knew it was because he didn't want Camillo hanging around the girls at the barn and getting himself into trouble—the kind of trouble that had brought me into this world.

I grabbed a plate from the cabinet. As I sank down across from Camillo, I realized I was starving.

"*La vi montando a caballo hoy,*" Camillo said. *I saw you riding today.*

Dad and I always spoke English, but Camillo's English wasn't so good yet, so he was always practicing. But at night, over dinner, at the end of a long day, he usually spoke Spanish and we answered him in English. "*Se veía usted muy bien.*" *You looked really good out there.*

"You didn't see me mess up, then," I said.

"No," Camillo replied.

Camillo was pretty good-looking. In fact, I'd overheard some of the other girls saying they thought he was hot. He had peach-colored skin and longish dark hair that he usually tied back in a ponytail. He must have done push-ups in addition to the barn work because he was also pretty built.

"I completely messed up and Rob made me stay behind after the lesson was done," I said.

I wouldn't say anything more. It was the closest I'd come to complaining about Rob. No one forced me to ride with him. I'd been the one who had begged Dad to let me, and I knew I could quit anytime I wanted to and he wouldn't care. He didn't pressure me to ride like some of the other parents at West Hills. And since Rob was the best trainer in the country, the one who coached all the winners, I didn't care how tough he could be, because it was all worth it.

I devoured all of the food on my plate. When all three of us were done, I took our plates to the sink and washed them, plus the pot from the stove. Dad and Camillo rattled on in Spanish about how the vet was coming tomorrow to give shots. Every week the horses each got a shot of a special joint fluid, to the tune of 100 dollars a pop. Joint fluid was perfectly legal, unlike some of the drugs other trainers gave their horses. It was hard to believe that such a small amount of what looked like milky water would do anything, but if they didn't get their weekly fix, the horses were creaky and stiff.

Camillo thanked me for washing up, thanked Dad for dinner, and said he'd see us in the morning. As he eased the screen door shut behind him, I told Dad I was going to my room to do homework.

"Whoa, whoa, whoa, not so fast, young lady," he said.

"Young lady?" I teased.

Dad patted the chair next to him. "Come here. Sit down. Take a load off."

Dad's hair had started to gray, but only in the front. The rest of it was still shiny black, but unlike my hair, his was straight. The only thing I seemed to have gotten from Dad was my skin, which looked tan even in the winter. My annoyingly thick, wavy hair, which I kept shoulder length so it would fit up neatly into my riding helmet and always wore back in a ponytail, and my green eyes must have come from my mother.

Even though I knew what was coming, I sat down next to Dad as he grabbed the manila folder that held the college brochures he'd been requesting for months. Besides promising to do well in school if he let me ride with Rob, I'd also promised I'd go to college. I'd held up my end of the bargain with my grades—I was one of the best students in my class. But college was another story. For someone who wanted to ride professionally, college only put you four years behind all the other riders who got riding jobs right out of high school. Or at least that's the way I saw it.

"I want you to apply to at least five," Dad said.

"But we've been through this."

Dad took out a brochure for Sweet Briar College. He pointed to the rider on the front and said, "Oh my God! What's that? It's a horse! They have horses at this college!" Dad opened the brochure and pretended to read a few lines. "Look here—it even says you can have a horse for a roommate if you want."

"Dad," I moaned.

He slid the brochure away and turned serious. "How many people ride in the Olympics in show jumping?" he asked, even though he knew I knew the answer. "Four, every four years. You can go to a school with a good riding program. I'm not saying you have to give up on that dream. I'm just saying you need to have a backup in case it doesn't work out the way you hope it will."

I could tell from his pained expression Dad hated throwing cold water on my dreams. And I knew, like always, he was just looking out for me. Dad believed that education was the most important thing in the world. When I was little, he'd taken ESL classes at night to learn how to speak English better and how to write so he could order grain, talk to the vet about any problems the horses were having, talk to the farrier about the horses' shoes, and fill out entries for the shows. Without those skills he wouldn't have been promoted to barn manager, which meant a steady salary and health insurance for us, instead of just a couple hundred bucks a week as a groom. He dreamed I'd be the first person in our family to go to college—not counting my mother, that is, which I never did. I wasn't even sure she had gone to college. All I knew about her came from two sources: Dad and a Christmas card addressed to Rob that I'd happened to see when I collected the mail for the farm one day a few years back.

From Dad, I knew that when he'd come to West Hills, he'd fallen in love with one of the girls who rode with Rob. He was twenty and she was eighteen, so it wasn't creepy or anything like that. They'd had "a relationship"—that was how Dad put it—but in normal terms I knew it was more like an affair, the product of which was me. When her parents found out their daughter was pregnant and that the father was a Mexican groom, no less, they freaked out. Still, despite their protests, they got married and had me. But then after only a few months she went back to her parents, eventually divorced Dad, leaving him with me, and, as far as I knew, never looked back.

I had two pictures of her, both of which Dad had given me. One was her holding me at the hospital. She wasn't smiling, and she looked totally overwhelmed. The other was her on a bay horse. She looked happier in that photo. I'd always thought it was strange that Dad hadn't given me a photo of him and her together, but a couple of years ago I'd realized maybe they didn't have any. Both photos were completely outdated but good enough so that when the Christmas card showed up at West Hills, I knew it was her. I had stared at her face, her sharp nose, her wavy hair, trying to see myself in them long enough to know without a shadow of a doubt. The card showed a perfect little family—mother, father, son, and daughter—all beaming. The note below it read: *Rob, All the best for a wonderful New Year!* That exclamation mark killed me more than anything. Oh yeah, and the fact that all of their names began with the letter *E*. Elaine (my mother) had married Eliot, and maybe that was just coincidence, but then they'd named their kids Emily and Ethan. That had to be on purpose, and it was enough to make me want to puke.

So I knew she had remarried, as I'm sure Dad knew too, and she had two kids. I had a half brother and a half sister. But I didn't know anything else about my mother—whether she'd gone to college, whether she worked, whether she ever thought about me. I wish I could say I didn't care. Why should I? I couldn't even remember her, and Dad had raised me fine all on his own. But part of me still wondered.

I could understand why Dad wanted me to go to college—he wanted me to have the opportunities he didn't have, maybe the happiness he didn't have. He wanted me to have that exclamation mark. But all I wanted was to ride professionally, to make it to the Olympics. And I knew I couldn't do it halfheartedly. I wasn't naive. I knew how many Hispanic riders and trainers there were in America: none. This wasn't Major League Baseball, where practically every player's last name ended in *-ez*. If I wanted to make it to the Olympics, especially since I didn't have the money to buy some great horse and would need sponsors to buy me the horses to ride, I had to prove I was the best. I had to dedicate every inch of my life to it, which was what I'd been doing up until now.

"But college is expensive," I said. We didn't exactly have heaps of money lying around.

"I hear there's a discount if you agree to have a horse for a roommate," Dad teased.

"Dad, be serious."

"I've saved some," he said. "And with your grades you can get a scholarship."

"Leslie Burr Howard didn't go to college," I argued. Leslie Burr Howard was one of the best grand prix riders in the country. She'd won the World Cup Final, ridden in two Olympics, winning the gold medal in L.A. and the silver medal in Atlanta, and she'd also won the Medal and Maclay Finals.

"And last time I checked, you're not Leslie Burr Howard," Dad replied.

"Not yet," I said, standing up. I would have been mad if I thought Dad meant I would never be as good as Leslie Burr Howard, but I knew he just wanted me to have options besides riding. "There's something else for you," Dad said. "I left it on your bed, and don't worry, it's not a Sweet Briar sweatshirt."

I went through the TV room to my bedroom. A garment bag from the local tack shop lay on my bed. Dad had followed me and was leaning against the door frame. "Dad—" I said as I quickly unzipped it and pulled out a brand-new, beautiful navy riding jacket, which had no doubt cost a minor fortune. Most of my riding clothes were either from the secondhand part of the tack store or castoffs from some of the other riders in the barn. I could count on my fingers the things I'd gotten new. "Now we'll never be able to afford college."

"Keep dreaming," he said.

Chapter Four

At school I was known as "the horse girl" or the girl who was MIA most of the time. That's not to say I didn't have friends. I had a few, but none I was really close to. It was pretty hard when I was away at horse shows so much of the year, including two months in the winter, when we went to Florida for the winter circuit and I did my courses through correspondence. And even when we were training at home, I went to classes, studied during any free periods, and left the minute the final bell rang.

I saw Becca, one of my friends, before first period since our lockers were only five lockers apart. Becca's locker was filled with pictures she'd cut from magazines, the latest hot movie star, an ad for perfume with this gorgeous guy sprinting after a gorgeous girl on a beach with the ocean lapping at their feet. There was also a picture of Becca and the rest of the soccer team after they'd won the state championships last year. I'd never bothered to put up pictures in my locker. It would have just felt forced.

"Guess what?" Becca said. I noticed she was practically beaming.

"What?"

"Doug and I hooked up at the party at Tanner's this weekend," she gushed.

Becca had been obsessed with Doug Frantollo since, oh, let's see, about the second week of freshman year. Doug was Mr. Football Stud. Football was big at our high school. Everyone went to all the games, and lots of people, even parents, painted their faces the school colors, blue and white. I guess it was the same with certain parents who got all into riding, though I couldn't imagine any of the parents at West Hills painting their faces. Doug was the star running back. As far as I could tell, he didn't seem to have much more going for him other than his ability to carry the ball for a gazillion yards, but I'd give Becca this: he was gorgeous. Tousled dark brown hair, blue eyes, and a killer smile. Becca was definitely pretty enough for Doug—she had long brown hair that she "Clairoled" Summer Berry, and her skin was so even and clear that when she got one zit, it was a traumatic moment. But she had always been the kind of girl who was too nice for someone like him to be interested in since he was known as much for being a player off the field as he was for being one on the field. Too nice, that is, until senior year, when he'd worked his way through all the other eligible bachelorettes.

For the longest time, Doug had never known how Becca felt about him. But all that changed two parties ago, when Becca had too much to drink and lipsticked the bathroom mirror BECCA ❤ DOUG. Word got back to Doug pretty quickly. Of course, I wasn't there—but that was what a mortified Becca had reported anyway.

"That's so cool," I told Becca now.

"I can't believe it. After all this time. It's like my dream is finally coming true, you know?"

"Yeah," I said, but then I came up blank. I had a hard time relating when my dream was about winning the finals and then the Olympics and hers was about a guy, and not even a very nice guy at that. I guess Becca's other friends would probably have asked how far they went, but I didn't feel right asking that. I guess because we just weren't that close.

"How was your weekend?" she said. "Good lessons?"

I shrugged. "Pretty good."

Of everyone at school, Becca knew the most about my riding. Most of the kids thought I "raced" horses, if they even knew who I was. Becca always asked how I did at shows, but she'd never come to watch one. Most shows were at least a few hours' drive away, and anyway Becca was always busy hanging out with her other friends, going to parties, or doing homework. She'd never brought up the idea of coming and I'd never invited her, since I was sure it would just feel weird to have her there. She did invite me to parties, though. Or rather she used to try to get me to go all the time. After I said no so many times, she'd stopped asking. I actually kind of missed her asking. There were some weekends when we were home and I could have gone out, but she never asked anymore.

There was an awkward silence where Becca and I just looked at each other. I fiddled with the zipper on my backpack and she ran her fingers through her hair. There was tons of stuff I could have told her about my weekend—how we had to jump the hardest course ever and how Gwenn fell off twice. But Becca didn't ask any more questions, and I wasn't sure she really cared. And she could never understand what happened at the barn in the same way that I couldn't relate to most of

30

what happened at the parties. Still, I decided to put an end to the awkward silence by asking, "So what else happened at Tanner's?"

Part of me did want to know the scoop—who hooked up with who, who booted, who got up on a table and sang "Rainbow Connection" in a Kermit-the-Frog voice. Becca kept me informed, so even though I wasn't really in the loop, I sort of was. But there was also always a part of me that didn't want to hear because then I'd just wish I'd been there.

"Oh my God." Becca laughed. "Wait till you hear this one. You have Mrs. Meyer for world civ, right?"

I nodded. Mrs. Meyer had a thick knobby bun of gray hair and a tendency to say things like, "Simmer down! Simmer down!"

"You're gonna love this, then. Pete Young gets wasted—no big surprise there—but then he goes and gets the keys to his uncle's pet shop—you know, the one in town?"

"Cam's Critter Corner."

"Right. So he gets the keys and he busts out all the hamsters, takes them to Mrs. Meyer's house, and puts them through her mail slot."

This was the punch line, and I knew I was supposed to be laughing hysterically. But it just sounded mean—to the hamsters and to Mrs. Meyer. I thought about the award for community service at graduation that was named after Mrs. Meyer's late husband and I couldn't help but feel a little bad for her.

"It must have been at least a hundred hamsters. . . . Can you imagine her face the next morning when she came downstairs and saw them all?"

Becca giggled, and I tried to make myself laugh too. She was still laughing when Tracy strutted in. She was wearing dark jeans, a tight black shirt, and sunglasses. She looked like she was pretending to be a model on her day off.

"I was just telling Francie about what Pete did," Becca said, wiping her teary eyes. She always cried a little when she laughed really hard.

Tracy slid the sunglasses onto the top of her head and faced Becca, so I was left staring at her back. "Have you talked to him?"

Tracy came to our school in ninth grade when her family moved from New Jersey. She and Becca were co-captains of the soccer team, so they spent a lot of time together. She reminded me of Tara in more ways than one.

Becca shook her head. "When I see him, should I act like nothing happened or act like it did happen?"

As I stared at the frayed ends of Tracy's hair—clearly from too much blow-drying and styling—I wished Becca had asked me. But what would I have said? I had absolutely zero experience when it came to guys. And I mean zero. As in *Never Been Kissed* zero.

"Wait and see what he acts like," Tracy advised. "If he's into you and it wasn't just a one-night thing, you'll know."

Brilliant. Even I could have come up with that.

"And what if he's not into me?"

"Then act like you don't care and he *will* be into you."

Before Becca responded, and without really thinking, I blurted out, "He likes you, Becca. How could he not like you?" I didn't even *want* him to like her, but I wanted to say something and not just sit there staring at Tracy's deep-fried hair while they talked like I was nonexistent. But the second I said it, I knew I sounded like a total optimistic loser, which was funny, because most of the time I was a complete pessimist. But it was easier to be an optimist when it came to someone besides myself.

Tracy opened her mouth to speak but then stopped, like my comment was so stupid she wouldn't even bother.

Becca smiled. "I wish."

I saw Becca again after last period. "Did you see Doug?" I asked her.

"Just once in the hall," she said. "But I'm sure he'll be around after practice."

As we slammed our lockers and headed out the main door together, I wanted to tell her to call me to let me know what happened, but it would have been weird since we hardly ever talked on the phone. Instead I said, "Good luck," which was completely stupid. What was I wishing her luck for? I quickly added, "See you tomorrow."

"Yeah, have a good ride," she said.

Becca mixed in with the kids straggling across the quad to the gym and I headed the other way. But then I stopped and looked back at what was now a sea of blue-and-white varsity jackets. I could still make out Becca, Tracy, and a few other girls from the soccer team. Their voices carried over the field.

"Double sessions." Abby Morin.

"I can't take it." Trish Baker.

Tracy said something else, and this time they were too far away and I couldn't make out anything but the laughter that followed. As I turned back the other way, for a second I wondered what it would be like to be heading to the gym, throwing on shorts and a T-shirt, and doing double sessions. What it'd be like to talk in the locker room about guys and about the party that had just happened or was about to happen and about going out for Coffee Coolattas after practice. But it was no use wondering, really. I'd decided a long time ago that riding was more important than best friends, parties, and boyfriends.

I rode the school bus back home to West Hills. The driver's name was Foxy, and he wore a tweed cap every day. His father used to work for one of the biggest stables in Newport, and he always greeted me with, "Here comes the champion!" Today was no different.

"Hey, Foxy," I mumbled without much enthusiasm. It was cuter the first few hundred times.

When he dropped me off at the bottom of the road West Hills was on, he called after me, "Go get 'em!"

I walked up the hill toward the farm. The temperature had dropped to the low sixties, and I wished I'd worn a sweatshirt or a jacket. I walked faster, all the while keeping my eyes peeled for any interesting finds on the road. Looking for abandoned stuff was something I did all the time. If you kept an eye out, it was amazing the kinds of things you'd come across. And not just loose change or a few bucks, which I did sometimes find, but pieces of people's lives that they'd lost somewhere along the way. I kept all my best finds in a shoe box at home—grocery lists, wallet-size photos, love or hate notes. I had my favorites, like the ticket stub to a Pearl Jam concert with some girl's name and number on the back and the words *you rocked my world* in slanted script, or the torn page of a lined notebook with four sentences in angry block print: *I can't believe you. You said you'd be here. I needed you. You suck.* My favorites were lost love notes that seemed like they might have come straight from one of those romantic books we read in English: *Wuthering Heights* or *Pride and Prejudice.* I knew most people would think I was pretty strange for collecting stuff that was essentially trash, but I loved finding a slice of someone's life and imagining the rest. Maybe it was my way of, for a few minutes, if only in my head, living the lives I could have had if I wasn't riding all the time. But today I came up empty. Not even a drugstore receipt.

After dropping my backpack full of books, including my mammoth chemistry book, in my room, I changed into my breeches and navy fleece West Hills jacket. I wore my jacket any chance I got. Sometimes I even dressed in a T-shirt just so I could wear it. I remembered when I first started training with Rob and got my jacket. Before then I'd always admired how the other riders looked in theirs and desperately wanted one of my own. Dad ordered mine as a Christmas present, and for the first few months I never took it off. I even wore it around the house.

I grabbed a quick PB&J and trudged up to the barn. By the time I reached the top of the hill, I felt like I could collapse on the pavement and fall into a deep sleep. I'd stayed up way too late cramming for my economics test. I had wanted to do especially well since econ was my favorite class. It was an elective that only the best students got to take, and the teacher, Mr. Roth, was really cool. He always used examples from real life that we cared about to explain the principles and theories we were learning.

The minute I stepped inside the barn, the smell of the fresh wood shavings, sweet hay, and horses' sweat jolted me awake. Everything—Becca, seeing her walk to the gym, school, homework, even Rob and the finals—faded away.

"*Hola,*" Camillo called from where he was brushing Stretch on the cross-ties in the middle of the main aisle. "*¿Cómo era la escuela?*" How was school?

"*Asi asi.*" So-so.

Camillo grabbed Katie's saddle to put on Stretch and I checked my watch. I only had twenty minutes before our lesson. I went to Tobey's stall and he shuffled toward me. He snuffled my breeches' pockets for a treat and I pulled out a peppermint, his favorite, which he lipped from my hand.

I slid his halter on and picked the shavings out of his feet, then led him out of his stall to the cross-ties. I curried him first—putting all my weight into it—and then brushed the unearthed dirt away with a medium-bristle brush. Tobey was dark brown and looked almost black, but not shiny black like the Black Stallion, and he didn't have any markings, not even a small white sock on a back leg. Because he didn't have Riley's thick blaze or Stretch's striking white coat, most people probably thought he was plain-looking, but I still thought he was beautiful.

I finished grooming him and then went to the tack room to grab my saddle and Tobey's bridle. I passed a group of pony riders, their braids bouncing on their shoulders. Even though they were only eleven or twelve, they had ponies that cost as much as houses. Katie was looking at the qualification chart posted by the tack room door. The chart had the names of all the equitation riders who were training at West Hills that year and boxes for all the finals—the USET, the Medal, and the Maclay. When we placed in the top four at classes throughout the year, we earned points toward each final. Once we had the required number of points to qualify, we got a big Q next to our name. Now all the names had Qs. Pretty soon the chart would be coming down and next year's chart would be going up. Without Katie's, Tara's, and my names, that is, since we were all about to turn eighteen and age out of the competitions.

"Remember that show when I got my last points for the Maclay?" she said.

How could I have forgotten? Susie, Katie, Pablo, and I had driven six hours to some nowhere part of New York State because the deadline was looming for Katie to qualify and she had still needed ten points—or the equivalent of first place. Then this girl who wasn't even trying to qualify got called back first in the test and we had to beg her to make an intentional mistake so Katie could win. This wasn't unheard of at the end of the qualifying period, but usually it was someone in your own barn who was willing to make a mistake so you could qualify.

"I'll be on in a minute," I told Katie as I headed down the aisle to Tobey.

"No prob," she said. "I'll wait."

Katie and I rode down to the ring together. Rob had set up a new course in the indoor like he did every day during boot camp. This time he told me to go first and, thank God, I didn't lean up the neck or do anything else stupid.

"Good," he said. It was the most positive thing he'd said to me in weeks. I wished he would say something more, but I figured "good" was better than nothing. It was certainly better than getting yelled at.

Afterward Katie and I rode up to the barn. I asked her if she wanted to walk the loop around the rings to cool the horses down. Stretch was still huffing, and if she didn't walk him, Dad or Camillo would have to.

Katie glanced at her Rolex. "I can't."

"Tutor?" I asked.

"No, sports shrink."

Katie wasn't the only girl on the show circuit who saw a performance psychologist. Lots of other girls did, and sometimes I wished I could. I could talk all about Rob and how he thought I could never win the finals.

Just then someone I'd never seen before walked out of the barn. He was wearing boots and breeches and looked like he was waiting to mount up.

"Who's that?" Katie asked.

"No idea."

"I didn't think anybody else was coming in for the finals."

"Me neither."

Most riders trained with Rob all year, but every once in a while someone from the West Coast would show up for the finals just for Rob's finishing touches because there was no coach quite as good as him out there. He saw us looking at him and started walking our way. As he came closer, Katie whispered, "He's kind of cute."

She giggled, and I tried not to laugh too because he was only a few strides away. The thing was—he *was* kind of cute. And any guy at West Hills—cute or not—was a big deal since hardly any guys rode. A Sacramento Kings baseball hat sat low on his head, and hair the color of a golden retriever peeked out from its edges. He had a barely noticeable cleft in his chin and big, goofy ears that together made him look kind of hot in a not-perfectly-perfect way.

"Let me guess," he said when he reached us. "Tara and Katie."

Before I could say anything, Katie said, "Right. I'm Katie and this is Tara."

"I'm Colby."

He even had a cute name. And I couldn't be sure, but it seemed like he was looking at me more than Katie.

"You're here to ride with Rob?" I said, and immediately regretted it. He was standing right in front of us in breeches and boots. Of course he was there to ride with Rob.

"Yeah," Colby answered. "I'm from L.A. You guys from around here?"

"I'm from New York City," Katie said. "And Tara's from Pennsylvania." I waited for her to crack up and tell him who I really was, but she didn't. Dad came out of the barn leading a chestnut mare that Colby must have brought with him, because I'd never seen her around the barn before. Colby traded his baseball hat for his riding helmet. Dad gave him a leg up and wiped off his boots with the rag that always poked out of his back pocket.

"*Muchas gracias,*" Colby told him, making me shudder. Dad hated it when people tried to talk Spanish to him. "I can speak English perfectly fine," he always said to me, although he would never say anything in front of the clients. "I've only been in this country for twenty-five years."

Colby rode up to us and said, "Maybe you guys can give me the quick tour?" It seemed like he was talking to me more than Katie, and I couldn't figure out why. Did he think I was pretty? Could he possibly?

"I can't," Katie said, clearly bummed. "I've got an . . . appointment."

"How about it?" Colby said, looking at me again.

I shrugged, trying to act like I didn't care one way or the other. "Sure."

As Katie slid off Stretch and handed him over to Dad, Colby and I headed out on the loop. I didn't have to look back to know Dad was watching us for a minute before he led Stretch inside.

We headed away from the barn. I pointed out the main ring and the gymnastics ring, which were both pretty obvious. I racked my brain for something to tell him that only the riders knew so I'd seem in the know, but I came up blank. Colby nodded to a building site next to the main ring where workmen were busy laying a foundation. "What's going on there?"

"That's the new indoor Rob's putting up."

Over the years Rob had slowly rebuilt West Hills. It had once been a grand estate and farm, but the person who had owned it before Rob had let it fall apart, which was why he had been able to afford it.

I glanced over at Colby, hoping to check him out for a second, but he caught me. My stomach fluttered like it usually only did before I went into the ring.

"So, I hear you're pretty good," he said.

And that was when it hit me. He wasn't looking at me because he thought I was cute or pretty but because he thought I was Tara. I wanted to kill myself for being so stupid. Of course he'd heard of Tara; everyone had. He was scoping me out, seeing if he thought he could beat me. So I decided to say something Tara would say. "I'm the best. Isn't that what people in California say about me? That I'll win?"

This was exactly what the real Tara would have said. Although the words felt odd coming out of my mouth, they also felt kind of good. As much as I hated Tara for saying things like she'd said to Rob the other day after his lecture—*I won't let you down. . . . I'm going to win*—I really wished I was the one saying them. Humility might be a virtue, but in riding it got you nowhere. You had to believe in yourself—absolutely and completely. You had to walk into that ring thinking, *I'm going to win.* Something Tara did every time and something I was still working on.

Colby halted his mare. I walked a step farther and then stopped Tobey and swiveled in the saddle to look back at him.

"I don't know about the rest of the world, but I'd never

heard of you before Rob told me who I'd meet today," he said. "So get over yourself." Then, as he turned back the other way, sarcastically: "Thanks for the tour."

I hesitated—feeling like the biggest idiot ever. Why couldn't I have just been normal around him? I hated myself for being so uncool. I legged Tobey into a trot and caught up with him. I rode alongside him at the walk, but he wouldn't look at me.

"I'm not Tara."

Still nothing.

"When you came out and said, 'Let me guess, you're Katie and you're Tara,' Katie just went along with it and so I did too."

"So the other girl *was* Katie?" Colby asked, staring between his mare's pricked ears.

"Yeah," I said, relieved that he seemed to be talking to me again. I wished we could back up and start all over.

Finally Colby turned to me. "And that makes you?"

"Francie."

I thought Colby might ask me why I kept pretending to be Tara and why I was so rude, but instead he said, "What's Francie short for? Francis?"

"Francesca."

"Well, Francis, what else do you have to show me that I need to know around here?"

There wasn't much else to show him, but I didn't want the tour to end, not when things were getting good between us again. "I guess there's Rob's house," I said.

"Okay."

I steered Tobey away from the barn. Rob made sure that the grounds were immaculate. The lawns were lush green even now in September, and all the hedges were trimmed to perfection. He lived in the restored farmhouse, a brown brick colonial draped in ivy. Pablo was washing Rob's black Escalade in the driveway while Mexican music played from a nearby radio.

"*Hola, señorita!*" he called to me.

"*¿Es que lavar coches es mejor que lavar caballos?*" I asked. *Is washing cars better than washing horses?*

"*Al carro no hay que decirle se quede quieto,*" Pablo quipped. *No telling the car it has to stand still!*

"That's cool you speak Spanish so well," Colby said. "I've been taking it for four years, and I can still hardly say more than 'hello,' 'thank you,' and 'where's the bathroom,' and that's just because Señorita Sanchez won't let us go to the bathroom unless we ask in Spanish. Even if you're about to piss your pants, if you don't ask in Spanish—no go."

I knew I should have told him right then the real reason I spoke Spanish so well. He would figure it out sooner or later. But for some reason I didn't. And it wasn't because I was ashamed of who I was either. Maybe I just wanted to see what he acted like around me without knowing so I could see if it would change when he did know. Life for me was kind of weird that way. When I was with Dad or any of the other grooms, I was Mexican. I could banter with them in Spanish and I knew all about where they'd come from and what they'd lived through to get here. But since I grew up in America, I was also comfortable around people like Katie, Tara, Becca, and Tracy. It was like hovering between two worlds. Sometimes being able to choose whichever world I wanted to be in was nice, but sometimes it made me feel like two entirely different people.

"What's your horse's name?" I asked Colby, hoping to change the topic of conversation.

"Ginger." Colby patted her neck. "I think she's still a little wiped from the plane ride here, aren't you, girl?"

"This here's Tobey," I offered.

"He yours?"

"No, he's Rob's. I get to ride him because everyone thinks he's, well, kind of mildly insane."

I wasn't exaggerating. Rob bought Tobey thinking he was going to be as good as Stretch, and he had all the talent to be. But someone must have treated him badly or maybe he just had some loose cables in his brain, because he was incredibly temperamental. Like sometimes when he saw another horse coming at him in the ring, he'd leap to the side. Or other times at shows he got so nervous that he sweated profusely and wouldn't walk or trot but would only canter. When Rob saw he wasn't going to be able to lease Tobey out or sell him for anything, let alone the price he had had in mind, he gave him to me to ride. "Maybe you can figure him out," he said at the time. I wasn't really sure I'd figured him out, but we got along and most of the time he was good for me. Since I cleaned his stall and groomed him every day, I knew him well and he trusted me. I tried never to make him do anything he hated, like ride in a ring with lots of other horses going in all different directions, and if he got upset, I didn't get mad at him, because I'd found that only made it worse. Instead I just kept going and tried to make the best of it.

"What's down there?" Colby asked, taking his reins in one hand and pointing to the dirt road that led to where Dad and I and the other grooms lived.

"That's where the grooms live," I said.

"Can we go down there?"

"There's not much to see."

43

"It's not nice?"

I shrugged. "It's fine."

"Are they all illegal?" Colby asked. "At my barn at home a lot of them are."

Them—I knew Colby didn't mean anything by it, but I couldn't stop thinking how *I* was one of *them*. I shook my head. "No, Rob won't hire anyone who doesn't have their green card."

Some barns did hire illegals because they'd usually work for even less money. Every now and then there were raids at the shows. There was even a code that shows used when INS was on the grounds. If you ever heard the announcer say, "Elvis is in the building," over the PA system, you knew half of the grooms would be jumping in cars or hiding in the bushes.

"I'm not sure how I feel about it," Colby said. "I mean, if people can't get work where they're from and want to work hard why not let them in, but then again, what about all the people here that need work?"

Not really wanting to discuss the finer points of immigration with Colby, I said, "We should probably head back."

"Yeah," he said. "I'm a few minutes late."

"Late for your lesson?"

I must have looked completely horrified because he added, "What?"

"It's just Rob doesn't like it when people are late." Actually, Rob had refused to teach people because they were a few *seconds* late. No one had ever dared be a few *minutes* late.

"He'll just have to deal," Colby said.

Rob—deal? Colby sounded like a rule breaker in the making. "I should let you in on a few important things," I told him, and explained the rules. I was glad to be able to fill him in.

"Who made these up?" he asked.

"No one. We all just know them. Mostly because we learned the hard way. I thought I would try to save you getting yelled at."

Colby shook his head and smiled. "Thanks," he said. As we headed back to the barn, he asked, "So what else can you tell me about yourself?"

"What do you want to know?"

"Just anything."

I took a breath and pondered the question. I felt like I was in school and the teacher had asked about some book I'd read but suddenly couldn't remember anything from, not even the main characters' names. What was it about Colby that made me feel so clueless? "Well, I've been doing the equitation and riding with Rob for six years. I've gotten ribbons at the regionals, but I always manage to mess up at the finals. This is my last year."

"Okay, that's a start; what else?"

"What do you mean? That's pretty much it."

"I don't know, like, what else do you do?"

"Not much. I mean, I go to school; I come here and ride." I wasn't sure how I was supposed to do more. I was already exhausted from working at the barn, riding, and doing my schoolwork.

"Are you starting to think about college?" Colby asked. "Where do you want to go?"

"What are you, my dad?" I asked.

Colby dropped his reins and held his hands out in front of him, stick-'em-up style. "Jeez, touchy."

"My dad wants me to, but I want to ride professionally," I explained. "What about you?"

"I'm definitely going to college. Riding's fun, but it's not my life, that's for sure."

"So what else do *you* do, then?" I asked, turning the question back on him.

"Let's see—I run track. I'm obsessed with graphic novels, especially those of the genius Alan Moore. I've written a screenplay. I can juggle." Colby paused and then added, "Oh yeah, and I'm a killer Scrabble player."

"Quite an impressive résumé," I said.

"Thanks," he said with a grin. "I like to think of myself as a well-rounded individual."

I didn't want to stop talking, but we had reached the front of the barn. Plus, he was already late for his lesson.

"Your lesson's at four?" I asked. I checked my watch—it was 4:07.

"Yeah," Colby said, still not leaving.

"I guess I didn't really show you much," I said. "Sorry for the bad tour."

"There's always tomorrow," he called as he finally turned and trotted off.

I watched him trot away for longer than I should have. I was glad no one was there to see the goofy grin plastered on my face.

Chapter Five

The next day when I got to the barn after school, Dad was in Finch's stall with his ear pressed to his side, checking his gut sounds.

"Again?" I asked.

"Yup," Dad answered.

Finch was a chronic colicker. When it came to horses, colic was the one thing people feared most. Horses have a complex intestinal system, and if something throws it off—moldy grain or hay, improper worming, or even just a drastic change in weather like the one we'd had in the past few days—it could spell trouble. Sometimes colic was just kind of like a tummy ache and it passed with the aid of a concoction of Pepto-Bismol and baking soda or a little pain medication. Other times the intestine could twist or rupture and the only chance the horse had at survival was surgery. Even then, sometimes they didn't make it. By listening for gut sounds, which in a healthy horse you could hear just by putting an ear to their side, you could get a sense of whether things were working or not. Some horses never colicked their whole lives, some colicked only every now and then, and others, like Finch, colicked what seemed like every other minute.

"He wasn't eating," Dad said. "Pablo said he hadn't picked manure out of his stall all day and then I found him lying down."

Usually when a horse colicked, its system blocked up and it stopped eating and passing manure.

"Any gut sounds?" I asked.

"Minimal," Dad said.

He clipped a lead rope to Finch's halter and led him out into the aisle. "Can you go get Rob?"

I jogged down to the indoor, where Rob was teaching four women that Katie liked to call the Horny Housewives. They were middle-aged, wealthy women who lived in Boston, didn't work, and were completely bored. Their children were either off at boarding school or college and their husbands were always working or playing golf. To relieve their boredom, the HHs spent their time riding. They weren't very good, but they took the sport incredibly seriously and burned outrageous amounts of money on horses, lessons, and riding clothes. They also tended to fawn all over Rob, buying him expensive polo shirts as presents and always bringing him espressos from Starbucks. Katie said she was sure they all fantasized about having torrid sex with him in the hayloft.

"Sitting trot, ladies!" I heard Rob holler as I made my way down the hill to the indoor. "Come on, Marcia, stop shaking and baking. Sit still up there!"

I waited at the door for Rob to acknowledge me per rule number one—*Wait until Rob tells you to.*

"What's up, Francie?" he said. Sometimes Rob just saying my name like that, acknowledging me and me alone, even if it was only because I was there to ask him a question, was enough attention to keep me going for days.

"It's Finch," I said. I didn't need to say anything more.

"How bad?" Rob asked.

"Not too bad, but Dad said to come get you."

"All right, ladies," Rob called out. "Take a quick break. I'll be back in a few minutes."

The women brought their horses down to the walk, a jumble of sighs and "whews."

"Don't stay away too long," Marcia purred to Rob. With her blond hair, trim legs, and pink Lily Pulitzer shirts, she was the best-looking of the bunch. She was also the most outwardly flirtatious. "We'll miss you too much," she cooed.

The rest of the ladies giggled and Rob grinned. I got the feeling he kind of liked them drooling all over him.

I followed Rob up the hill to the barn, lengthening my stride to keep up with him. I was usually so shy in front of Rob. We didn't ever talk to each other, except for him to tell me something I needed to do in the barn or in a lesson. But the quiet between us was killing me. I knew if I was Tara, we'd be talking. So I said, "Susie better watch out for that Marcia." I felt like I was stealing a line from Katie, but I didn't care. I just hoped it would go over okay with Rob.

In fact, he laughed. He actually laughed. "No kidding," he said.

I found myself smiling too. When we walked into the barn, Rob took in Finch's drooping head and glazed-over eyes. "How is he?" he asked Dad.

"Weak gut sounds. And he hasn't manured since the morning."

"Did you give him anything?"

"Pepto and baking soda earlier, but I wanted to check with you before I gave him anything else."

"What are you thinking?" Rob asked.

Dad and Rob had a great working relationship. Dad handled everything to do with the horses, and Rob trusted and respected him completely. I'd even heard him say once that West Hills wouldn't be what it was today if Dad hadn't come to work for him when he was just starting out. It was pretty amazing that Dad had become a barn manager. Most barn managers were white and only the grooms that worked under them were Hispanic. And it was also amazing that Dad had been working for Rob for so many years, since most people—Hispanic or white—hopped from barn to barn. Most of the grooms that worked for West Hills stayed for long periods too, but I think that was more because of what it was like working with Dad than anything.

"Let's give him ten cc's of Banamine and see if it'll pass," Dad said. "If he hasn't manured within another hour, I think we better get the vet here."

"Sounds good," Rob said.

Dad went to draw up a syringe of Banamine, the pain medication. When he came back, I held Finch's head while Dad whispered, "Easy, boy," and slid the needle into the vein in Finch's neck. He pulled back the syringe to make sure he'd hit blood, and therefore the vein, and then injected the clear fluid. As Dad led Finch out for a walk with the idea that it might jump-start his system again, I tacked up Tobey. Tuesday was our day for flat lessons. We didn't jump, but that didn't mean we got off easy.

"No stirrups today," Rob said as he headed back to finish teaching the Horny Housewives. "Tell the others."

Riding without stirrups makes your leg muscles incredibly strong but hurts like hell. You feel it for days afterward.

I was in the tack room pulling on my riding boots when

50

Katie walked in. Besides Tobey's stall, the tack room, with all its gleaming brass hooks and the smell of glycerin soap and well-used leather, was my favorite place at the barn. A big wooden sawhorse stood in the middle of the room and a four-pronged hook dangled from the ceiling. Wooden tack trunks, each engraved on top with WEST HILLS FARM, lined the walls.

Katie was sipping a chocolate smoothie, one of her meal-replacement drinks. She was on Weight Watchers. She wasn't fat, just chubby. But in the riding world anything less than slim was a problem because all things being equal, the equitation was a beauty contest. Weight Watchers meant she had to keep track of everything she ate. She received a score for each item she ingested, like an apple was one point and a piece of chicken the size of a fist three. When she was at the farm, she mostly ate Weight Watcher meals for breakfast, lunch, and dinner. She could only eat twenty points a day, and when she was at home, she had to get weighed every week.

"No stirrups," I told her.

"My poor VG," she moaned, using her pet term for "down there." An unfortunate but frequent side effect of riding without stirrups was that you could feel pretty sore. "I finally just recovered from last week." Katie sank down on a tack trunk and sipped her smoothie. "Where's Colby?" she asked.

"I don't know. Haven't seen him yet."

"How was the tour yesterday?"

"Fine."

I knew Katie wouldn't let me get away with that, and I was right.

"That's it?" she said. "You've gotta give me more than that. Did he figure out you weren't Tara?"

"Yeah, he didn't even know who Tara was."

"Everyone knows who Tara is," Katie said.

"That's what I thought."

Katie furrowed her brow. "Interesting," she said. "This boy is very interesting. Needs further exploration."

I grabbed my saddle off the rack and started pulling off my stirrups. Katie still seemed to be in a daze thinking about Colby. "No stirrups, remember?" I reminded her.

"Do you think if I tell Rob I can't because of my VG, he'd understand?" she joked.

I just shook my head. "Come on," I grumbled, starting for the door.

Rob worked us for forty-five minutes straight. We even had to do ten minutes of half seat, where you lift yourself forward out of the saddle into your jumping position, which is nearly impossible without stirrups and not at all good for the VG. Katie kept looking over at Colby throughout the lesson, and it was so obvious even Rob noticed. "Katie, what are you looking at?" he yelled at her at one point. "I know having a member of the male persuasion in our lesson is distracting for you girls, but keep your eyes straight ahead of you."

When the lesson was over, Katie told me to come by her room later. "I have a plan," she said.

"A plan for what?" I asked. I already knew it had to do with Colby. With Katie, everything was always about boys.

"Just a plan. I've gotta go finish a math assignment that was due, like, a week ago and e-mail it in, but come by, okay?"

"I don't know," I said. I wasn't sure I wanted to be involved in whatever plan Katie had in mind. I didn't really want Katie getting all interested in Colby, although I was pretty sure it was too late for that.

"Francie!" Katie practically screamed.

"Okay, okay," I said as I went off to do my barn work.

I was emptying the last wheelbarrow from picking out stalls when Dad came back in with Finch. "Success," he said, meaning Finch had finally manured.

Finch already looked more upbeat—the sparkle in his eyes was back. Dad led him into his stall. I'd taken his hay away, since it wasn't good to add anything more to his system for now except water.

"I want to wait a little while to feed," Dad said. "Make sure he's really out of the woods."

"I was going to stop by Katie's," I said. "I could come back after and feed."

"Sounds good. Then I'll check back in on him after dinner."

Knowing Dad, he'd also probably be setting his alarm clock for once or twice in the middle of the night to drive up to the farm and check on him. When a horse was really sick, Dad often slept in the barn so he could get up every hour if necessary.

As Dad headed home, I went to Katie's room. I found her sitting at her desk. "Ugh, I detest math," she groaned.

Without her riding helmet, Katie was what most guys would consider cute, but not beautiful. Short brown hair she tucked behind her ears and a round face. She always wore a silver chain with a heart on it around her neck, and her fingernails were perfectly shaped and painted from weekly manicures. This week's color was hot pink.

"How's Finch?" she asked.

"Better. He seems to have come out of it."

Katie's cell phone rang, and she located it under two pairs of jeans and a shirt on her bed. Clothes with designer labels covered every inch of Katie's room. A bunch of ribbons from past horse shows lay in a heap in the corner, and above her bed hung pages torn from fashion magazines of models mid-strut.

Katie was a total clothes junkie and dreamed of someday being a famous fashion designer like her idols Stella McCartney or Miuccia Prada the way I dreamed of going to the Olympics.

"Hello, Dad," she said. She didn't even need to check the caller ID—her father called every evening to ask about her lesson.

I sat down at her desk and went to work on the math problem that had stumped her, which was really just simple algebra. I finished it in about two seconds and then opened the bottom drawer, where she kept her not-so-secret supply of junk food, including Twix bars, Kit Kats, Reese's peanut butter cups, and my personal favorite, Oreos.

"Yes, it was fine," she told her father. "No, I haven't eaten a candy bar in a week."

Katie tapped me on the back and motioned to the junk food drawer, a defiant grin on her face. I handed her a Twix and pulled out a package of Oreos for myself. The one good thing about mucking stalls every day was it meant I could eat pretty much whatever I wanted and still stay thin.

"No, I swear," Katie assured her father. "You can even ask Francie if you want. She's right here."

I waited to see if Mr. Whitt would want to talk to me. It wouldn't have been the first time he had me vouch for Katie's eating habits. Supposedly Mr. Whitt had never lost a court case, and it was obvious it just about killed him that Katie had no talent when it came to riding. Since he couldn't make her a better rider, even though he tried by sending her to West Hills and getting her the best horses, he focused on keeping her from eating.

Katie held up the Twix to the phone. "All right, Dad, I've gotta go." When she finally hung up, thankfully without her father talking to me, she tore open the Twix and bit off a huge chunk. "This is probably like twenty points, but I don't really care right now," she said through a full mouth. "I swear I should just stick my finger down my throat like Tara does. It'd be a lot easier."

"You don't know she does that," I said.

"Then how does she stay so freaking skinny? You've seen what she eats."

It was true. Tara was always ingesting inconceivable things like Big Macs and supersize sodas, yet if anything she only got skinnier.

"Your dad didn't want to talk to me?" I kidded. "I'm hurt."

"No, he had some function to go to—thank God." Katie bit off another hunk of the Twix. A devious look came over her face. "So, we're going to visit Colby."

My stomach plummeted. She liked him—I knew it. *Why Colby?* I thought. Why did she have to like *him*?

"I have to go back and feed and check on Finch," I told her. "You go ahead—you don't need me to go with you." Even though I really wanted to see Colby again, I wasn't exactly dying to have it slip out that I was a groom. I wished I'd told him before because now it just seemed weird that I hadn't.

"No way, I'm not going alone. I'll help you feed and then we'll both go."

"Okay," I agreed, shoving the last Oreo in my mouth and standing up. "By the way, I did your math problem for you."

Katie looked at her notebook and chirped, "You're the absolute best."

At the barn we looked in on Finch, who met our concerned gazes with a curious gaze of his own, which was a good sign. I quickly took his pulse just to make sure it was regular and listened to his stomach. Then Katie helped me mix up the grain in the feed room. I scooped out the pellets and sweet feed and Katie sifted in the powdered supplements like glucosamine and vitamin E. Each horse got a different mixture of grain and supplements depending on whether it was naturally fat or thin, energetic or lazy. Dad had told me to mix up a small bran mash with extra water in it for Finch, to help keep things moving.

The minute we came back out into the aisle, the horses started whinnying. Stretch, the most impatient of the bunch, stomped his hooves and paced his stall. I brought out flakes of hay in a wheelbarrow and threw each horse one of the chunks, then went stall to stall with the grain buckets.

"All right, it's coming!" I hollered to Stretch, who I always fed first.

Out in the barn Katie didn't help. Not because she wasn't willing or didn't want to get hay all over her Michael Kors sweater, but because if anyone saw her helping, especially Rob, even if she'd volunteered, they'd freak out. Katie's parents didn't pay thousands of dollars a month for her to throw hay—we all understood that.

When I was done, Katie and I walked across the farm to the pool house, where Rob had put Colby. Nobody supervised what went on at night. Rob's only attempt at propriety was making the boys stay in the pool house and the girls in the gardener's house. But even that didn't really mean anything. A few years ago when Bobby and Celia were riding at the farm, Celia practically lived in Bobby's room in the pool house.

Away from the stable it was easy to forget West Hills was a horse farm. That is, except for the occasional mounds of manure that hadn't been picked up yet and the signs that read: PLEASE KEEP HORSES OFF THE GRASS.

We passed Tara sitting on the front steps of the camper she and her mother stayed in, her pink cell phone pressed to her ear.

"Hello, Brad," Katie cooed as we walked by. Tara shot us

a dirty look. Brad was Tara's boyfriend and had won the Medal Finals two years ago. Now he worked as an assistant trainer for a grand prix rider and was even getting to show in some small grand prix classes himself. He traveled all over the country to compete and had been in Europe a bunch in the summer, where show jumping was almost as popular as baseball or basketball is in the States. All this meant he hadn't seen much of Tara. But they talked plenty—she called him at least five times a day.

The pool house was much smaller than the gardener's house, since it wasn't intended for someone to live in but really just for people to change for swimming. Rob had converted it into two bedrooms, a bathroom, and a little kitchenette for nuking hot dogs or cans of Chef Boyardee.

We were still ten yards from the door when we heard music playing. I recognized the band from hearing them on the radio in the barn. When Camillo and Pablo weren't playing tapes of their Mexican music, we listened to this independent rock station that played newer, less well-known bands.

Katie knocked on the door. Colby opened it, dressed in a T-shirt, scrubs, and Tevas. Instead of saying "hello" or "hey" like a normal person, he said, "Do you know what 'cop' stands for?"

"What do you mean?" Katie said.

"Constable on patrol. How about 'drag'?"

Katie shook her head.

"Dressed as girl."

"Huh," she said. "Who knew?"

Without really being invited, Katie walked in and sat down on a stool at the kitchen counter. I wasn't as comfortable just walking in and plopping down, so I decided to stand. Colby's iBook—the source of the music—sat on the counter.

"So," she said. "We just came by to see if you survived your first Rob Renaud flat work extravaganza."

"Barely," Colby said.

"It must be even worse for guys. . . . I mean, down there," Katie said.

"You mean the penis or the testicles?" Colby asked, deadpan and looking her right in the eye.

Katie turned red and I stifled a laugh. It served Katie right. She was always trying to be so outrageous, and this time her outrageousness hadn't fazed Colby in the slightest. He'd not only called her on it, he'd raised her. I had thought I'd liked him before, but now he was really growing on me.

"I guess both or either," Katie said, trying to recover.

"They're not swearwords," Colby said. "They're just names for body parts, like elbow or arm."

"Not quite," I said.

"Okay, well, not quite," Colby admitted. "And yes, it's not all that comfortable riding without stirrups if you're a guy, but I think I'll still be able to have kids someday."

"What's with the scrubs?" Katie said, trying to change the subject. She glanced down at Colby's legs but then looked right back up again—I guess it was too soon after Colby's comments to be looking anywhere below his waist.

"My dad's a doctor," he said.

"Oh, what kind?" Katie asked.

"Plastic surgeon. But not the good kind that helps victims of tragic accidents or anything like that. The tummy-tucks-and-boob-jobs kind."

"So, Francie said you really don't know who Tara is?" Katie asked. She was certainly giving him the third degree, but he seemed to take it all in stride.

"No," he said.

"Don't you read the *Chronicle*?"

The Chronicle of the Horse was a weekly magazine that ran coverage and photos of all the horse shows throughout the year. It was pretty much every rider's bible.

Colby shook his head. "Not really. I kind of try and stay away from all that and just do my own thing."

Katie looked intrigued. "Kind of like a Zen approach?"

"I guess so," Colby offered.

"That's cool," Katie said. "I should try that." She nodded to Colby's laptop. "What are you listening to? It sounds familiar."

Colby and I said at exactly the same time: "It's Guster." Then he turned to me. "You know Guster?"

I shrugged, trying to act like it was no big deal, but really I was so happy I knew the band he liked, especially since Katie, who went to concerts in New York City, didn't. For once I seemed like the cool one. "Yeah."

"This is their first CD ever. When they were called Gus? I guess there was another band called Gus, so they had to change it. Do you have this one?"

"No," I said. We didn't exactly have extra money lying around for music—not with new breeches costing 200 dollars.

"If you give me your e-mail, I can send you a copy if you want."

"That's illegal," I blurted out, and then wished I hadn't. I was back to being totally uncool again. I wouldn't have usually thought much about it being illegal, but we had just talked about the free-rider principle in economics, which is when someone pays for something and then others piggyback on and get it for free. Mr. Roth had even used the example of music sharing.

"I might break the law for you," Colby replied. Was he flirting with me? I wasn't sure I even knew what flirting was, but I sure hoped so. When I didn't respond, he added, "Immigration law, copyright law . . . did you ever think about going to law school?"

"Immigration law?" Katie asked, clearly confused.

"Yesterday we were just talking about the grooms and whether they're legal," Colby said.

"Francie and her dad—" Katie began, but I cut her off.

The longer Colby didn't know I was a groom, the more I didn't want him to find out. Being a groom seemed like the most uncool thing of all. "I told him Rob only hires people with their green card," I said.

Thankfully, Katie changed the subject to the regionals. She asked how Colby could show in our regionals if he was from L.A. He explained that he just had to register and then earn the number of points required for our regionals.

"If I don't make it this year, my dad is going to freak," Katie said.

"Yeah, my dad wanted me to go last year, but I'd just gotten Ginger and it was such a long trip," Colby replied.

Katie's eyes were wide. "You mean you qualified for the Garden and you didn't come?"

"My dad wanted me to, but I said no." Colby shrugged, like it was nothing. "The power of no."

"What?" Katie said.

"The power of no. It's just this saying from these weird self-help tapes my older sister listens to. Two little letters: big impact."

"Hmmm, the power of no," Katie said. "We should try that with Rob."

"Yeah," I added. "I can just see it. 'No, Rob, we're not riding without stirrups today.' That would go over well."

We all laughed pretty hard thinking about saying no to

Rob. Like that would ever happen. I began to feel some cool factor creeping back in. When we stopped laughing, I looked at my watch to find a whole hour had slipped by.

"I better get going," I said.

Dad would be wondering where I was and if Finch was okay. He wouldn't be thrilled either if he found out I was hanging out with Colby. "So I saw you've met the new boy," he'd said to me after I'd given Colby the tour yesterday. I could tell from those few words alone that he didn't love the idea of me spending time with Colby.

"So you two are both staying on the farm too?" Colby asked.

Before Katie could explain how she lived here temporarily and I lived here permanently, I said, "Um, yeah."

"Great, so I'll see you guys tomorrow. Thanks for coming by."

"No problem," Katie said. "Just think of us as the welcome wagon."

When we were far enough away from the pool house to be out of earshot, Katie said, "He's really cute, huh? A little weird, but cute, don't you think?"

"I guess so." I didn't want to let on that I thought he was beyond cute and interesting too. He wasn't just a dumb football jock like Doug. But I was sure there was no way he would be into me.

Katie shook her head. "You know, Francie, someday you're going to actually *like* a boy."

"Maybe someday," I said. Katie might not know it, but I was pretty sure that it was already happening.

Chapter Six

Day nine of boot camp and I was so sore that I soaked in the tub every night, downed two Advil before bed, and still could barely walk the next morning. Only three more days to go before the regionals, but I wasn't sure I would live that long. By fourth-period English, I was already so exhausted I didn't think I'd make it through the rest of the day. At the end of class Mrs. Hanson passed back our papers.

"How'd you do?" Becca asked as we straggled out of class.

I knew I'd done better than her—I always did. "A-minus," I told her. "How about you?" I didn't really care so much what she'd gotten, but I knew it was the right thing to ask. Tracy would have asked.

Becca showed me her paper: a C+. I would have been devastated with that grade, but she just shrugged. "After all that's been happening with Doug, I couldn't care less about grades right now. Did I tell you we hung out after the game this weekend?"

"That's so cool," I said. I thought about telling her about Colby, but it just seemed stupid because nothing had happened at all. In the past few days we had talked more, but that was about it. I was sure that anything I might have felt between us was a figment of my imagination.

As we headed downstairs to the cafeteria for lunch, I could already smell the American chop suey. Becca groaned. "Not again. Gross."

"We can just get salads," I offered.

"Definitely."

I loved Tuesdays and Thursdays because Becca and I had English right before lunch and ended up eating together. On the other days, she had sixth-period lunch and I had fifth, which meant I often ended up eating alone.

The salad plan shattered, however, when Doug turned the corner, shrugging on his football jacket.

"Hey, we were just going into the cafeteria for lunch," Becca said.

"No, we're going *out* for lunch," he announced.

"Um . . ." Becca wavered, casting me an "okay?" glance.

I wasn't sure if her look meant "okay, you wanna come?" or "okay, I've gotta go." Then Doug said, "Come on, Peters and Pepper are already in the car," and somehow I was swept up in the whirlwind and walking with them to the parking lot.

Billy Peters and Billy Pepper were linemen. Besides playing the same position and sharing the same first names, both also had red hair. One was never far from the other, and people called them the twins; even though they weren't related, they should have been.

Peters was in the passenger seat of Doug's Chevy Nova. Pepper was in the backseat. Doug climbed behind the wheel as

Becca and I slid into the back. I was in the middle next to Pepper, who sat with his legs splayed, taking up a good two-thirds of the bench.

"Who're you?" Pepper grumbled, looking at me like I was an exotic animal yet to be classified.

I wasn't sure how I should respond, and I wanted to just disappear. Thankfully, Becca answered for me. "This is my good friend Francie."

After Pepper's warm welcome, I was content to remain mute while they argued over whether to go to McDonald's or KFC. We ended up at KFC and then hit Dunkin' Donuts for Coolattas. The whole time I hardly said a word, but just being with them was kind of cool. Doug and the twins recounted their top ten worst practices. Number one was when their coach made them run hills piggybacking each other.

"And I get Pepper here," Doug said. "What do you weigh, Pep?"

Pepper looked up from his bucket of wings. "Two-oh-five."

"I'm carrying two-oh-five up the hills. And I weigh one-seventy."

Pepper grinned. "He was light as a feather."

"But we won against North that year," Doug said.

There were two high schools in town—Attleboro and North Attleboro—and the big matchup always came the Saturday after Thanksgiving.

Becca spoke up. "Did you know Francie's like this amazing rider?"

At the sound of my name I almost choked on my biscuit. I had been so happy just being a fly on the wall.

"She's ranked in the top ten in the country." Becca turned to me. "Right?"

"Um, we don't exactly have rankings," I said. I was very

aware that Doug and the twins were staring at me. I knew they couldn't care less about my riding, and I wished Becca hadn't brought it up.

"But you're one of the best, right?" Becca said.

I shrugged. "I guess so." No one was there to say otherwise, and what was I supposed to say, "No, actually, I'm not good at all"?

There was a moment's pause. Then, to my complete surprise, Doug said, "That's cool." I wondered if I could have heard him right.

"Yeah," Pepper added. "I loved *Seabiscuit*."

"That was that one we saw about the racehorse?" Peters said, and Pepper nodded. "Me too, man, I loved that flick."

I smiled. Who knew the twins had a soft spot for horse movies?

On the way home Doug blasted the radio. It was a song I usually hated, but Doug, Becca, and the twins started singing along, and all of a sudden I got the urge to sing too. I couldn't believe I even knew the lyrics. I opened my mouth and sang the chorus very quietly, testing if anyone would notice and tell me to shut up. They didn't, and I sang louder.

Doug tapped out the beat on the steering wheel. "This song totally rocks," he said.

And right then, it did totally rock, because I almost felt a part of things. For a second, I wasn't just the horse girl.

As we pulled into the campus parking lot just in time for next period, Becca asked me, "What do you have next?"

"Chem. You?"

"Spanish," Becca said.

It always felt a little weird that people took classes in Spanish or, really, that I didn't because I already spoke Spanish fluently.

Doug groaned. "I have math."

"You studying, man?" Pepper asked.

"No, I'm failing," Doug reported. "Test next week. I'm totally dead."

"You can't fail, man." Pepper again.

"We'd be totally screwed against Natick without you." Peters.

"There's gotta be a way. We gotta get you a tutor or something." Pepper.

That's when Becca chimed in. "Wait—Francie's like a god in math."

I elbowed her. "I am not." It was bad enough that Becca had gone on about me being such a great rider, but a math god? Very uncool.

To me: "You totally are." To them: "She took precalculus as a *sophomore*." From the backseat Becca placed a tentative hand on Doug's shoulder. "Maybe Francie could help you. She keeps all of her tests and assignments. She's like the most organized person on the planet. She could totally tutor you."

I didn't really have time to tutor Doug, but I couldn't help wanting to say yes, to be a part of things again.

"Wait, who'd you have for precal?" Doug said, suddenly all interested. "Please say Zorba the Greek."

"Mr. Yannakopoulos?" I ventured, not sure what he was talking about.

"Zorba the Greek!" Doug cried. "Score!"

"That's what they all call Mr. Yannakopoulos," Becca explained.

"Oh," I said, feeling incredibly out of it again.

"You still have the tests?" Doug asked. He didn't wait for me to reply. "Well-known fact: the Greek only changes one or two questions from year to year."

I waited for Becca to speak up. To say something like, "I said she can tutor you, jerk, not help you cheat." But she didn't say anything, and in case we didn't get it the first time, Doug offered again, "If I fail, I'm off the team."

I never agreed to help "tutor" Doug. He just assumed it was a given. I guess he was used to getting whatever he wanted. We got out of the car and Doug reached for Becca's hand. "Your friend is so awesome," he told her.

I knew this had nothing to do with me being awesome. It only had to do with me having the tests. Suddenly, being in the car, going out with them for lunch, feeling part of things didn't matter. There was no way I could give Doug one of my tests. That was cheating.

When we walked into school, we ran into Tracy coming out of the cafeteria. "Where were you guys?" she said.

"We went out to lunch," Becca said. "Sorry, I didn't see you anywhere before we left."

Tracy looked at me like she couldn't believe I'd been invited. "You all went?"

"Yeah," Becca said.

"Oh," Tracy answered, sounding surprised.

When I headed off to class, Becca called out, "See you later."

"Later," Doug added, and the twins even waved. I would say I walked away, but suddenly it was more like floating and I had forgotten all about the test. All I could think about was how I'd gone to lunch instead of Tracy.

But that didn't mean the test stayed out of my mind altogether. Pretty soon I was back thinking about it again. For the rest of the day I kept thinking about what I would say to Becca when I saw her again. I had decided that honesty was the best policy. I would just say that I didn't feel right about giving

Doug the test, that then he wouldn't be learning anything. If she really wanted, maybe I could somehow find time to tutor him during a free period.

I finally saw her after last period at our lockers. I took a deep breath, ready to launch into my explanation, but before I could say anything, she said, "I'm sorry about that, earlier in the car with Doug. The calc test thing . . ."

"No big deal," I said, totally relieved that she'd finally come to her senses and I wouldn't have to give her my whole lame speech about him not learning anything.

Becca pulled her jacket out of her locker. "You wouldn't mind, though, would you?" she asked. "Just giving him the test?"

I paused, my tongue suddenly on strike. Then I managed, "That doesn't really seem fair."

Becca put on her jacket and turned to me. "But how are you supposed to know Mr. Yannakopoulos gives the same tests? It's his fault if he doesn't change them."

I tried to remember everything I had planned to say, but the only thing that came out of my mouth was, "Well . . ."

"Come on, Francie," Becca pleaded. "If you don't give it to him, I'll look like a total loser and I don't want to ruin this. You know how long I've been in love with him."

I knew I should have said no, but all I could think about was back in the car when we were all singing that song—how it felt to be a part of things. And how Becca had introduced me as her good friend. And how Tracy had looked when she'd found out I had gone with them to lunch. "Yeah, okay," I said. What was one test?

On the walk home I came across a gum wrapper (gross, left it there) and a penny (picked it up, boring, but at least good luck). Not a banner day all around. I couldn't believe I had said I'd give Doug the test. What if Mr. Yannakopoulos found out? I could lie to Becca and say I'd checked for my old tests and actually my dad had raided my room on a junk-purging spree and had thrown them all out. Or that Bandit had mistaken them for chew toys. But she'd never believe me, and it would be obvious I was lying. She'd end up thinking I was a total loser, and then I'd eat lunch alone every day, not just on Monday, Wednesday, and Friday.

During our lesson my mind was still on the test and I was totally distracted. Rob asked me to go first, and I went off course.

"Stop," he said after I'd jumped a wrong fence. He shook his head. "Two days left and you're going off course. Come on, Francie, you should know better."

"I'm sorry," I told him.

"Don't be sorry. Just get it right. Maybe watching a few more will help."

He told Tara to go, and then I had to sit through everybody else's rides before he gave me another chance.

"Guess I know not to go off course if I can help it," Colby said to me afterward when I was sweeping the aisle. "You should add 'never go off course' to the rules."

I had the impulse to throw the broom across the aisle and pretend I wasn't working, but I decided there was no point. So he knew I was a groom? I didn't really think I had a chance with him anyway. And if it mattered to him that I was a groom, then I wouldn't like him. Or at least that's what I told myself.

When I got home that night, I looked through my old class notes and tests. I had them all organized in file folders and labeled, so it was easy to find the test that Doug wanted. I had gotten only one answer wrong, for a 98. Even now, seeing the grade filled me with pride. As I looked at the test, I wondered if Doug could be wrong: maybe Mr. Yannakopoulos didn't recycle his tests. Or maybe one or two questions would be the same, but not the whole test. I took out a Magic Marker and blacked out my name. Then I stuffed the test in my book bag.

Chapter Seven

The morning of the regionals, the hotel wake-up call rang at four o'clock. I was already wide awake and doing the dream. It wasn't a real dream, because I wasn't asleep. It was more like a daydream. I always did the same one, and if I did it with people around or if I was in class and someone interrupted me, I had to start over from the beginning. It had to be the whole thing, even though each time it was exactly the same. I guess maybe it was like the visualization Katie said she did with the sports shrink.

It started just before I headed into the ring, when Rob told me to "nail it." I nodded and cantered off like I knew I was going to put in the ride of my life. I rode the course flawlessly. The crowd got quieter with each jump, and Rob locked his eyes on me. When I jumped the last fence, Rob whooped and clapped. As I was leaving the ring, he said, "Nailed it." He was grinning at me.

After the first round in a final, there's usually a second round and then a test of the top few riders. In the test the judges ask the riders to perform special moves, like a halt, or trotting a jump, which is harder than you'd think. Sometimes the judges even ask verbal questions about horse care, to see if riders know how to take care of their own horse, which most don't because they figure that's the groom's job. In my dream I nailed the second round. I went back in first place for the test and all Rob's other girls had messed up, even Tara. I was it. Rob's only shot. I rode the test and I nailed it again. In my dream I don't feel nervous at all; I'm all confidence, just like Tara. The last jump was a hand gallop, which some riders never do. They're too scared to risk it and never really gallop. But I went for it, top speed, finding the perfect distance. When I was riding my closing circle, Rob said to the trainer next to him, "That's it; I just won." Of course, if it were real life, I wouldn't have heard him say that part, but since it was my dream, I got to.

In the winner's circle, I said to Rob, "You didn't think I could do it, did you?" He didn't say anything back but just smiled and the cameras flashed. The photo would run in the next issue of the *Chronicle*. "*Francie Martinez brings Rob Renaud another Maclay win.*"

This time the wake-up call interrupted the dream right before I went back for the test. Dad rolled over in the bed next to mine. I headed into the bathroom, ran the water full blast, and, thanks to my nerves, threw up what was left of last night's pizza into the toilet. So much for being all confidence.

We pulled into the show grounds at four-thirty. The horses were stabled in a tent—the kind people like Katie's parents put up for parties or weddings, only bigger. The tent was divided into aisles, twelve stalls to an aisle. Each stable had its own aisle. We had spent the day before setting up a makeshift tack room and decorating it elaborately with a hunting motif—hanging hunting prints of foxes and hounds, a dark-framed wooden mirror, and an old hunting horn on the walls. Each barn displayed a banner with the farm name. Some also hung ribbons and horse blankets that their riders had won at other shows throughout the year. But Rob didn't have to show off like that to attract new riders—everyone knew how much his kids won.

The tent was soon busy even though it wasn't yet light out. Not busy with the riders, though, because most wouldn't show up until six-thirty. Dad handed me a pitchfork and I grabbed a wheelbarrow. I passed Stretch's stall on the way to Finch's. Camillo was mucking it out and had already put the magnetic blanket on Stretch. They cost a few thousand dollars and were supposed to stimulate the circulation in his muscles so he wouldn't be stiff. Katie's father also paid for Stretch to have weekly treatments with a chiropractor and a masseuse. The treatments did seem to help, but at the same time it all seemed a little ridiculous. Sometimes I wished I had Stretch's life. In the next stall, Randy, a professional braider with bundles of yarn looped through her belt, hunched on a stepladder over Finch's neck. The horses' manes and tails had to be braided for every competition—a complete makeover.

When I finished cleaning Finch's stall, I moved on to Tobey's. He was standing with his head hanging low. He perked up when he saw me and nickered softly.

"Good morning," I said, stepping into his stall. Before I started cleaning, I leaned close to him and mumbled into his neck, "Today's the big day, Tobe. We've made it through every year before, and we can't not make it in our last year. Okay?"

He flicked his ears back and forth as I talked like he understood every word. All I cared about right then was making it through. I didn't have to win. I didn't have to be amazing. I just had to get my last shot at the Garden.

"Okay," I answered for him.

After I finished Tobey's stall, I braided his mane and tail. We couldn't afford Randy's rates, and over the years I'd gotten pretty good at it. Sometimes I even braided other people's horses to make some extra cash for entry fees. Next I emptied and refilled Tobey's water buckets, took off his leg bandages, and brushed him.

"Francie," Dad called from down the aisle. "Ginger's got a stain that needs work."

"Be right there."

Yes, she did. A whopper of a manure stain on her right flank. Manure stains were the bane of my existence. (I'd once heard Mr. Roth use this expression and I kind of liked it.) Luckily Ginger was chestnut, not white like Stretch, so the stain would be easier to get out. Stretch and manure stains were a whole other story involving lots of hot water, whitening shampoo, and sometimes, when nothing else would work, even bleach. I grabbed a rag and spot cleaner from the grooming box and was in her stall furiously trying to rub it off when Colby walked in.

"I can do that," he said, reaching out for the rag.

I hesitated. I had assumed he'd figured out that I was a groom from seeing me at the barn the last few days, and as much as I hated manure stains, it was my job. Only now I wasn't so sure he knew I was a groom. Before I could speak, Dad poked his head into the stall. "What's up?" he asked. "Francie, do you need help?"

"No," I said. "I'm fine."

Dad eyed me once more before retreating and Colby reached for the rag again. "Let me do it."

"It's my job," I answered, now annoyed by the whole situation even though I'd kind of brought it on myself.

74

"I don't mind," he said.

I stopped rubbing and stared at Colby. "No, I don't think you understand. If I don't do this, then I don't get to ride. Okay?" Why was I flipping out when I was the one who'd lied in the first place? I just wished that things could be normal between us and that I didn't have to explain about who I was. I wished *I* could be normal.

"I'm sorry I even said anything," Colby muttered, and walked out of the stall.

I sighed and turned my attention back to the stain. First Becca, Doug, and the test and now this . . . not what I needed right now. Becca had been so happy when I'd given Doug the test Friday morning. So had Doug. "I owe you," he'd said. "When we go out for lunch today, I'm buying."

"I can't," I told him. "I have fifth-period lunch on Fridays."

"So skip fifth period," he said, like it was nothing.

"I can't." I knew lots of kids skipped classes, but I had never. The thought of skipping was completely out of the question.

"Then next week, okay?" As he and Becca walked away, she mouthed, "Thank you."

So I had made Becca and Doug happy, but I was living in fear. For the rest of the day on Friday all I could think was, what if Mr. Yannakopoulos found out? Wouldn't he get suspicious when Doug went from failing to doing well? Doug wouldn't be so stupid as to get every answer right, would he? He'd have to be smart enough to know to get some wrong on purpose. Why would Mr. Yannakopoulos suspect me, anyway? Doug and I weren't friends. But what if Mr. Yannakopoulos questioned Doug? I'd blacked out my name from the test in case he somehow got ahold of it, but what if Doug caved and told him it was mine? I could already see Mr. Yan-nakopoulos's confused and disappointed expression. I had been one of his best students.

When I finally rubbed the stain off Ginger, I changed into my show clothes, including my new jacket, which fit perfectly. Other trainers let their riders wear pin-striped or colored shirts and green or brown jackets, but Rob had a standard dress code: navy jacket, white shirt. He also required that each of us be in our show clothes for the course walk, no matter if we went first or one hundred and first in the order. The only thing we could wear other than our show clothes was our West Hills jacket over our show jacket, which I didn't mind. When other riders looked at me, I could feel them noticing my jacket and thinking, *She rides with Rob Renaud.*

Katie was fixing her hair up in her helmet in the tack room when I came in to pull on my boots, which I'd polished to a shining black the night before using the hotel courtesy shoe shiner. I was relieved to see Colby was nowhere in sight. I needed to concentrate on riding now—I couldn't be thinking of Doug and the test or Colby.

"Hey," Katie said. "When do you go?"

The order was posted that morning and I drew twenty-second. Twenty-second wouldn't be bad except that Tara went nineteenth. It was my curse. I always ended up going within five riders of Tara, which meant Rob was busy with her and I was stuck with Susie. Since Susie used to be an equitation rider like us, she knew what it was like to do the finals, but she still wasn't Rob. She wasn't why everyone came to West Hills.

"How about you?" I asked Katie.

"Fifty-fourth."

"That's good."

"I hate my hair," Katie groaned, tearing off her helmet and

pulling the hairnet from her head. We all wore hairnets under our helmets, which in the real world is completely gross, but in the riding world is completely normal. She stretched the hairnet out on her fingertips like she was playing cat's cradle. "Another hole. This is my third hairnet this morning. Do you think that could be bad luck or something?"

Before I could answer, Tara strutted in. She leaned in front of Katie to check herself in the mirror. Her hair was perfect. She wasn't beautiful, though, at least not in a model kind of way. But she was the type of pretty that came from being tall and skinny and from knowing she was the best.

"This is it," Tara said. "Last year for all of us . . . our last shot at the Garden. Who's gonna make it?"

"We all are," Katie replied, even though in three tries she'd never made it through.

"Everyone doesn't always make it," Tara scolded, grabbing her West Hills jacket from the back of a nearby chair. "You of all people should know that, Katie."

Tara turned and headed to the ring. In her wake, Katie huffed, "Maybe she'll be the one who won't make it."

But it wasn't even worth hoping—there was no way Tara would choke.

Gwenn and her mother trailed into the tack room with Susie. Tears streamed down Gwenn's face even though the class hadn't begun. Thankfully, Rob wasn't around to see it. Gwenn's mother stood behind her and draped her arms over her shoulders. I hadn't thought it was physically possible for anyone to be more nervous than me, but clearly Gwenn was. She shouldn't have been nervous, though. It didn't matter if she made it through. Not like it mattered for me. At only thirteen, Gwenn had plenty of chances left. This was my last shot.

"Rob's at the ring," Susie said. "The course is posted. You

girls better head up. I'll be there in a minute. Katie, you do okay with the Ace bandage?"

"Yeah," Katie said.

Katie was fairly well endowed, which might have been a good thing when it came to boys but wasn't when it came to riding. Rob had made Susie tell Katie to Ace-bandage down her boobs so they wouldn't bounce when she rode.

"You're lucky you're flat," Katie said as we headed out of the tent and up toward the ring. "I can barely breathe in this thing."

We passed the schooling area, with riders already practicing and trainers yelling. We passed grooms holding saddled horses, parents with steaming coffee cups, and yippy Jack Russell terriers straining on leather leashes.

"I hope we both make it," Katie said.

"Me too," I agreed.

Rob was at the in gate, dressed in jeans and a white button-down shirt. "Learn the course, girls," he said.

Katie and I gazed over other riders' heads at the laminated course posted next to the in gate. More and more riders converged at the in gate and pushed their way to the front, blocking our view. I spotted Colby, but I quickly looked away and pretended I hadn't seen him.

Finally the announcer's voice boomed out over the PA system, "The course is open to walk," and all the riders and trainers flooded into the ring. Rob strode ahead with Susie second and all of us behind.

The course was an array of colored rails, rolltop boxes with a carpet of fake grass on them, and brush boxes filled with pine branches. It looked like something out of a video game, only you had to navigate it for real. We walked the course to determine how many strides to do in the lines—four human strides equal a horse stride—and to plan our approaches to the jumps. Rob explained how to ride every jump, and it differed for each of us, depending on our horses' strides or tendency to drift right or left. As we walked, I could feel other riders looking at us because we rode with Rob. I loved how it felt to be one of Rob's students. Tara and Katie probably took it for granted now, but I never would.

After we'd walked the whole course, Rob stopped in the middle of the ring. We circled him with Tara glued to his side, as she'd been for the whole course walk.

"Any questions, girls?" Rob asked.

Colby cleared his throat.

"Any questions, girls *and* boy," Rob amended, cracking a smile.

No takers.

"Good. Then you're all gonna nail it." He slung an arm around Tara. "Right?" he asked, and I wished more than anything that his arm was around me instead.

She looked him dead in the eye. "Right."

"Okay, let's do it. Tara goes first out of all of us, so she'll watch the first few and then get on. The rest of you watch Tara to see how it's done and be up to the schooling area fifteen trips before you go."

I turned away. Rob had forgotten me. I went right after Tara. I couldn't bring myself to remind him. I didn't say anything—I shouldn't have had to—but Susie did: "Francie goes early too."

Rob glanced at me like he was noticing a sweater in his closet that he'd forgotten he even had and never really wanted to wear again. I wished Susie hadn't said anything—it only made it more painfully clear how much of a nothing I was to him. "Right. So watch a few and then get on too."

The stands were pretty much empty; nobody really came to watch except parents of the riders. I sat with Katie, her parents, and her younger brother, Brian. Brian was stuffing his face with a Boston crème doughnut while furiously pounding on his Game Boy. My stomach was already a mess, and the sight of the white crème caught in Brian's braces tossed the burn of my wake-up vomit back into my throat. I looked out at the ring and went over the course in my head, trying to push Rob from my thoughts.

"How's the course look?" Katie's father asked. Mr. Whitt was tall and thin with dark, slicked-back hair that he must have dyed, because it didn't have a touch of gray in it. He wore jeans that looked like they'd been ironed and a blue button-down shirt.

"I don't know. Okay, I guess," Katie mumbled.

"Okay? This is your year, Kate," Mr. Whitt said.

Katie shrugged as her mother shot Mr. Whitt a look that screamed, "Lay off!" Even though she didn't work, Mrs. Whitt was always dressed like she was going to an office—long skirts and blouses or pantsuits. Sometimes when I looked at mothers like Katie's or Gwenn's, I couldn't help but wonder what my mother was like. Was she one of those soccer moms in jeans and sweaters? Or did she dress more like Mrs. Whitt? Whenever I started wondering about her, though, I always tried to tell myself not to bother. Especially now, when I needed to concentrate.

"You'll do great, Katie," Mrs. Whitt encouraged. "I know you will."

When Kelsey Larson entered the ring, the whole stadium

quieted. Usually this only happened for the best riders, but it also happened for the first rider. Going first was probably even worse than going after Tara, although I wasn't sure *anything* could be worse than going after Tara. But going first meant you didn't know how the course rode, and the judges usually started out scoring low.

Kelsey turned in a decent trip, no major mistakes, but it would take more riders to go to tell how she'd stack up—whether or not she'd get through. I watched three more riders, getting more and more nervous, before I decided I couldn't take sitting still any longer and headed back to the barn. Out of habit I kept an eye out for any finds on the way, but in general, shows were a bad place to look. For one thing, people at shows hardly ever littered. And if they did drop anything, it was usually nothing worth keeping—an order-of-go sheet, a braiding list, a receipt for a feed order. Those things I could easily decipher—I liked finds with more uncertainty and mystery to them.

At the barn, I took my time brushing Tobey and tacking him up. Doing something made me feel a little bit better. I led Tobey out of the aisle, buttoned my new coat, and straightened my number on my back. Then I asked Dad for a leg up. I was so used to seeing him give other girls legs up that it always felt strange for him to give me one. He wiped Tobey's mouth and my boots with a rag and then placed a steady hand on my knee. "Good luck out there. Have fun."

As I rode up to the schooling area, I prayed this time would be different. That somehow Rob would fuss over me like he did over Tara. That he'd school us both, finish Tara, and then shuttle her up to the ring with Susie instead of going up with Tara and leaving me behind with Susie.

Tara was already jumping. "One more time at this height, Tara, then we'll go up," Rob called to her from his position with Susie next to the jump. "Keep it even. Keep your pace."

Tara cantered the jump perfectly and Rob raised it two holes.

The in-gate announcer's voice charged out over a loud-speaker into the schooling area: "Carla on deck, Angela in one, Tara in two, Jessica in three, Will in four, Francie in five."

Rob pointed to a lower jump across from him. "Get to it, Francie. Canter the vertical."

I cantered the vertical, hoping Rob was watching me. But Tara jumped his fence and he said, "Good, Tara, just like that."

Susie's voice followed. "Again, Francie. A little more pace to it."

"Once more, Tara," Rob said, and I found myself sneaking looks at Tara instead of concentrating on my jump. I knew I needed to focus on myself, but I couldn't help thinking how if I rode like her, Rob would be paying attention to me too.

"You're on it," he praised Tara. "Let's do it."

Rob and Tara headed out of the schooling ring. I knew he'd forgotten me again. Then he stopped abruptly and swiveled back to Susie and me. "Have her canter the vertical a few more times and then the oxer," he told Susie. "Come on up when you're ready."

I watched Tara and Rob walk out of the schooling ring. Rob was leaning close to her, gesturing. A part of me was hurting so badly from seeing them, but I reminded myself I didn't have time to hurt. Not if I wanted to make it to the Garden. *Concentrate*, I told myself. *Get with it.*

"Okay, Francie, the vertical again," Susie called.

I cantered to the vertical. I saw a long spot, leaned for it, and ended up chipping in. So much for concentrating. This was exactly the confidence-shattering jump I didn't want to have before going into the ring.

Rob would have killed me if he'd seen it, but Susie didn't make a big deal about it. She seemed to know it would only make me more frazzled. "Try it again," she said.

Somehow I managed to pull myself together and find a better distance this time. I finished warming up with Susie, and we walked up to the in gate just as Tara was jumping the last line. I hoped that somehow she had made a mistake, but as she finished, everyone started clapping. Rob clapped so hard his hands must have been stinging.

Tara rode her finishing circle and the stadium sprang back to life. People trickled out of the stands to get a cup of coffee or a bacon-and-egg sandwich. Dawn Longren came down from the stands and said to Rob, "Nice ride." She trained Karen Bay, who besides Tara was the favored rider to win this year. A few years ago Karen had come to the farm and taken a lesson with Rob, but she'd decided to ride with Dawn instead. I was pretty sure it killed Rob that Karen chose to ride with Dawn; not only was Karen good, but her family also had a ton of money—her father was some potato chip tycoon.

Dawn's politeness was just an act. As much as the trainers pretended to be friendly, they were just as competitive as us.

"Should do it, shouldn't it?" Rob said.

Rob was so busy gloating over Tara's ride that I was sure he'd forgotten I was on deck. Susie started going over the course with me. I tried to concentrate on what she was saying, but I kept being distracted by Rob gushing to Susie, "Tara was beautiful . . . beautiful."

"Francie schooled well," Susie said, which was nice since it was a total lie—we both knew my warm-up had been awful.

"You ready, Francie?" Rob asked, finally acknowledging me.

I barely nodded.

"Don't bother coming out of that ring if you make a mistake," he warned.

I swallowed and legged Tobey forward. *Concentrate,* I told myself. *Forget about Tara.* But all I kept hearing was Rob's voice. *Beautiful.*

I made it halfway around the course without a mistake. I came out of the corner to the last line and saw a long distance, maybe too long. If I pushed for the long one and ended up chipping in, like I had in the schooling area, it would flat-out kill our chances of making the Garden.

Instead I pulled Tobey together and fit in the extra stride. It wasn't seamless or as smooth as it could have been, but the bottom line was it worked. We finished the course with just the one tight distance.

Rob clapped and gave a few small whoops—nothing compared to what he'd done for Tara. But as much as I craved his praise, I knew I didn't deserve it, not with the round I'd had.

I came out of the ring, gasping for air like I'd just swum the length of a pool underwater. "You're in," Susie said to me. "Don't you think, Rob?"

I looked at him, hopeful.

"We'll see," was all he said.

Chapter Eight

Dad wasn't at the in gate when I came out of the ring, but I knew he had watched me. Somehow he always found a way to watch. Pablo or Camillo was usually happy to cover for him, since he always helped them out when they needed him.

"Good ride," he said when I trailed back to the barn area.

After the lukewarm response from Rob, I was glad to see Dad's face. At least someone cared about how I'd done.

"I almost choked," I said.

"Well, there was that," Dad teased.

"Did it look bad?"

"Horrible," Dad kidded. He always tried to keep it light by joking. I guess he knew I put enough pressure on myself and didn't need any more. But underneath I knew he wanted me to do well.

"Dad—" I said.

"You were great. You'll make it—relax."

"I don't know," I said.

"Well, I *do* know."

I slid off Tobey, still jittery from my round. One minute to decide everything. One minute to decide if I earned my last shot at the Garden. And then Rob had to go on about Tara's *beautiful* round right before I went in the ring, which only made things worse.

I put Tobey away in his stall but didn't take out his braids because we still had to ride in the flat phase. I grabbed the hose to top off water buckets, but Dad said, "Go on up and watch. We're all set here."

"You sure? I don't have to—"

"Go," Dad said. "We'll need you later. Katie and Gwenn ride at about the same time."

I headed up to the ring and found Katie in the stands next to Colby. After our exchange that morning I didn't really want to sit with him, but I had no choice. Katie had seen me, so I couldn't just go sit somewhere else.

"You were great," Katie said.

"Hardly."

"It'll get you through," Colby added.

"How about you?" I asked him, trying to reform and be polite. I had been such a jerk earlier about the stupid manure stain, of all things. I guess they really were the bane of my existence, in more ways than one. "Did you go yet?"

"He was so good," Katie answered for him.

"I was okay," he said.

"No, you weren't. You were really good."

I'd ridden in a couple of lessons with Colby that week and he *was* good. He had a natural style and feel—something you couldn't teach someone—they either had it like Colby or didn't like Katie.

"How've the rounds been in general?" I asked.

"Pretty good," Katie said. "I think Kelsey's trip is still

holding up. Katrina van Amsterdam was good. Oh, Anna Silver was a disaster—she did three in the two stride."

Katie and I knew most of the riders, since they were from the region we showed in all year. Even if we didn't know them to say hello or good luck to, we knew who they rode with, where they were from, how they'd done at the finals last year, and, most important, whether we thought we could beat them.

Katie turned to where her father sat behind us keeping score on a legal pad. "Dad, who else was good?" she asked.

He scanned his list. "Kim Greene, Alison Morris."

We watched a few other riders go, none great, and then Colby stood up to get something to eat. "Want anything?" he asked.

"I'd love a coffee with lots of milk and sugar," Katie said, digging into her pocket and extracting a twenty. Her father caught her eye and she added, "Skim milk and Equal if they have it."

"Francie?" Colby asked.

"I can't eat anything when I'm riding," I said.

"Last time I checked, you're not riding right now," he quipped.

I rolled my eyes. "I'm sorry, but I get too nervous."

"You get that nervous?"

"Oh my God, she gets totally nervous," Katie said.

"You're one to talk, Miss Hyperventilation," I said. When Katie got really worked up, she started breathing so fast she came close to making herself pass out.

"Why do you get so nervous?" Colby asked.

"I just don't want to mess up," I said.

"Now there's a positive attitude if I've ever heard one,"

Colby said in the sarcastic tone I'd noticed he was very good at.

"What do you mean?" I asked.

"I mean, if you're so worried about messing up, you probably will. Ever heard of a self-fulfilling prophecy?"

"Thanks for the Psych 101," I said.

When Colby was halfway down the aisle and out of earshot, Katie leaned close so her father couldn't hear. "So I've decided I totally have a thing for him."

"For Colby? He's a total pain in the ass with all his questions and snide comments." I didn't really think he was a pain in the ass. In fact, the more time I spent with him, the more I liked him. He was sort of like a new song on the radio—the first few times you heard it, you weren't sure about it, but then pretty soon you wanted to buy it so you could put it on continuous replay. But I wasn't about to admit any of these feelings to Katie.

"I think his questions are cute, plus don't you think he's totally hot?" she said. "He could make me forget all about you-know-who."

You-know-who was this guy, Mike, who worked on the jump crew. He and Katie'd had a thing all last summer until Mr. Whitt paid him to break up with her. Apparently a college dropout who was setting jumps wasn't his idea of the perfect boyfriend for his daughter. To Mike it wasn't a big deal, since he was a guy in a sea full of girls, but it had pretty much devastated Katie. She still hadn't quite gotten over the fact that he would choose a few hundred bucks over her, and she had made me promise never to utter his name again.

"Do you think I have a chance?" Katie asked. "I mean, have you heard him talk about having a girlfriend back home or anything?"

"Not that I know of."

"Good," Katie said.

Great—it was definite—Katie liked Colby too. How could I ever compete with her? For one thing, she was much more comfortable and experienced around guys than me. For another, she wasn't a groom.

After the twenty-fifth rider, the judges broke to announce the standby list and a man in a tractor smoothed the footing between the jumps. Colby had returned with two coffees, a bagel, and a hot chocolate for me that I hadn't asked for. "I wasn't sure if drinking was off-limits too," he said as he handed it to me. It seemed like he was still trying to make up for earlier that morning, but I was pretty sure I was the one who needed to make amends.

"Thanks," I said.

I spotted Rob at the in gate with his order-of-go sheet out. Sometimes when I looked at him, I still had to remind myself that I rode with him. That I was one of the girls at West Hills. He passed the list to Susie, who stood poised with a pen. In the stands around us, parents took out pens too, including Tara's father a few rows back. He was bald and had a big red nose. I'd heard someone say it was red because he drank too much. He delivered appliances for a living. Katie's father won at everything and so wanted his daughter to win too. I had the feeling that with Mr. Barnes, it was the fact that he'd never won at anything that made him so hungry for Tara to win. Tara's mother—a large, squat woman, who made me wonder where Tara's long legs came from and gave credit to Katie's bulimia theory—sat next to him, arms crossed.

"And after twenty-five riders have gone, we have a preliminary standby list for the flat phase," the announcer called.

I held my breath. My stomach churned like I was about to

ride all over again. Only now it was different because there was nothing I could do anymore—my fate was already decided. It was kind of like waiting for a test to be passed back at school—not that I wanted to think much about tests.

Quiet blanketed the stadium as all the riders, trainers, and parents waited breathlessly. The announcer ran down the numbers of the riders in a bland tone devoid of any emotion. I knew my number and I knew Tara's, which was the first called. I closed my eyes. After Tara's number, there was one, two, three numbers; I counted each number, four, five. I opened my eyes. I was sixth. There were twenty-five more riders left to go and a few would slide in front of me, if not in front of Tara. Then the judges would call back twenty for the flat phase. Eventually they'd select twelve for the Garden, probably four to test for the top ribbons. I only had six spots leeway, which wasn't much.

"Francie, you're sixth," Katie said.

"I know."

"Were you in there?" she asked Colby, as if she hadn't memorized his number too.

"Eighth."

"That's awesome."

"Who's on top?" Colby asked.

At exactly the same time, Katie and I answered, "Tara."

"You ready, Katie?" Rob asked as I quickly wiped off Katie's boots and Camillo slapped oil on Stretch's hooves to make them shine. The last rider had already left the ring; the judges were waiting on Katie. She'd been late coming to the in gate because she'd kept missing distances in the schooling area. Now she looked sickly pale and like she might start hyperventilating.

Katie didn't acknowledge Rob but just pressed Stretch forward.

"Good luck," I called out, but I wasn't sure if she even heard me.

Mr. Whitt's voice followed: "Come on, Kate!"

Katie was halfway through her course and doing fine when Colby joined me leaning over the railing to the ring. "How's she doing?"

"So far, so good," I said, holding up my crossed fingers.

Colby nodded to where Mr. Whitt was moving his weight from one leg to the other. "He's a little intense, huh?"

"A little?" I said.

"I guess I shouldn't talk. You haven't met my dad yet."

"He couldn't come this weekend?"

"Nope. Some boob conference. He'll be flying in for the USET, though, you can count on that."

Five more good fences and Katie would probably make it. Five more fences and Mr. Whitt wouldn't freak out at her. I saw Camillo watching too. He was no doubt praying just as hard as I was that Katie would keep it together, for her sake but also because he took care of Stretch and so he took pride in Stretch doing well. Katie found a steady distance to the next jump, which Stretch made look good, but as if she were trying to make up for it, she started speeding up, pushing Stretch too fast.

"Slow down!" Rob called out to her, sounding beyond angry.

At the next jump Katie caught what people call a flyer—a really long distance, which was usually my specialty. Some horses would have stopped, sending Katie straight over their head and onto the ground, or added a stride and chipped in like Tobey would have. But, of course, Stretch stretched. Still, it looked awkward.

"Goddamn it!" Rob said, but I knew he wasn't that upset for Katie, more because of the hell he would probably catch from her father.

Katie pulled herself together for the last few jumps, but the damage was already done. Rob still clapped loudly, trying to sway the judges into somehow overlooking that one jump. When Katie came out of the ring, her eyes were locked on Stretch's neck. She knew what was coming.

"How many times do I have to tell you not to make a move?" Rob asked. "Let the jump come to you."

"I thought I was under the pace," Katie said.

Rob shook his head. "Don't think out there." He pointed to Stretch. "Let *him* do the thinking."

Rob turned away and Katie moved Stretch out of the in gate. Camillo was waiting for her with a sugar cube for Stretch. Whenever Stretch came out of the ring, Camillo had a treat for him.

Gwenn had been schooling with Susie while Katie was on course and now she was waiting on deck. I moved away to help Dad shine her boots and put oil on Finch's hooves. I was just grabbing the can of hoof oil when I heard Mr. Whitt bark, "Don't feed him that! No wonder he wants to bolt by the end of the course. He knows he's going to get fed when he comes out. I can't believe this!"

I turned to see Camillo mumbling an apology, his eyes set on the ground. "Get Gwenn's boots," Dad said to me. He jogged over to where Mr. Whitt was staring at Camillo.

"He was just trying to reward the horse," Dad said.

"I don't care what he was trying to do," Mr. Whitt snapped. "He shouldn't be doing it."

"Dad, it was my fault Stretch was going fast," Katie tried. "Not Camillo's."

"Mr. Whitt, it won't happen again," Dad promised.

Sometimes I didn't know how he did it. I was sure that more than anything, Dad wanted to tell Mr. Whitt he was out of line and on top of that a bad father who was cruel to his daughter. But he wouldn't say any such thing. He'd smooth things over and calm Mr. Whitt down in the same way that he'd smile politely and act like he didn't care when without even so much as a thank-you, a rider handed him a horse that was still hot and blowing hard and that he'd have to spend an extra half hour cooling down.

"It better not, or else I want someone more competent taking care of the horse," Mr. Whitt said.

"It won't happen again," Dad repeated. "Right, Camillo?"

"Not ever," Camillo managed in his shaky English. "I want to take care for him. To me this horse means so much."

This seemed to be enough for Mr. Whitt to leave Camillo alone, but he wasn't done yet. He turned his disappointment toward Katie. "How could you do that?" he demanded as I shined Gwenn's boots.

"I thought I was going too slow," she explained again.

"How could you be so stupid? You'll never make it through with that round, never!" He shook his head and stalked away.

As Gwenn entered the ring, I went up to Katie. "Hey," I said gently.

She turned, tears streaming down her face. "Jerk," she choked out.

Katie cheered up somewhat when she was called back thirteenth for the flat phase. If she rode well enough, the judges might move her up and she would make the Garden. Tara still

held the lead. I stood eighth, Colby tenth. Gwenn was twentieth and had no prayer of making it.

Rob cautioned us to be conservative. "It's just walk, trot,
and canter in both directions. Maybe a lengthening of stride,
counter-canter, or halt depending on what the judges need to
see to make a decision. This isn't the time to go for brilliant at
the lengthening of stride at the trot, break into the canter, and
get tossed to the end of the pile." He wagged a finger at us. "I
know you don't think it can happen. But let me tell you, it's
happened. Solid and correct. That's the way."

We entered the ring and spread out along the rail. With the
jumps removed, the ring looked huge. The judges didn't ask
anything complex, which meant they decided quickly. They
lined us up and we stood for a few minutes that stretched out
endlessly. Other horses stood statue still while Tobey bobbed
his head and pawed the ground in impatience. I could tell he'd
reached his limit and just wanted to go home. To keep him
calm, I scratched his withers in front of the saddle until the announcer finally excused us and we shuttled out the in gate.

"Tara, don't go anywhere. Francie, Colby, you too, just in
case they test more than four," Rob instructed. "Gwenn,
Katie, you can head back to the barn."

I waited with Tara and Colby until the announcement came.
They were testing only the top four. Tara was testing, still hold-
ing first place. Colby and I'd eked in at eighth and eleventh.
Katie hadn't moved up—she wasn't going to the Garden.

"Tara, get ready," Rob called.

"I'm ready, Rob," she answered.

Rob looked at me, but probably just because I was next
to Tara, so I blocked his line of vision. Still, even the little
acknowledgment felt nice, like a small, warm ray of sunlight

after a week of cold rain. "Francie, you made it by the skin of your teeth," he said.

"I know."

I took a deep breath and then exhaled, letting go of all my tension. I had made it. That was the most important thing. I was going to the Garden.

Susie walked over. I leaned down from Tobey to hug her. "Good job, kiddo," she said.

"Want to head back to the barn?" Colby asked me.

"Sure," I said.

We walked side by side and didn't speak for a few minutes until Colby offered, "So we both made it."

"Yeah," I said, surprised by my own lack of excitement. Suddenly making it didn't seem like enough.

"You don't seem happy."

"I guess I just wish I was testing." I knew it wasn't right to feel disappointed in making it when Katie and Gwenn hadn't, but I couldn't help it. I wanted to be up there at the ring with Rob like Tara, getting ready to test.

"You're so hard on yourself," Colby said.

"How do you know?" I said. "You don't know anything about me." Even though he was probably right, I felt annoyed that he thought he could size me up so fast. He didn't know the first thing about my life. Of course that was in part because I hadn't told him. Part of me liked the feeling of being just like him, of being just a regular rider. I was always different from the other girls. I always had to go back to the barn after lessons and work. It was kind of nice to feel, if only for a few seconds, what it might be like to be one of them.

"You're right, I don't. But it doesn't seem like you want me to either."

95

"It's not that—" I started to say. Why did everything always come out wrong when I was around him? "It's just—"

I was planning to finally come clean right then and explain about my being a groom, but he jumped in. "I'm sorry if you're still upset about this morning. Why didn't you just tell me you were a working student?"

"I don't know," I said, still not managing to tell the truth. So now Colby thought I was a working student, which was still something entirely different from a groom.

Colby sighed. "It seems like one of us is always apologizing to the other. Maybe we should just agree to have an ongoing apology or something."

"Sounds good," I offered.

"So from here on out instead of saying hello when we see each other, we'll just say I'm sorry, okay?"

I smiled. "Okay."

"You mean, I'm sorry."

"Yeah, I'm sorry," I said, laughing.

At the barn I slid off Tobey. Colby dismounted from Ginger. Dad came to take Ginger from him, and Colby offered to bring her back to her stall.

"I got it," Dad said, and this time Colby didn't argue.

"I guess I'll see you later," he said to me.

I untacked Tobey. After I gave him a handful of carrots, I took him to the wash stall to sponge him down with warm water. The whole area smelled like menthol from the liniment Dad was using on Ginger. Dad put a wet hand on the side of my head, pulled me close, and kissed my forehead. Then he passed me the bucket and sponge. "You made it," he said.

"Dad," I moaned. "Gross."

"Oh, I know, a kiss from your father—gross!"

"No, you got me all wet," I said.

As Dad squeegeed the excess water off Ginger with a sweat scraper, I started sponging Tobey's neck. "How's Katie?" I asked.

Dad shook his head. "That man is unbelievable. I'd like to put *him* on a horse and see how he would do out there."

"I know, and what about Camillo?"

"Don't get me started," Dad said.

After I sponged Tobey off, I brought him back to his stall and cut the yarn from his braids with a seam ripper. I expected to see Katie at some point, but she wasn't around, which meant her dad was probably tearing into her somewhere.

The announcer's voice crackled over the loudspeaker into the tent, reporting the final results of the class. I hardly listened, because I knew how it would go and I didn't want to hear Tara's name in first place. When I heard it in second place, I was sure that they'd made some kind of mistake and that a correction would follow. But it didn't. Karen Bay had won. That would drive Rob crazy. I knew it wasn't nice of me to root against someone in the barn, but I was so glad Tara hadn't won.

As I finished with Tobey, I saw Dad pull the West Hills trailer up in front of the tent. Tara's parents and Rob came back from the ring with outraged expressions, mumbling something about Karen Bay having slept with one of the judges. I helped Dad, Camillo, and Pablo take down the stalls and load up all the equipment—tack trunks, water and grain buckets, wheelbarrows, saddles, and bridles. The whole time we lugged things out, Tara fumed in a director's chair in the tack room. Outside, Rob dragged on a cigarette and talked to his mother on his cell phone. "So don't go out for the mail, Ma," he said. "Not if you can't get enough air."

Rob's mother suffered from bad emphysema, which you'd think would be enough to make him quit smoking. She had been in and out of the hospital for the past few years. Rob kept saying she couldn't live alone anymore, but there was no way he was having her move in with him.

Camillo carried a forty-pound bag of shavings out on his shoulder like it weighed nothing and opened it onto the floor of the trailer. "You're going to the Garden!" he said.

"Yeah," I said, wishing I felt happier about it. Maybe Colby was right. Maybe I was too hard on myself. But, at the same time, I had to be. Things would never come easily for me. Not like they did for Tara or Katie.

As Camillo left to get another bag of shavings, I grabbed a pitchfork. I was spreading out the shavings when Mr. Whitt's Porsche Cayenne with the license plate WTT2 pulled up. WTT1 was a vintage Porsche that only made appearances when rain wasn't forecast for weeks. WTT3 was Katie's BMW. Mr. Whitt slid out and marched toward Rob.

"Yeah, Ma, I gotta go," he said.

I could see Mrs. Whitt in the front seat. The back windows were tinted, so I could only make out shapes that I assumed must be Katie and Brian.

"Thirteenth, Rob," Mr. Whitt said. "Thirteenth, not twelfth."

Rob threw his cigarette on the ground and stamped on it, grinding it with the heel of his paddock boot. "What can I say? She rode well. She deserved to be in there."

"I wanted the Garden this year. How do we get them to take thirteen, just one more?"

Rob shook his head.

"Don't tell me there isn't a way," Mr. Whitt said.

"There isn't."

"There's always a way, Rob. You know that as well as I do."

Rob pulled out his pack of Marlboros, fumbled for another. "We've still got the USET and the Medal Finals."

"See what you can do," Mr. Whitt said. "I'll make it worth somebody's while. And don't forget that bonus we talked about."

He got back in the car, and I watched Rob watch the car pull out.

Back in the tent Tara was still sulking in the tack room. I got out the stepladder and starting taking down the curtains while she sat there pouting. Colby came in as I was stretching to get to the top part of the West Hills banner that was just out of my reach. "Can I help?" he offered.

I should have just asked Camillo or Pancho for help, but I didn't want to offend Colby, especially after we seemed to be getting back on better terms. "Sure," I said, getting down off the stepladder.

He climbed onto the ladder and undid the banner. As he was bringing it down, he said to Tara, "You know, you could have gotten off your butt and helped." Colby started folding up the banner. "Just because she's a working student doesn't mean she should have to do everything."

There was this moment when everything stopped. I knew my lie was about to catch up to me and it was going to be ugly.

"Working student?" Tara looked from Colby to me. "Is that what you're calling it these days, Francie? Funny, I call it groom." Tara stood up. "Where's your father, anyway?" she said. "I need someone to pull off my boots." She looked around and called out, "Juan?" Then to Colby she said, "Francie's dad is the absolute best at pulling boots off."

I felt like I'd been kicked in the stomach. Maybe it served me right for not telling Colby on my own, but Tara didn't have to be so mean about it. I barely managed to say, "He's busy getting the trailer ready."

Tara clucked and said, "I guess I'll just have to try the bootjack, then."

She walked away, leaving me and Colby alone. I wasn't sure how I could make him understand about wanting to be like all the other riders, but I knew I had to come up with some sort of explanation.

"Colby—" I began.

Before I could say anything else, Rob walked up. "Colby, you ready?" he said. "We're leaving."

Apparently Colby was catching a ride back to the farm with Rob. I looked at Colby again, trying to say I was sorry with my eyes.

"Yeah," Colby said. "I'm ready."

Chapter Nine

At school on Monday, Becca took me aside before English. "Guess what?"

"What?" I asked.

"I just saw Doug. He said the test was exactly the same and he totally aced it!"

"Aced it? Like he got a hundred?" Even I hadn't gotten a hundred.

"No, he got a few wrong on purpose, but he probably got a B." From the way Becca said it, I had the feeling Doug hadn't seen many B's in his life. I was glad to know he was at least smart enough to have made sure to get a few questions wrong.

"That's great," I told Becca.

I looked into the classroom. Most of the other kids had taken their seats. Mrs. Hanson was writing on the board.

"Once Coach hears about how he did, he'll be totally set to play this weekend."

"That's great," I said again. Suddenly the only word I knew was *great*.

The bell rang. We walked in and sat down. Becca leaned

over to me and whispered, "Oh yeah, Doug asked me to invite you to the game on Saturday."

"He did?"

Becca nodded. "And the party afterward. Can you come?"

"I have a lesson and I have to work at the barn. . . ."

"What about the party?"

Becca hadn't asked me to a party in forever. I guess she'd given up hope of me ever going. Now she looked at me all excited, and I desperately wanted to say yes. We didn't have a show that weekend, so it was even possible. Even though I wanted to say yes, I held back. I couldn't imagine going to the party—how would I get there? Would I go with Becca and Doug? And after all, even if we didn't have a show, we *were* in the middle of boot camp. It was hardly the time to start going to parties.

"I probably can't," I told her.

"Why not?"

I started to give my excuses when Mrs. Hanson turned around to face the class or, really, me and Becca. "Girls, this isn't social hour," she said, and I dropped my eyes to my notebook.

The day after a show we always gave the horses a day off, so when I got home from school, I went straight to Katie's room, where a pity party was in session. Katie was lying on her bed with a tissue box at her side. She was wearing sweatpants, which for her is as bad as it gets.

"I can't believe I didn't make the Garden," she whined.

"You still have the USET and the Medal," I said, trying to cheer her up. She reached for a tissue. She wasn't even really crying, just sniffling, but the minute she so much as pressed the tissue to her nose, she crumpled it up and tossed it in the huge pile by the side of her bed. I didn't think I'd ever used as many tissues in my whole life history of being sick or sad.

"It's just that my dad is totally freaking out," she said. "You don't know what he's like. I mean you kind of do, but he's even worse than you think. All the time it's, 'Why can't you get it right?' and 'How can a daughter of mine be such a loser?'"

Katie didn't need to convince me. I had seen enough of her father to know how bad he was. One time a few years ago when she was called back on top in a class at a big horse show and blew the test, he screamed at her at the in gate for a full ten minutes in front of the whole horse show.

"I don't even care about the stupid Garden," Katie said. "I just wish I could ride for fun, you know? Like not even do the finals."

"Did you ever think of just telling him you wanted to quit?" I asked. "The power of no?" As I said it, I thought about Colby. I hadn't seen him since the regionals. I had no idea whether he was still pissed at me for lying to him or just thought I was really weird or pathetic.

"Quit?" Katie said. "Whitts don't quit. He actually says that. It's like his motto—Whitts don't quit! Whitts don't quit!"

I laughed.

"It's not funny," she said. "This is my life."

Tara knocked on the door and stuck her head in. "You're cordially invited to the fifteen-millionth annual West Hills Film Festival," she announced. "Rob said we all have to go."

"Great," Katie said. "Just what I need—reliving the regionals all over again. I hope he got the part on tape where my dad tells me I'm stupid."

Rob made us watch videos of our rounds throughout the year. Like Katie, I wasn't sure what was worse—making a mistake or seeing it over and over again with Rob telling you what you'd done wrong.

Katie and I followed Tara and her mother to Rob's house. Susie greeted us at the door. Even though she'd lived with Rob for a few years now, it was always kind of strange seeing her there. We went into the living room, where Gwenn, her mother, Rob, and Colby were already huddled around the wide-screen TV. Gwenn and her mother were squeezed into one armchair even though there were plenty of open seats. They had the same thin, mousy brown hair and pale skin. They might as well have been Siamese twins; I had yet to see Gwenn without her mother hanging all over her.

"I would die if that was my mother," Katie had said once when we saw Mrs. Curtis waiting outside the bathroom for Gwenn. "She doesn't give her a minute to herself. Look—it's killing her that she can't be in the bathroom with her. Someone better tell her to chill out or that girl's going to be permanently scarred for life, if she isn't already."

I had laughed at the time because it was pretty true, but it was different for me than for Katie. Katie had a mother, which meant she could joke about what a pain her mother could be. Even though a mother like Mrs. Curtis might be a little overbearing, at least she cared about her daughter. Something my mother had forgotten to do.

Katie and I sat down on the couch next to Tara. Everyone was watching Gwenn's trip from the regionals. Rob said, "See that?" and then rewound the tape to show Gwenn horrendously chip a jump once more.

"She didn't ride out enough in the corner and came in completely crooked to the line," he explained. "How are you going to meet the jump well if you come to it crooked? Steering,

Gwenn—what do I keep telling you about steering and looking at the middle of the jump?"

As Rob rattled on, Colby glanced over at us from his perch on a nearby ottoman. He held up a hand, fingers spread, a modified wave.

Katie whispered, "Oh my God, he's cute."

He was wearing baggy khakis and a T-shirt that just said COLLEGE. Katie looked away. Colby caught my eye again. "Sorry," he mouthed.

"No," I mouthed back. "*I'm* sorry."

Katie elbowed me. "What was that all about?"

Rob heard us whispering and stopped berating Gwenn for a second to turn and stare at us. "You girls like to participate here?" he snapped.

When he finished with Gwenn, it was Colby's turn, then Katie's, then mine, then Tara's. While he found plenty to criticize in Katie's, Colby's, and my trips, with Tara's, he just shook his head and said, "If anyone can explain to me why that didn't win, I'd love to hear it."

Rob finally clicked the TV off and we milled around, snacking on the carrots and celery and what tasted suspiciously like fat-free dill dip that Susie had put out on the coffee table.

"I think I've lost about five pounds since I've been here," Colby said, joining Katie and me and surveying the carrots and celery with apathy. "Are you sure this isn't fat camp instead of a training stable?"

"It's basically both," I said, crunching down on a carrot. Colby didn't seem mad, but I wished we had a few minutes alone so I could talk to him and try to explain why I had lied. It was impossible with everyone else around.

Colby shook his head. "I need some real food."

"I could hook you up," Katie offered.

"Really?"

"I've got a whole stash back in my room."

"It's true. She's got everything," I said, and then wished I hadn't. Why was I sending Colby off with Katie?

"Cool," Colby said.

"We can go now if you want," Katie told him. "Looks like the director's cut edition of the regionals is thankfully over."

Colby looked from Katie to me. "You coming, Francis?"

I was glad he'd asked, but I knew I couldn't go with them. I had to do my barn work. "I can't. I have to go back and help finish up at the barn."

"Come on," Colby cajoled. "It'll only be a few minutes."

"Really, I can't."

"Then we'll go with you—we'll help."

It was a nice offer but completely out of the question. Colby helping had already gotten me in too much trouble. Katie shook her head. "Rob doesn't like riders helping."

"Why not?"

"I don't know. It's just the way it is," Katie said.

"That's stupid," Colby proclaimed.

We all walked out together. When I headed to the barn, Colby still looked semi-reluctant. I desperately wanted to go with them or at least ask them to wait for me. But then Katie chirped at Colby, "Come on," and he said to me, "See you."

In the barn Camillo was grooming Stretch for what must have been the third time that day. Camillo had taken care of Stretch since he'd come to West Hills, and Stretch was his favorite horse. Since Camillo's family was back in Mexico, Stretch meant a lot to him. Even though he'd never sat on his back,

Stretch was his baby, and Camillo worked on him whenever he got a free moment, so Stretch's white coat gleamed as bright as a full moon against a dark sky.

I grabbed a pitchfork and was on my way to snag a wheelbarrow to pick out the stalls when he stopped me. "I already picked out," he said.

"You didn't have to do that." Picking out the stalls was always my job.

"I know. I wanted to. I fed too."

"So everything's done?" I asked.

"*Sí. Tu papá* go home already."

I thought about going after Colby and Katie, but I knew Dad would wonder where I was. So instead, Camillo and I walked home together. The air had cooled, and fall felt like it was here to stay. Even the leaves overhead were starting to change.

"Too cold," Camillo complained. "I hate the cold. In my country, always is warm."

"Do you miss things other than the weather?" I asked.

"Also I miss my family," he said.

"Do you have brothers and sisters?"

"Three little sisters. You want to see a photo?"

"Sure."

Camillo pulled out his wallet and took out a small, faded snapshot, worn on the edges. He moved a dirt-embedded fingernail over the photo. "This is María; she is the most old. This is Rosita and this is Carmen." He looked up at me with a huge grin—Carmen must be his favorite. "She is the most young. She has six—" Camillo paused again. "—eight years old. She has six when I leave my home."

Dad had left family behind in Mexico too. His mother and younger sister still lived in the same town that he'd been born in. His father had died when he was young. Dad wrote to his mother and sister all the time and sent them money whenever he could. He also had an older brother, who had come to the States before him and now lived in California. We'd seen him once in Florida when we were there for the winter circuit and he was just passing through. I was pretty young at the time, so I don't remember him too well. Dad had been back to Mexico to see his family twice since he left, but both times he'd said it would be easier if I didn't come. I think he didn't want me seeing how they lived there, but I was determined to go the next time. I'd grown up my whole life with only my father. It was always just the two of us, the two of us against the world. And even though we had all the other grooms, who were a certain kind of family too, I couldn't believe I had other real family— a grandmother and an aunt, not to mention some cousins— that I'd never met.

"It must be hard not seeing them," I said as Camillo slid the photo back in his wallet. "Can you go back and visit?"

"Maybe," he said. "One day I earn money and I bring them to America. I always tell them—America is the best. Here, you work a lot, you get everything. House, car, school for the childs."

Dad had thought about bringing his mother and sister here too. But his mother was pretty frail, and they were worried she wouldn't survive the trip. His sister had said she wouldn't go without her, which made sense.

We came out of the woods into the clearing in front of the cottage. Dad and the other grooms were already at the picnic table. In the good weather we would eat outside together. We would either barbecue or Dad would cook up a feast for everybody. Bandit was always underfoot too, waiting for the scraps that inevitably came his way.

"How were the videos?" Dad asked as I sat down next to him and picked up an ear of grilled fall corn off the plate in the middle of the table. There was also a plate of chicken.

"You know. Same as always. Tara won the Oscar and the rest of us lost out in the Best Supporting Actor/Actress category."

"But how was her acceptance speech?" Dad asked.

"Moving," I said.

"The horses okay? Finch?"

"All fine."

I had just bitten into the ear of corn when Katie and Colby pulled up in Katie's red BMW. She had sunglasses on and propped them onto her head as she put the car in park. Colby had his baseball hat on. He looked incredibly cute, and I felt a pang of jealousy that he was with Katie.

"My junk food wasn't enough for Colby," she said to me. "We're going out for dinner—wanna come?"

"I don't know," I said, looking at Dad. "Can I?" *Please say yes,* I thought. I couldn't stand the idea of them going out without me.

"We'll be back really soon," Katie told Dad. "And you know I'm a safe driver, right, Juan?"

"As long as she's better driving a car than she is riding a horse," Pablo mumbled so only we could hear. A few of the other grooms stifled chuckles.

I could tell Dad wasn't nuts about the whole idea, but he said, "Be back by eight—it's a school night." He reached into his back pocket, pulled out his wallet, and handed me a ten.

In the car I asked if we were going to Amelia's, the Italian place Katie and I usually went when we went out. Amelia's had yummy garlic bread and also a really good pasta prima-vera that was $7.99 and was big enough that I had some to bring home.

"I thought we'd try this new sushi place Susie was talking about," Katie said. "I'm sure it's not as good as in the city, but I'm having massive sushi withdrawal."

I had never had sushi before and the thought of eating raw fish grossed me out, but I certainly wasn't going to object, in case Colby liked it too.

"There must be really good sushi in L.A.," Katie added.

I got the feeling she was trying to impress Colby, but it didn't seem to be working. "I guess so," he just said.

The sushi place was a few towns over. Katie blasted the radio the entire way, so we hardly had a chance to talk. As the music blared, I thought of riding in the car with Doug, Becca, Peters, and Pepper. Katie was so different from them. For one thing, she drove a BMW, not a Chevy Nova. And we were going out for sushi—a far cry from KFC. In some ways I felt more comfortable in Doug's car going out for KFC. But at the same time I was better friends with Katie.

When we sat down at the booth in the restaurant, I scanned the menu. Katie was already oohing and aahing. "This looks so good," she said. "Yum, I love yellowtail." I was completely grossed out by all the strange stuff that was supposed to pass for food: seaweed salad, sea urchin, fatty tuna. Then I looked at the prices. They were outrageous. I thought of the ten Dad had given me and felt my body flush warm. It would never cover dinner. I had a few bucks of my own with me, but I would still have to order carefully. The good thing was I saw hardly anything I would eat. Katie and Colby ordered all this crazy sushi—eel, octopus, and giant clam. I settled on two rolls, a shrimp one that said the shrimp was cooked and a mixed vegetable roll.

"That's all you're getting?" Katie asked.

"I'm not that hungry," I lied. Actually, I was starving. It pained me to think about the normal food I'd left behind at the cookout.

"So," Colby said after the waitress had taken our order. "Tara's a piece of work, huh?"

"You're not kidding," Katie said. "She keeps going on and on about the regionals—*to me of all people*—about how the judges stunk and she should have won."

"Has she always been like that?" Colby asked.

"Ever since I've known her," Katie said.

Colby picked up the pot of steaming tea the waitress had left and poured us each a cup.

I thanked Colby for pouring the tea and then said, "Tara wasn't always so bad." It was hard to believe, but Tara and I had actually once been friends. She came to ride at the farm years before Katie did. Back then I wasn't taking lessons with Rob. Tara had been nicer to me. She'd even invited me to watch *National Velvet, International Velvet,* and my favorite horse movie, *Pharlap* (much better than *Seabiscuit*), with her in the camper. "It's like the better she got, the meaner she got," I told Katie and Colby. "Maybe it's just her way of staying mentally tough. Her parents are pretty hard on her."

Katie took a sip of her tea. "You're cutting her way too much slack." She glanced at Colby. "If you haven't already noticed, Francie's too nice to people."

"Being nice isn't a crime," Colby said, looking up and meeting my gaze.

"Thank you," I said.

"You always have to look out for number one," Katie replied. "That's what my dad says, anyway."

"Since when do you go around quoting your dad?"

Katie shrugged. "Maybe in this case he's right."

The waitress brought our sushi in a big wooden boat. I immediately took mine onto a separate plate. I didn't want my pieces even touching their giant clam and octopus. Katie ate hers with chopsticks. I hesitated, both because I wasn't sure I could handle chopsticks and because I wasn't sure I even wanted to eat mine. Even though the rolls were vegetables and cooked shrimp, they still smelled fishy. I eyed my chopsticks and was relieved when Colby picked up a piece of sushi with his fingers. I decided to go with the fingers too.

"What do you think?" Katie asked after I'd cautiously bitten into a piece.

"Oh, I've had sushi before," I said. Another total lie. In fact, it wasn't as bad as I had thought it would be. I even kind of liked the rice.

I was doing fine and feeling quite proud of myself when Colby had to go and offer me a piece of his.

"She won't eat it," Katie said.

"Maybe I will," I said. "What is it?"

"Eel."

"You don't even like olives," Katie pointed out. "And now you're going to eat eel? I don't think so."

I wasn't sure I could stomach it, but just to prove Katie wrong, I reached out, grabbed the piece of sushi, and popped it into my mouth. I hardly chewed but just swallowed. I wasn't sure it was going to go down. Then I wasn't sure it was going to stay down. Thankfully it did. I reached for my water to wash it down.

"I'm impressed," Katie said. "Okay, now try the giant clam."

I swore I could feel the eel twisting in my stomach. "No way."

I had pretty much lost my appetite and barely managed to

finish the rest of my sushi. When she was done, Katie stood up and grabbed her Kate Spade purse. "I have to go to the ladies' room," she said.

She eyed me like I was missing something crucial, and when I just said, "Okay," she finally left.

"I think you were supposed to go with her," Colby said. "You know, girls always go to the bathroom together."

"Oh," I said. Oops. I had missed the boat on that one. But I was glad to have a few moments alone with Colby. I could finally talk to him about what had happened at the regionals. I cupped my hands around my tea, which so far was my favorite part of the meal. "I'm sorry I didn't tell you the truth about Juan being my dad."

"Why didn't you?"

"I don't know. I guess I liked the idea of being just one of the other riders."

Colby made a face. "You are just one of the riders."

"No, I'm not."

"Did you think it would make me act differently to you or something?" he asked.

I looked down into my cup of tea. "I guess I wondered if it might."

"Well, I'm not like that," Colby said.

Katie came back from the bathroom, her lipstick refreshed and her hair brushed. Colby refilled our tea and we stayed a little while longer. When the waitress brought the check, Katie reached for it. "This one's on my dad," she said.

"No way," I said, pulling out the ten Dad had given me and my few rumpled ones. But Katie wouldn't take it.

"Absolutely not," she said, whipping out her American Express card. "He doesn't care. He doesn't even look at my statements. His accountant pays the bills."

"Thanks," I said.

"Yeah, thank you," Colby said.

Katie shrugged. "Don't thank me, thank Daddy War-bucks." She sipped at her tea. "So this weekend we should to-tally go out for dinner again. I mean, since we don't have a show. I heard about a good Thai place in Providence, or we could even drive into Boston."

"I'm actually going home for a few days," Colby said.

"Oh," Katie said, her excitement fading.

"I've gotta catch up on some schoolwork."

"When do you leave?"

"Tomorrow," Colby said. "I'll be back Sunday, though."

"Well, maybe we can go then," Katie suggested.

We all downed the rest of our tea and headed to the car. On the way out I saw a piece of paper in the parking lot. The paper looked thick, like it might even be a photograph. I had found photos before: a snapshot of a grinning baby with the words HENRY, SIX MONTHS written on the back and even a prom pic-ture, a girl in a poofy dress and a boy in a white tux. Even if it might be something as good as a photograph, I knew I should walk right past and not embarrass myself in front of Colby, but I couldn't resist picking it up and putting it in my pocket.

"People who litter suck," Colby said, looking at me all ap-provingly.

Katie laughed. "It's not about being a good citizen. Francie has this little obsession."

"It's not an obsession," I said.

"Fine, then what is it? You explain it."

I was very aware that Colby was looking at me, waiting. "It's just people throw away all this stuff and some of it's really interesting. I pick up things and sometimes I keep them."

"In a box in her room." Katie made a face like I'd just told Colby I believed in UFOs.

"Okay, so I'm weird," I said. I was sick of pretending to be somebody I wasn't. I was a groom, I'd never eaten sushi, and I collected random scraps of paper—so what?

On the ride back, Colby offered me the front seat.

"So chivalrous," Katie said.

I couldn't wait, and once we were in the car, I took out the piece of paper from my pocket. I'd been right—it was a photo. It was the kind you get in a booth at an amusement park. Two girls, good friends or maybe even sisters, sat scrunched together on the stool. In the first shot one was sticking her tongue out and the other had blown up her cheeks. In the second shot one was looking at the camera and the other was looking somewhere outside the booth, like something had distracted her. In the third shot it became clear that the something was actually a someone: now both girls had turned and you could see part of a boy's face. I wondered who he was to them. I had the feeling he wasn't their brother.

"So what is it?" Katie said, glancing over. "Anything good?"

I held up the photo so she could see it. Colby leaned forward from the backseat. "What makes something good?" he asked. He sounded genuinely interested, not like he was giving me a hard time, so I handed him the photo.

"Huh," he said. "Who do you think the guy is?"

"I suppose they could be sisters and he could be their brother, or he could be one of their brothers and maybe the other one's having a thing with him."

Katie reached for the photo. "And the sister doesn't know, but she's starting to figure it out," she said.

"Or maybe they aren't even related," Colby offered. He

snatched the photo from Katie and looked at it again. Then he handed it back to me.

"That's what makes something good," I told him. "When you have to wonder about it."

"But you'll never know," Katie said. "There's no way to find out for sure."

"Exactly," Colby said.

I turned and smiled at him. He totally got it.

When we got back to the cottage, I thanked Katie again, hopped out, and headed to the door. But I only got halfway when Colby called out, "Wait a sec!" and came after me. "I almost forgot," he said, jogging toward me with something in his hand. "I made a copy of that Guster CD for you."

I glanced toward the cottage and waited for Bandit's bark, but he must not have heard the car pull up. "Thanks," I said.

"You said you liked Guster, right?"

"Yeah." I looked at the cottage again. Any second Dad would be calling my name or, even worse, coming outside. He wouldn't like seeing me out here with Colby.

Colby must have thought my looking back meant I was dying to go inside, because he said, "Wait, did I do something wrong again? Should I be saying I'm sorry for something again?"

"No," I said. "It's not that."

"It's just that I'm getting the distinct feeling you're being weird right now."

Before I could say anything else, Bandit took that moment to decide he'd been delinquent in his watchdog duties and barked.

"It's just my dad. He doesn't always like me hanging out with the riders."

"What's this whole thing with the riders? *You're* a rider."

When I didn't answer, Colby added, "He lets you hang out with Katie."

"That's different."

"Why?"

"She's a girl."

"Oh, I get it. He doesn't want you hanging out with boys."

"Yeah," I said, although it wasn't just any boys Dad didn't want me hanging out with.

"Well, you better go, then," Colby said. "I'll see you when I get back."

We stood there for a few seconds, staring at each other. I had the feeling he didn't want me to leave as much as I didn't want him to. Finally I thanked him for the CD and I went inside. Dad was jabbering away in Spanish. *"Bueno,"* he was saying. *"Tengo que irme ya. Sí, sí, ahora la hago."*

I came into the kitchen to find him just hanging up the phone. "How was dinner?" he asked.

"Good." I handed him back the ten he had given me. "Was that Abuela you were talking to?"

"Didn't you eat?" Dad said, pocketing the ten and avoiding my question. He never liked to talk about my grandmother or my aunt. He always called them when I wasn't around and put me off when I asked to talk to them or about going to visit them. It was like he wanted to keep that part of his life from me.

"Katie put it on her credit card," I told him.

"Francie," he protested.

"I tried to pay, but she wouldn't let me. She wouldn't let Colby pay either." I knew that would make him feel better.

He looked at the CD in my hand. Before he could even ask, I explained, "Colby gave it to me. I said I liked the band and he made a copy for me."

"He made it special for you?"

"It's nothing," I assured him.

"A CD doesn't seem like nothing."

"Kids at school share music all the time," I said.

He moved to sit down at the kitchen table and nodded to the chair across from him. "I think we need to have a talk."

I sighed. I didn't want to have a talk. All I wanted to do was go to my room, look at the photo I'd found, and then maybe think about Colby. But if Dad insisted on talking, I wasn't going to make it easy. "I know," I said. "We need to talk about when we're going to Mexico."

"No, we need to talk about boys."

"Dad," I said. "I know all about the birds and the bees . . . where babies come from."

"Do you?"

"Yes."

"So you know they come from that?" he teased.

"From what?"

"That—what I just saw outside."

"So you were spying on me?"

"I was talking on the phone and just happened to look out the window."

"Why can't you just admit you were spying?"

"Fine," Dad said. "A little spying."

"So then you saw we were just talking."

"Exactly," he said.

"So what? I'm not supposed to talk to boys? No boys at all? I better reconsider where I'm going to apply for school— pick out some all-girls colleges. . . ."

Dad held both of his hands out in front of him like he was making a scale. "Boys," he said, moving one hand higher than the other. "Clients," he said, moving the other up.

"But what if a boy just happens to be a client?" I asked.

"Then you stay away from him," Dad announced, like it was easy.

"Okay, okay, I get it," I said, borrowing a bit of Colby's sarcasm. "I can do whatever I want with other boys. Stay out all night, sleep over at their houses, just not the clients; that's cool." I glanced at my watch. "Actually, I've gotta go. I've got a hot date tonight. I'm not sure when I'll be back. . . ."

"Francie," Dad said.

"Dad," I came back.

Dad sighed. "Okay, talking's fine. But just talking. Promise me you'll be careful."

"Just talking, I promise," I said.

For right then it seemed like a safe enough thing to promise. But just maybe, I hoped, that would change when Colby got back from L.A.

Chapter Ten

"Okay, Tara first, then Francie, then Katie, then Gwenn, trot the low side of the bank," Susie called to us. She was teaching our lesson because Rob was taking his mother to look at a nursing home.

I fell into line behind Tara, leaving enough room between us. We were riding outside because next was the USET Finals. USET stands for United States Equestrian Team, and the USET Finals is different from all the other finals because it's held outside on a grass course with natural obstacles like the ones we were practicing.

The bank was a raised platform that you jumped either lengthwise—in which case you jumped up one level, then up another, and then off—or widthwise, which is how we were jumping it now. Widthwise it was only about two feet up onto the platform and then one stride on top and two feet down.

I stayed back with my upper body and let Tobey jump to me. Then I made sure not to grab the reins as he popped back down to the ground.

"Good," Susie said. "Just remember, stay back a little more coming down."

It was beautiful out in the field where we were practicing. The leaves on the trees were at their brightest colors, just before they tinged brown and fluttered to the ground. It was crisp out, but not yet cold. Even at four o'clock the sun still hovered high in the sky. In a few more weeks, after the clocks had been turned back for daylight savings, it'd be too dark to jump outside at this time. Usually I wouldn't have noticed how beautiful it was out on the field or whether it was getting dark, but with Susie teaching, things were much more relaxed and it was possible to stop and smell the roses, so to speak.

We trotted the bank again widthwise, cantered it lengthwise. Next it was time to jump the water, one of the hardest types of jumps. The rail above the water was only a foot off the ground: what made it difficult was its width. At ten feet wide, it forced you to gallop to clear it. It was also a spooky jump because horses were often scared of the reflective surface.

This time Katie went first, and Stretch sailed over like the star he was. Tobey and I were next. Since he could be a little skittish, I whispered to him as we approached, "It's the water. You know what to do."

Tobey pricked his ears and surged forward. He judged it perfectly and soared over. I patted his neck and told him he was brave. After Tara and Gwenn jumped the water fine and we practiced the grob, a sunken road with two ditches a few strides apart, Susie said, "Good enough. Let's quit with that."

Tara and Gwenn headed back to the barn right away, but Katie and I lingered. We walked Tobey and Stretch around the field and talked to Susie, who had sat down on the edge of the bank.

"So how's school?" she asked us.

"Fine," Katie said. "Especially since I'm never there."

"Francie?"

I shrugged. "You know. The usual." Of course, ever since the test, school had been anything other than the usual.

"Your father said you're deciding which colleges to apply to."

I reached down and patted Tobey's neck. "That's what he thinks, yeah."

Susie knew I wanted to ride professionally. I figured if anyone would understand me not wanting to go to college, it would be her. But she said, "You should go to college. I wish I had."

"Why?"

"Just because . . . I'd have other options besides this."

"Okay, so my dad begged you to talk to me," I said. "That much is clear."

"I'm serious," Susie said, ignoring my hunch.

"Like what else would you do?" Katie asked.

It was the exact same thing I had been thinking—it was hard to imagine Susie doing anything besides horses.

"I always liked photography," she said. "I would have taken some photography classes . . . see where that led me. Katie, I know you want to go into fashion design. Francie, what do you think you would do if you weren't riding?"

I tried to think about what else I might be interested in besides horses. I'd never really considered there might be anything else.

"What are your favorite subjects in school?" she added.

"Economics is pretty cool," I said, thinking of Mr. Roth. But I wasn't sure what job economics could lead to—maybe something in business.

Just then Rob pulled up in his Escalade. He rolled down the window and called out, "Lesson over already?"

"They were awesome," Susie called back. "How was the nursing home?"

"It was like the Taj Mahal of nursing homes. Ma loved it."

"That's great!"

"Yeah, if you happen to have a couple hundred thousand dollars lying around. You want a ride back to the barn?"

"Nah," Susie said. "I'll walk back with the girls."

"Suit yourself," Rob said, and drove off.

On the walk back Susie asked, "Are you guys planning anything for the big weekend without a show?"

Katie shrugged. "Maybe we'll go see a movie or something."

Before I could think it through, I blurted out, "Or there's this party . . . one of the guys from my school is having."

"That *you* got invited to?" Katie said it like I was some total loser who could never possibly be invited to anything, least of all a party.

"Yeah," I said, all defensive.

"When is it?"

"Tonight."

"Oh my God, we are *so* going," Katie said.

Susie laughed. "Whatever you guys decide, just be careful, okay? I think it's great—you deserve to have some fun, take your minds off the finals. I won't tell Rob. But just be careful."

Back in the barn Katie handed Stretch over to Camillo and followed me to Tobey's stall. "Let's go to the party," she pleaded.

I undid the curb chain on Tobey's pelham bit. He hated it to be too tight and was always grateful when I undid it altogether. In fact, it had to be loose or else he would flip his head on course.

"I'm not sure it's a good idea," I said.

"Why not? Susie even gave us her blessing."

Why not? It was a good question. I couldn't graduate from high school without going to at least one party. Doug had invited me, and Becca really seemed to want me to go. Maybe this was my shot to finally see what it was like and if I was really missing out. Why not? I asked myself again. What would be so wrong with having a little fun? Like Susie said, we deserved a break.

"Please?" Katie tried again.

"Maybe," I said.

I thought I might have a harder time getting Dad to let me go to the party. But he almost seemed happy I was taking an interest in something besides the barn.

"A party at school and you want to go?"

"It's not at school," I said. "It's at someone's house."

"But someone from school?"

"Yup."

He made me promise to be back by eleven-thirty, which I knew Katie would think was insanely early, but she would have to deal. At least we were going. "How are you getting there? Do you need the truck?" he asked.

"No, Katie's driving."

"Will there be drinking?"

"Probably."

"But you won't be drinking?"

"Of course not," I said.

Going to a party was one thing, drinking was another altogether. I never drank and I wasn't about to start. Dad didn't drink either, not even a beer with the rest of the guys after a long day at the farm. Maybe it was because he never knew when one of the horses, like Finch, might get sick and he would have to drive the trailer to the vet. But I was pretty sure it had more to do with the fact that he'd seen too many grooms turn to drinking to try to cure their loneliness from being so far away from their home and their families. Too many times we'd witnessed grooms dragging themselves into the barn an hour late in the morning, hung over and reeking of booze. If Dad noticed it before Rob, he'd immediately take the person aside and try to help him. He'd even taken a few guys to AA meetings over the years. Sometimes they'd clean up their act, but it didn't always last. And if Rob found out, they'd be gone that day. He didn't tolerate drinking around the horses. I guess Dad knew that it might be easy for him to fall into the same trap. Even though we had each other and he'd been in the States for so long now, there had to be times he missed home. I'd seen how drinking could ruin a groom's chance of making a life for himself. I felt I owed it to Dad—and how hard he'd worked to get us where we were—not to even try it.

"And you won't get in the car with Katie if she drinks," he said. "You'll call me and I'll come pick you up."

"Yup," I confirmed.

"Okay," Dad said.

So it was settled. I was going to my very first party. When I thought about it, I got all jumpy inside. Better late than never, I figured.

I went over to Katie's room at around eight. She was bent over, blow-drying her hair upside down—to give it volume, she explained.

"Hey," she said, righting herself. She had on a skirt that

fell mid-thigh and a black scoop-neck shirt that revealed a little too much cleavage if you asked me, which Katie didn't.

"Do you want to borrow some clothes?" Katie asked, eyeing what I had on.

"Why? This isn't cutting it?" I looked at my jeans and hoodie sweatshirt. Okay, so maybe it wasn't exactly glam.

"It's all right," she said, turning to look at the mess of clothes on her bed. "But I have all these clothes—"

I walked over and picked up a glittery shirt. "I don't know."

"That would look so cute on you," Katie said.

"I don't think I can do glitter."

Katie grabbed the glittery shirt from me and tossed it back onto the pile. "I promise this won't be one of those teen movie makeovers," she said. "You know, where I do your makeup and your hair and you change from the girl with glasses and paint-splattered overalls to a teen model."

"I don't wear glasses or overalls," I said.

"Exactly." Katie grabbed a shirt off the bed. "So just put on this shirt. . . ." She grabbed a pair of pants. "And these . . ."

"No glitter," I repeated.

"No glitter."

After I was dressed to Katie's satisfaction and she had put on her makeup and a finishing squirt of Gucci Envy perfume, we called Becca to get directions.

"You're coming?" she asked.

"Yes."

The line was silent for a moment before Becca said, "Really?"

"Yes."

"Oh my God, how many times have I tried to get you to go out?"

Becca's voice was full of excitement, and it felt nice that she really wanted me to come. I remembered how she'd introduced me to the twins as her good friend. That had meant a lot to me too. After all, she had other friends, like Tracy, and didn't need me.

"This is going to be so much fun!" she added.

"I'm bringing a friend from the barn too," I told her.

It struck me as strange right then that Becca didn't know more about Katie. And for that matter that Katie didn't know more about Becca. But that was the way it was with my two worlds. Neither really had much to do with the other. Only tonight they were about to converge.

When we pulled up to the house, cars already lined the street. "Butt-ugly house," Katie said. "It looks like Martha Stewart threw up all over it."

The house, a pink ranch, wasn't very attractive. Especially compared to the penthouses on the Upper East Side and beach houses in the Hamptons that Katie was used to.

I'd assumed we would take a moment before we went in to make a game plan, but Katie was out of the car and headed up the cement walkway before I could stop her. I had no choice but to follow her inside. Music blared from a stereo in the living room, and people stood in clumps drinking from plastic cups. I had watched this very scene on TV and in movies plenty of times before, but I still felt like I was entering uncharted territory. I looked around—I didn't see anybody I knew. And even if I recognized someone from a class, it wasn't like I had actually ever spoken to them.

While I was feeling awkward and out of place, Katie seemed right at home. She marched up to the first person she saw and said, "Where's the keg?"

The guy pointed to the back of the house. "Kitchen."

I followed Katie while trying to keep an eye out for Becca. I had the idea that once I was with Becca, I wouldn't feel so out of place. In the kitchen a bunch of guys from the football team stood huddled around the keg. Besides the fact that most of them were huge, they were easy to identify because of their letter jackets. Unfortunately the few people I would know tonight—Doug and the twins—weren't among them.

"Hey," Katie said to Tom Deacon, who besides Doug was one of the other stars of the team. Like Doug, he also happened to be one of the cutest guys in the entire school. "What does a girl have to do to get a beer around here?"

"Depends," he said, taking in the sight of Katie and her cleavage. "What are you *willing* to do?"

She cocked her head, all flirtatious. "What do you have in mind?"

I couldn't believe Katie. If only she was this assertive in the ring. As Tom handed her a beer, I spotted Becca through the open door into the living room. She was with Tracy, but at this point I'd take what I could get.

Katie tried to pass me a beer, but I shook my head. "I see Becca," I told her. "Come on."

I expected Katie to protest leaving Tom, but she followed me into the other room.

"Hey," Becca said. "I can't believe you're actually here!"

"Becca, this is Katie, my friend from the barn; Katie, this is Becca, my friend from school." Tracy glared at me. I don't think she was used to being left out. "Oh yeah," I added. "This is Tracy."

"So I can't believe you got Francie to go out," Becca said.

"It wasn't easy," Katie answered, and took a sip of her beer.

"I bet," Tracy added.

I wanted to point out that Katie hadn't really needed to convince me. I had wanted to go, which now seemed like it might not have been the best idea.

"Where's Doug?" I asked, trying to change the subject.

"He's coming with Peters and Pepper. They're not here yet."

"Who's Doug?" Katie asked.

"My boyfriend," Becca said, practically beaming.

Katie leaned in closer. "Okay, so tell me everything about that total hottie in there."

"Who?" Becca asked.

"Tom Deacon," I supplied.

"Oh, totally cute," Becca said.

"And single too," Tracy added.

Becca looked surprised. "Since when?"

"Just last week. Ginny broke up with him."

"Who's Ginny?" Katie said. "And why'd she dump him?"

Becca nodded to where Ginny Sanders was standing across the room. She was pretty in a fake, anorexic kind of way: thin with bleached-blond hair. Tracy explained, "That's her, and I don't know why she dumped him. Probably just wanted a little drama in her life."

"Oh, the old break-up-so-you'll-want-me-back thing," Katie said.

Becca took a sip of her beer. "Probably."

As Katie was checking Ginny out, a guy with a buzz cut and glasses who was in my economics class came by with a tray of what looked like little paper cups of Jell-O. I had always thought he was a geek like me, but apparently he was much cooler than I was.

"Hors d'oeuvres, anyone?" he asked.

"Hmmm," Katie said. "My favorite kind. Right up there with caviar."

"Jell-O?" I said.

"Jell-O *shots*," Tracy informed me. "They're made with vodka, not water."

They all giggled at my cluelessness and my face burned. I was glad they all seemed to be getting along, but I didn't need them bonding anymore over me not having a life outside of the barn. Becca and Tracy reached for a cup. Katie grabbed two.

The guy offered me one, and I politely shook my head. "Hold everything!" he said, seemingly noticing me for the first time. "You're the horse girl, right? You always miss class because you're off racing or something?"

"Yeah," I said, wishing he would keep his voice down. "That's me."

"Cool! The horse girl escaped from the farm."

He started to walk away, but Katie stopped him. "Wait," she said, downing the second of her Jell-O shots and reaching for a third from his tray. "I hate to fill up on hors d'oeuvres, but what the hell!"

When he had left, Katie said, "He was kind of cute in a future Wall Streeter kind of way."

"Look out, she's on the prowl," Tracy said.

"I'm allowed," Katie replied. "I go to an all-girls school."

We hung out talking a while longer. I wanted to tell Katie to slow down on the drinking, but I couldn't figure out a good way to say it without sounding like a complete loser. What with the three Jell-O shots and the beer she was fast on her way to intoxication, which became clear as she started going on about how much money her dad makes. It came up when she was explaining how he yelled at her all the time about her riding.

"My dad does the whole live-vicariously-through-myprogeny thing," she rattled on, talking fast. "He's not like Francie's dad. Her dad is *so* nice. Have you met Juan? He's the absolute best. My dad . . . I swear sometimes I just want to say to him, if you want to win so badly, just go buy a grand prix horse and get one of the top riders to ride it and then you can win. I mean, it's not like he can't afford it. He makes a couple million dollars a year. . . ."

Becca was smiling, but I could tell from the look on her face she was just trying to be polite. People at our school didn't have parents who made millions of dollars. I tried not to shudder visibly as Katie talked. I hated when people talked about money, which horse people somehow always ended up doing. I was almost glad when Katie's attention turned to Tom and his crew, who had just come into the room.

"Oh, there's that guy, Tim," she said.

"Tom," I corrected.

"Whatever," Katie said, grabbing my hand and pulling me toward him. "We're going to say hello!"

Katie walked right up to Tom, stepping in between two other beefy football guys he was talking to, and said, "You relinquished your duties as keeper of the keg?"

"Who are you?" Tom asked.

"Who are *you*?" Katie shot back.

Tom looked at me. "Do you guys even go to Attleboro?"

"She does," Katie said. "I'm from New York *City*." She put the emphasis on the city part, like she was way too cool for all of us. Things were going beyond the embarrassing stage. I was seriously starting to wish I hadn't come. I felt completely out of place and I missed the barn, where I always felt at home.

"You go here?" Tom said to me. "I've never seen you around. What's your name?"

Of course he hadn't seen me around. First of all, I hardly ever *was* around. And second of all, we didn't exactly run in the same circles: Tom wasn't an honor student taking the high-level classes.

"You mean you don't know Francie Martinez?" Katie said.

I cringed at the sound of my name being blurted out across the room. Right then I wished I was just Francie Martin. That sounded good. Plain, old, white Francie Martin. The fact of the matter was there weren't too many Hispanic people at our school. Most everybody was white, and with my dark skin and funny last name I stuck out even for someone who wasn't around much.

"You really go to Attleboro?" Tom said.

Instead of answering Tom's question, I turned to Katie. "I'm leaving," I told her.

"What do you mean? We just got here."

"We didn't *just* get here. We've been here for almost two hours, and my dad isn't going to be happy if we don't get home soon." I realized that to Tom, talking about needing to get home sounded completely lame, but I was beginning not to care how I looked to these people anymore.

"Don't go yet," Tom said.

And that was all Katie needed. "Come on, Francie," she said. "Live a little."

But this wasn't about living. It was about Katie being drunk and annoying. So I just turned and walked away, leaving her to throw herself at Tom. Of course I didn't have a ride home without Katie and I wasn't calling my dad to pick me up—even though he'd told me to. I looked for Becca. She and Tracy were now talking with a bunch of other girls from the soccer team. I could have gone over and joined them, but I would have had nothing to say and I would have ended up feeling even more out of place, if that was even possible. Instead I ended up sitting outside the house on the front steps, shivering, since the night had turned cold. I kept checking my watch and with each passing minute getting madder and madder at Katie and her stupid idea to come to this party, which had really been my idea too. I was thinking about breaking down, calling Dad, and leaving Katie there, which I didn't want to do because she shouldn't drive, when Doug and the twins showed up.

"Hey, it's my tutor!" Doug called out as they lumbered up the path.

"Francie," I said.

"I know your name," Doug said.

Peters sat down on one side of me and Pepper plopped down next to me on the other side. "What's wrong?" Peters asked.

"You look sad," Pepper added.

"Maybe you could tutor me in Spanish too," Doug said. "You speak Spanish, right?"

"Actually, I take French."

"But come on, you speak Spanish, don't you? *¿Hablás español?*"

"Leave me alone," I said. Things were going from bad to worse. I couldn't believe I'd given a jerk like Doug my test.

"Whoa," Doug called out. "We gotta get this girl a beer . . . get her to lighten up a little."

"I don't drink," I told him. I don't cheat either—I wanted to add.

"What?" he shouted. "You don't drink?"

I was beginning to think that Doug, Peters, and Pepper had already had a little pre-party of their own.

Thankfully, before I had to take any more crap for not drinking, Becca came outside. "Hey, babe," Doug said, slinging his arm around her.

"I think you better go rescue your friend," Becca told me. "She's all over Tom, and I just saw them heading to one of the bedrooms."

"She can look out for herself," I said. "She knows what she's doing."

"I don't know. She had three more Jell-O shots. She's pretty wasted."

"Tom Deacon?" Doug asked. "Francie's friend is hooking up with Tom Deacon?" He said it like he couldn't believe Tom would ever be interested in a friend of mine. I wanted to point out that he was going out with a friend of mine.

"She's from New York City," Becca said, as if that explained everything.

"Cool," Doug said. "He needs to get his mind off Ginny."

At Doug's words I stood up and pushed past him and Becca back into the house. I wasn't going to let Katie get used like that. Not like Doug had used me to pass the test. I was sick of people getting away with things they shouldn't have. "You have to look out for people who can't help themselves," Dad always said. I thought about how he helped out the other grooms if they needed him: with money, with a ride. How he even tried to help the ones who started drinking.

Becca followed me inside. We found Katie and Tom in the hallway pressed up against the wall, kissing. Tom was groping her.

"Katie," I said.

She turned to look at me. "What?"

"We have to leave. My dad is going to kill me." This was only a partial lie. It was going on eleven, and if I wasn't home by eleven-thirty, Dad certainly wouldn't be happy.

"So leave," Katie said.

"I can't. You drove, remember?"

"You heard her," Tom chimed in. "Get lost."

Katie dug into her pocket and threw her keys at me.

"No," I said, catching her Tiffany heart-shaped key chain. "I'm not leaving without you." When this didn't seem to have any impact, I added, "If you don't come, my dad probably won't let me ride next weekend." I wasn't sure if this was true, but it could be, and anyway, I would have said anything to convince Katie.

We all stood there for a moment wondering what would happen. Tom, wondering if his chance at hooking up with a rich girl from New York *City* was going to happen; Becca wondering, I'm sure, why I was friends with Katie to begin with; and me wondering if Katie was going to listen to me and what, for that matter, I would do if she didn't.

"Fine," she said, wriggling out of Tom's grasp and taking a wobbly step toward me. "But I'm never going to forgive you for this."

I walked the few steps to meet her and linked my arm through hers. "Let's go," I said.

She called good-bye to Tom over her shoulder. We passed Doug and the twins in the hallway. I thought I saw Becca shoot Doug an' annoyed look, but maybe it was just wishful thinking.

Outside, Becca helped me get Katie into the car. I climbed into the driver's seat and adjusted the side mirrors.

"Look at you, driving a BMW!" Becca said.

Katie sulked in the passenger's seat. "You better not crash it," she muttered.

I had half a mind to open the door and roll her onto the sidewalk, but I kept trying to think of what Dad would do. So instead I started the car and slowly moved away from the curb.

"Drive carefully," Becca said. "Call me, okay?"

Katie was silent, staring out the window, for the whole trip back to the barn. I pulled up outside the gardener's house and killed the engine. I was about to get out and leave Katie in the car for all I cared when I heard her start crying. Then she said, "I'm sorry, Francie, I'm so sorry." She was really blubbering now. "It's just everything with my dad and not making the Garden. Do you know he offered Rob money to try to get me into the Garden—like to bribe someone? Not to mention the quarter million he promised Rob if I get a ribbon at any of the finals this year. And I'm still not over everything with you-know-who. I mean, he took money over me, you know? And that Tom guy . . . I don't know what I was thinking. I don't even like him. He's not like Colby. Colby's a guy I could see myself really having a relationship with, you know? Not just a one-night thing." Katie pressed her face into her hands. "If you hadn't come to get me . . . Oh God, I'm such a slut."

"You're not a slut," I said.

"I am. I'm a total slut."

"You were about to make a bad decision," I said. "That's all." If anyone could understand a bad decision, it was me. I hated myself for giving my test to Doug and for feeling cool just because he invited me to a party.

Katie looked up at me, mascara tracks running down her

face. "You're the best friend anyone could ever have. I love you, okay? I love you."

Right then I couldn't do anything but laugh. What a night it had been all around. One minute she hated me, the next she loved me. Poor Katie. She was a total mess. And I didn't feel too far behind her.

Chapter Eleven

I was in the tack room the next day cleaning a mass of bridles and saddles when Colby came in. I got all tingly when I saw him, and I wondered when that was going to stop. How many times would it be before seeing him didn't make my whole body jump? This time I was especially glad to see him after everything that had happened the night before.

"Okay, don't worry, I'm not going to ask whether I can help," he said, eyeing the dirty bridles. "I'm just going to sit here and talk to you, okay?"

I tossed my wet sponge at him. "No, you can help."

He caught the sponge and dunked it in the bucket of warm water, soaped it up, and started in on one of the bridles.

Although cleaning everyone else's tack and mucking ten stalls a day got old fast, I could never imagine not at least cleaning my own tack or taking care of my own horse. Not even if I was Leslie Burr Howard. It was part of riding for me, even if it wasn't for people like Katie and Tara.

"When did you get back?" I asked Colby.

"Just a little while ago. I was ravenous after the flight, so I stopped to raid Katie's junk-food stash."

"You should be careful," I said, sounding too much like Dad.

"Why?"

"You'll give her the wrong idea."

"Well, I didn't even get to see her," Colby said. "She was in the bathroom. I guess she's not feeling well. Some kind of stomach bug, Rob said."

After I had dropped Katie off, she spent the night throwing up. Worshiping the porcelain god, she had called it. I had stopped by that morning to check on her and found her sickly pale and guzzling bottles of Evian. She certainly couldn't ride—if she had, it would have been uglier than usual—so she'd told Rob she had the stomach flu.

"I hope we all don't get what she has," Colby added.

I glanced at Colby to see if he had any idea Katie was lying.

"What?" he asked.

"She's not sick," I said. "I mean, well, she is, but she's hung over. We went to this party some kid at my school was having last night. And don't say anything like, 'You at a party?' Okay?"

"I wasn't going to," Colby said.

I continued, "And Katie got really drunk." I decided to leave out the part about Tom. I didn't think Katie would want me telling Colby about that.

"What about you?" Colby asked.

"I don't drink. And don't say something like, 'That figures.'"

"Jeez, so defensive," Colby said. "So you're not big on parties or drinking. That's cool."

I put my sponge down. "Can I tell you something else?"

"Of course," Colby said.

"Okay, I have this friend at school who has this boy-friend. . . ." I told Colby everything about Doug and how I'd given him the test because I didn't want to lose Becca's friend-ship. I couldn't bring myself to tell him the other half—how I'd also done it because I had liked being part of things. "And now I'm so worried someone's going to find out that I gave him the test. I don't know what would happen then. I could get suspended or expelled. My dad would kill me."

It felt good to tell someone. I could have told Katie, but I knew she wouldn't think what I'd done was a big deal. For some reason, I knew Colby would understand why it was a big deal.

"I don't think you'd get expelled over giving someone a test from last year," Colby said.

"Still, even if I just got detention. You don't understand. . . ." Dad had worked so hard for everything we had. I could imagine how disappointed he'd be in me if he found out. Just the thought of it made me feel sick.

I sat down on one of the tack trunks and shook my head. "I can't believe I did something so stupid."

Colby sat down next to me and put his arm around me. "Hey," he said softly.

And that's when Tara walked in. I jumped up, which of course made it look worse than it was.

"Hope I didn't interrupt anything," Tara said. She de-posited another dirty bridle onto the rack and added, "Here's another for you, Cinderella."

She shot us a smug look and then left.

"I don't know how you guys put up with her," Colby said.

"Do we have a choice?" I sighed. "Now the whole barn's going to be talking."

"About what?" Colby said, and my heart sank. I had thought him putting his arm around me meant something, but obviously it hadn't. I wanted to disappear, but I got up and started in on the rest of the tack again. Colby helped, and with two of us working, we finished in no time flat.

"What's up now?" Colby asked.

"Heading home, I guess."

"I'll walk you."

I knew I shouldn't let him because Dad might see us, but I didn't want to say good-bye. I also desperately hoped that if we had more time together, something *would* happen between us. We walked close together on the dirt road that led to the cottage. We talked about school and where Colby thought he might like to go to college. He said his father wanted him to come east and go to an Ivy League school, but he wanted to stay out west. Then we talked about the barn and Tara and the other outrageous things she'd said over the years.

"Why did you pretend to be her the first day I met you?" Colby asked.

"I don't know," I said. "She just . . . she's got so much confidence in herself. . . ."

Colby reached out and grabbed my hand. Before I could say or do anything else, he had kissed me. Now this was certainly *something*. It was kind of good it happened so fast, because I didn't have a chance to worry if I was doing it right. Because it was so fast I also didn't really have a chance to analyze it, but the one thing I came away feeling was that it was much wetter and softer than I had expected.

"Sorry, but I just had to do that," Colby said when we had pulled apart.

I smiled and wanted to tell him there was nothing to be sorry about. Then for some reason I remembered Katie and how she'd said she liked Colby. It was like I couldn't let anything good happen without thinking of a way to ruin it. "What about Katie?" I asked.

"What about her?"

"She likes you. Isn't that obvious?"

Colby returned a smile. "And I like you. Isn't that obvious?"

I knew Katie said she liked Colby, but I wasn't sure how serious she really was about him. How could she be so into him and still have thrown herself at Tom? She'd even admitted to Tracy that she was on the prowl. Still, I thought of her last night, sobbing uncontrollably. As much as I liked Colby, I didn't want to hurt Katie. "She's really fragile right now with not making the Garden and everything," I told him.

"You know what?" Colby said. "I think we should worry about you and me and not about all these other people."

"What I need to worry about is the USET, the Medal, and the Maclay," I said. "That's all."

Colby stepped closer to me. "That's all?"

This time I kissed him back. We kissed for longer, and I had time to worry about my technique. I hoped I was an okay kisser. As far as I could tell, Colby seemed to think so.

"Why do you even like me?" I asked when we'd started walking again. "I mean out of all the girls."

"Man, you really don't believe in yourself, do you?" he answered, shaking his head. "You're fun and you're smart and you're not like other girls. That's why I like you. Oh yeah, and you're completely gorgeous—there is that."

Now my face was burning. Even with my tan skin I was sure Colby could see how badly I was blushing. "Please," I protested.

"I'm serious. You're totally hot."

"Come on," I said, looking away from him again.

"I'm just saying you got it all going on—the whole package."

This time I didn't argue with him. For once I wouldn't muddle up something good. We started walking again, closer together so our shoulders touched at times. I heard music playing before we came out of the woods. Outside the cottage Pablo, Camillo, and a bunch of the other grooms were gathered around the old hibachi, which was fuming black smoke. A radio sat on the picnic table next to a package of hamburger buns and paper plates. I didn't see Dad, and his truck wasn't parked in its usual spot by the cottage either.

"I hope you like well-done," Pablo said to Camillo as he poked at burgers on the grill.

"I like mine blackened!" I called out to them.

Pablo turned and called, *"¡Hola, chiquita fina!"*

"See, someone else agrees with me," Colby said.

I probably should have told Colby he had to go home, but Dad wasn't around, and when Pablo asked if we wanted to eat with them, I said yes.

"Where's my dad?" I asked as Pablo scooped one of the burgers off the grill and put it on a plate Camillo held out for him.

"He had to run an errand."

He pointed his spatula to the table and asked me to hand him some more plates, but Colby beat me to it. "So, are you making moves on my woman here?" Pablo asked as Colby passed him a plate.

"I think I might be," Colby said, unsure whether Pablo was serious or not.

"You better back off," Pablo said. Colby just stared at

him, and finally Pablo threw his spatula-free hand around Colby's shoulders. "I'm just kidding, man!"

Everyone laughed, and Pablo handed Colby a burger. We all sat down at the picnic table and talked and ate, and it didn't seem weird at all with Colby there. He drowned his burger in so much ketchup and mustard that Pablo teased him, "It's already dead, amigo, don't insult it!"

When we were finished, Pablo and Camillo arm-wrestled, and then Colby tried it and lost brutally. "You're making me look bad in front of my woman here," he said. "You gotta let me win one."

Pablo laughed and looked at me. "This one's okay," he said.

We kept talking and joking as the sun fell behind the trees. I should have told Colby he had to go, but I was having too good a time just hanging out with them. I forgot all about Dad. That is, until he pulled up.

"Uh-oh," Colby said.

"The boss don't like you?" Pablo asked.

"The boss doesn't like me messing with his daughter," Colby explained.

Dad got out of the truck carrying a bag from Home Depot. He put the bag on the steps to the cottage and walked up to the table, looking unamused.

"We saved you a burger," I tried.

"Don't you have homework to do?" he asked.

I nodded, and both Colby and I stood up. Dad turned back to the cottage and Pablo mumbled, "Man, he *doesn't* like you."

Before he headed back to the farm, Colby leaned close to me. I thought he might kiss me, which would have been way too much PDA too soon, but instead he whispered in my ear,

"Meet me at the pool at midnight. Be there!" I didn't get the chance to respond but could only watch as Colby jogged off to Pablo's hoots and hollers.

Back inside the cottage Dad said, "You can't bring him here."

"We were just hanging out—just talking and having a burger with the guys. You said talking was okay."

"And I probably shouldn't have. He's a client. He shouldn't be hanging out with the grooms, period."

"But I like him, Dad."

He sighed. "I just don't want you making choices that might hurt you later on."

"Like not going to college."

"Yes, and like getting involved with one of the clients."

"Which would be so bad because?"

"Because they live in a different world. We're the grooms, Francie; you can't ever lose sight of that."

"Dad, this isn't nineteen-sixty."

"Some things haven't changed."

But I was sure times had changed. Maybe even if what happened with Dad and my mother happened now, it would be different. Sometimes I found myself imagining a different version of my life, a life where they had stayed together and made it work. I knew I shouldn't, but I couldn't help imagining us living in a small house somewhere near the farm and coming home from the barn to have all three of us sit at the dining room table for dinner. She would tell Dad how great a cook he was. Maybe I'd even have a younger brother or sister. But then I'd think about reality—about my half brother and half sister who didn't even know I existed—and only feel angry and cheated.

I asked Dad, "What are you so scared of? I wouldn't make

the same mistake you and she made." She. I had never called my mother anything else. "I'm not you, and Colby's not her," I continued. It seemed crazy that Dad would think of me and Colby in that way—falling in love, having a baby, getting married. We were way too young for all that. But I reminded myself that Dad and my mother had been barely older than us. That seemed pretty hard to believe too.

"It wasn't a mistake," Dad said. "Don't ever call it a mistake."

"Well, whatever it was."

Dad set his gaze on me. "It was the greatest thing that happened to me, and don't you ever think otherwise."

"Okay," I said, glad that somehow we'd at least managed to get off the topic of Colby.

"I love you," Dad said, and he reached over to hug me.

I spent the entire night in my room doing a paper for world civ and trying to push Colby's words from my head: *Be there!* My room was about the size of Katie's at West Hills—not very big. Unlike Katie's, though, mine was neat and organized. A rainbow of ribbons hung from the walls, and trophies lined the sky blue bookcase Dad had built for me. I had decided there was no way I was sneaking out and risking Dad catching me or, even worse, Rob catching us at the pool, which was right next to his house. When I couldn't stop thinking about Colby, I put my paper aside and took out my shoe box, which included my most recent find: a page torn from a textbook with a note in purple Magic Marker. It read: *D., meet me after practice by the baseball field. F. won't find out, I promise. I'll be waiting. M.* If Becca had found it, she'd be trying to figure out who D., F., and M. were and worrying that D. was her D. But I preferred not knowing, so I could read it over and over and maybe even pretend I was D. or M.

At ten-forty-five I put the shoe box back in my closet and climbed under the covers, but I couldn't fall asleep. I kept turning to look at the glowing digits of the clock, thinking, one more hour till midnight, forty-five minutes till midnight, a half hour to midnight. Then it was midnight and I still wasn't anywhere near asleep. I got out of bed and then I got back into bed and then I got back out again and threw on shorts and a T-shirt. I just hoped C. was still waiting for me.

Sneaking out wasn't hard. Bandit was curled up on my bed and I told him to stay, then tiptoed out of the house, making sure to ease the screen door shut. The moon threw enough light for me to see where I was going, but it was still kind of spooky walking through the woods back to the farm. I broke into a jog, and when I saw the pool house come into view, the sudden fear that Colby wouldn't be there hit me. That he'd have forgotten or that he just hadn't believed I would come. Or more likely, since it was now twelve-twenty, that he'd given up and gone back to bed.

But when I went around the side of the pool house, he was sitting at the edge of the pool with his legs dangling in the water.

"I didn't think you were going to show. I was about to give up on you."

"Shh—" I said. "Rob's house is right over there."

"Relax," Colby said. "He's not going to wake up, and even if he did, he'd probably just get nostalgic for his younger days—oh, look, Colby and Francie are out there skinny dipping, how teenagerish."

"Who said anything about skinny dipping?" I asked, walking around to where he was.

"Well, what else would we be doing out here?"

"There's no way I'm taking off all my clothes."

"What if I go first?"

Colby stood up and pulled his shirt over his head. In the moonlight I could see his bare skin, and it made my heart skip several beats.

"You're not really going to—"

Colby answered by starting to undo his shorts. I couldn't believe him. He was so crazy and free of inhibitions.

"I'm covering my eyes," I told him.

"You don't have to," he said.

I waited with my eyes closed and only tentatively opened them when I heard a splash. Colby was looking up at me from the water. "Come on in."

"No."

"Come on!" he said, louder. "If you don't come in, I'm going to start screaming at the top of my lungs."

Knowing Colby even as little as I did, I knew he wasn't kidding. And the last thing I needed was for him to wake up Rob. "All right, all right," I said. I turned around so Colby wouldn't see and pulled my shirt over my head. Then I stepped out of my shorts. But that was as far as I was going. There was no way my bra or underwear was coming off. I turned back around, scampered to the edge of the pool, and slipped in. When I came up, Colby was swimming toward me.

"Isn't the water nice?" he asked.

I still couldn't believe I was here—in the pool with Colby in the middle of the night, and him totally buck-naked no less. In the last two days I'd done so much that I thought I'd never do. Go to a party, kiss Colby, sneak out at night. The pool wasn't very deep. The water reached just up to my collarbone. Colby swam right up next to me. "Hi," he said.

"Hi," I managed.

He kissed me and wrapped his arms around my shoulders, pulling me closer. The combination of his skin and the warm water felt amazing. As we continued to kiss, we pressed closer and I thought I felt fabric rubbing against my leg. I moved my hand down and felt the waistband of Colby's boxers.

He laughed. "I had you going, didn't I?"

"Yes, you did," I said, feeling a bit relieved and stupid at the same time.

"I would have ditched them in a second if you'd taken it all off."

"I don't doubt it," I said.

"So what made you decide to come?" he asked.

"I don't know."

"You *do* know."

"Because I wanted to see you," I admitted.

"And because you wanted to do something crazy."

"No, you're the crazy one," I said.

"It was a test," he said. "A test of the emergency rebellion system. To see if you were actually a real teenager."

"I gave Doug my test, remember? I think that counts as doing something I shouldn't have."

"That's different," Colby pointed out. "That was something you didn't want to do, but you did it because you were too scared to say no."

The truth of his words stung, and I looked away. "Thanks for making me feel even worse about it." All I could think was—the power of no.

Colby shrugged. "Last time I checked, you're allowed to make mistakes. Plus, what I'm talking about is going for something you really want. . . . Maybe there's this whole other Francie waiting to come out and you just don't know it."

"I thought you said I was perfect . . . smart, beautiful. . . ."

"You are, but I just get the sense that you don't always go hard enough for what you want. Like how you spend your whole life hoping you won't mess up."

"So what am I supposed to do?"

"Ever think about trying to win?"

I couldn't believe Colby. Mr. Who Cares How I Do was lecturing *me* about going harder for what I wanted. "What about you? You never even get nervous. It's like you don't care how you do. And the killer is you're a great rider. You could win if you cared at all about winning."

"To me, riding isn't everything," Colby said. "I decided that a long time ago."

"But if you aren't that serious about it, why do you even show at all?"

"I love it. It's fun. Why shouldn't I?"

"I guess," I said, but I still didn't really understand where he was coming from.

Colby and I stayed in the pool till just after one. When I told him I better go back, he said, "You sure you can't stay?"

"Positive," I said. Sneaking out and pseudo–skinny dipping was enough for one night. Sleeping over would be for sometime else, and probably not for a long time.

The air felt incredibly cold when we got out. Colby and I kissed good-bye, and I jogged the whole way home. I tiptoed back into the house and into my room. Bandit only barely lifted his head in a welcome. There was something to be said for older dogs. I changed into dry clothes and got into bed, my heart still racing. Sleep didn't come for a while, but I didn't mind. Instead of playing out my usual riding dream in my head, I rewound kissing Colby in the pool. I felt like I was watching a movie, and I had to keep reminding myself that it had been *me* kissing him. When I woke the next morning, I wondered if it had even happened, and I had to touch my clothes, still damp from the night before, to be sure it wasn't a dream.

Chapter Twelve

With each day that passed at school, I was more and more certain that Doug had gotten away with using my test. By the end of the week I was no longer walking the halls waiting for an announcement over the PA system calling me to the principal's office. While that made things calmer at school, at the barn I was more on edge than ever because of Colby. After our night at the pool, things didn't seem that different between us. I didn't know quite how to act in front of him. Was there something real happening between us or not? Suddenly I felt how Becca did after her first hook-up with Doug and, of all things, I decided to take Tracy's advice—wait and see what happens. If he was into me, I'd know it. Only, by the time we left on Friday for the USET Finals, I still wasn't sure.

Some people say New Jersey is the armpit of America, but those people have never seen Gladstone, where the United States Equestrian Team Medal Finals take place. It's picture-perfect horse country—grassy pastures lined with stone walls and brown post-and-rail fences. That is, after you spend six hours bumping along the highway to get there.

The show was held at the USET headquarters, where Leslie Burr Howard and all the other Olympians and Olympic hopefuls, Tara's boyfriend, Brad, included, trained before they went to Europe to compete. The barn was a beautiful old Tudor style with gables and a redbrick floor, more like a castle than a stable. Unlike the other finals, the USET takes place over two days. Dad, Camillo, and I got there early on Friday and unloaded the horses and the equipment and set up the stalls.

All the others were coming later: Tara and her mother were driving up, so were Gwenn and her mother, and Colby was catching a ride with Katie, which I wasn't thrilled about. They all weren't due to arrive for another half hour, so after we were done setting up the stalls, I wandered over to the main aisle, where all the Olympic horses were stabled. I walked down the rows of stalls with the horses' names on beautiful brass nameplates that I knew so well from reading the *Chronicle*: Grand Slam, Tiger Lily, Gunsmoke, Cotillion.

I was lingering at Leslie Burr Howard's horse's stall when I heard someone call my name. I turned to see Brad. He was dressed in jeans and a red, white, and blue jacket with a USA logo on the chest. He must have seen me looking around in awe, because he said, "Pretty amazing, huh?"

"Yeah," I replied. "So what's it like to practice with Leslie Burr Howard?"

"It's pretty surreal. Maybe next year you'll be here."

"I hope so," I said.

Brad dug his hands into his pockets. "Tara here?"

"Not yet, but she should be any minute."

"Cool. I'll see you later," he said. "Good luck this weekend."

I figured he was going to see if Tara had arrived, but instead he walked off in the other direction. After a few more minutes wandering around the main aisle, I headed back to our stalls. Tara was in the tack room, putting lip gloss on in front of the mirror. Katie was sitting in one of the director's chairs poring over *Vogue*. Colby sat next to her. He had the baggy khakis on again and a shirt with a picture of the earth on it that read LOVE YOUR MOTHER. He looked totally cute.

"Have you seen Brad?" Tara asked me.

"Yeah, I just saw him in the main aisle, but I'm not sure where he went."

"I guess I better go find that boy." Tara took one last glance in the mirror and smacked her lips together. "Give him some sugar."

Tara strutted off down the aisle. She must have found Brad because a split second later anyone in a five-mile vicinity could have heard her screeching his name.

"What's that all about?" Colby asked.

Without looking up from *Vogue,* Katie sang out, "Reunited and it feels so good." Then she added, "Tara just met up with her honey."

"You mean someone actually likes Tara?" Colby joked.

Katie finally looked up and smiled at Colby. "Yeah, it's still shocking to us too."

Katie put down *Vogue*. "Hey, anyone want to go shopping? I can't find my spurs," she said, making it clear that instead of looking for them, she'd just go buy a pair.

"I think I'll take a pass," Colby said. "I'm not much of a shopper."

"Who would have guessed?" Katie laughed, looking at Colby's tattered LOVE YOUR MOTHER shirt.

I said I'd go with Katie, since I always loved any excuse to wander around a tack shop and look at all the bridles, saddles, breeches, and jackets.

"How was the ride up with Colby?" I asked Katie as we headed over to the mobile tack store that had come for the show.

"Great," she said. "This weekend I'm totally making my move on him."

"What are you going to do?" I tried to sound normal, but my stomach was tying up in knots. I wondered if maybe Colby had said something to her about me. I had wanted to tell her about what happened in the pool, but I hadn't really had the right chance, and I wasn't sure it had meant anything either. Plus, the last thing I needed was the whole barn finding out. Now I wished I had told her about us—if there was an us.

"I haven't figured that part out yet, but something," she said. "Don't you think he likes me? I'm getting vibes that he does. I mean, why would he keep coming to my room all the time for food?"

"Maybe he's just hungry," I said. I knew this was my chance to tell Katie I liked him, but I couldn't bring myself to. Not when she thought he liked her. And anyway, what if he didn't really like me? He said he did, but maybe he hadn't really meant it or he'd changed his mind. I'd just look like a fool.

Katie shook her head and laughed. "You don't know the first thing about guys," she said.

"Maybe," I said, worried that she was right.

The Show Place was a big trailer outfitted to carry all kinds of tack, clothes, and equipment. It was a much fancier

155

tack shop than the one we went to at home, and as Katie went in search of spurs, I looked through the rack of jackets. I was surprised when I found the one Dad had bought me. I was looking for the price tag to see how much it was when an older woman with a neat blond bob who worked there walked up to me and asked suspiciously, "Can I help you with something?"

"I was just looking," I said.

She gave me this really hideous smile. I had never thought a smile could be mean, but hers was. "That's a *really* expensive jacket," she said.

As she said it, I realized I was still in my work clothes—jeans, sneakers, and a dirt-stained T-shirt. I hadn't changed into my boots and breeches. She thought I was a groom, not a rider. She thought I could never afford to buy the jacket and that I wouldn't have any use for it. I should have told her I had the exact same jacket, but I couldn't find the words. My face felt hot and my throat dry.

"No thank you," I managed, turning away. I hated that I could feel tears pressing at the backs of my eyelids. Even though Rob wasn't around I tried to remember rule number three: *No matter what, no crying.* I hated that some snobby woman was making me feel so worthless.

Katie came out from the other side of the shop. "Found a pair," she said, holding up the spurs.

"I'll meet you outside," I told her.

Katie came out right after me. "What was that all about? You look like you're about to cry, and I don't think I've ever seen you look like that."

"I'm not about to cry," I said, even though I was.

"Yes, you are. What happened?"

"It was nothing."

"It doesn't seem like nothing."

"Did she say anything after I left?" I asked.

"No."

I shook my head. "She just acted like I couldn't afford anything in there."

Katie slung an arm around me, and all of a sudden I was so glad I hadn't told her about Colby. "She's just some saleswoman. Who cares what she thinks?"

"Do you want to go back in for the spurs?" I asked her.

"Of course not," she said.

"But you need them."

"I can borrow yours, right?"

"Sure."

"Good," Katie said. "Then let's never go there again, okay?"

I wanted to hug her tight and never let go. "Okay," I said.

The USET had three phases, flat, gymnastics, and jumping, plus a final test of the top four riders. After the flat phase on Saturday, I stood tenth. I was really happy, since at the walk, trot, and canter, the tall beautiful-in-the-saddle riders, like Tara, usually did better. Tara was on top, and I was working hard not to let it bother me.

The next and last phase of the day on Saturday was gymnastics. Gymnastics are lines of fences, with hardly any space from one obstacle to the next. When we finished walking the course, Katie and Colby headed into the stands to watch, since they didn't go until the end of the class. I went back to the barn, because I was going eighth.

Back at the barn, Tobey's ears weren't pricked forward, but they weren't back either. Horses pin their ears back when they're angry, and the only time he ever got angry was when he saw another horse eating something when he wasn't. Now his ears were just floppy and pointed out to the side, which meant he was relaxed, hanging out.

I went into his stall and sat for a few minutes in a corner on a pile of fresh shavings. He leaned his head down and touched my face with his nose. At first he wasn't sure why I was just sitting in his stall, but after a few minutes he decided it was fine and went back to munching hay.

When the announcer called that the class was beginning, my stomach pulsed with cramps. I thought about what Colby had said about believing in myself. Maybe he was right. I had to be sure of myself, even if Rob wasn't. But I wasn't sure I could be.

As I led Tobey out of his stall, I heard Tara and Brad's voices coming from the tack room. Only it didn't sound like "Reunited and It Feels So Good." It sounded more like "Breaking Up Is Hard to Do."

"What are you saying?" Tara asked.

"I didn't want to tell you over the phone, but now's not the right time either."

I paused and listened, not so much because I wanted to hear what they were saying but because I had to pass the tack room to get out of the aisle and I didn't want to go by if they were having a major fight.

"It's the long-distance thing," Tara tried. "I know it's hard."

"It's not that—"

"Then what is it?" Tara said.

There was a pause before Brad spoke again. "There's someone else."

"So you've been cheating on me?"

"Tara—"

Before I could find a place to hide, Tara careened down the

aisle toward me, tears streaming down her face. I wondered if I should run after her, but what would I have said? We weren't really friends. And anyway, I had to head up to the ring with Tobey or I'd miss my spot in the order.

The judges had announced that in the gymnastics phase, you were to jump the course, and then if there was any part you didn't do well, you could do that section again. So before I entered the ring, I asked Rob, "And if I make a mistake and I think it's fixable? Should I do that line again?"

"If *you* make the mistake, don't bother. If you ride it decently and *Tobey* doesn't jump it the best, try it again so the judges see you know how to improve your horse. If it's your fault, it's too late for improvement. Got it?"

"Yes."

"But Francie—" Rob added.

I looked back at him.

"Let's try not to make a mistake, huh?"

Rob said it like I just didn't try hard enough, when in fact I was trying so hard all the time. How could he not notice that? I entered the ring and pushed thoughts of him away to concentrate on the course.

My first and second lines whizzed by. Jumping gymnastics was like being on a pogo stick. You jump, land, stride, jump, land, stride, and jump. I came in a little too forward to the next line, a bounce to two two-strides. A bounce is where you don't even put in a stride between the two jumps. It's just jump, land, jump. Tobey hit the second part of the bounce and the top rail thumped to the ground. I headed to the next line, thinking, *Should I go back after and redo that line?* I still hadn't decided when I finished. Rob started clapping, no whoops, and that's when I turned back to the line with the bounce. I wasn't settling today. I wasn't letting the regionals happen again. I was going for great. This time Tobey snapped his knees up in perfect form, six inches above the top rail.

As I exited the ring, it started sprinkling.

"Was that okay?" I asked Rob.

"Fine."

"I mean that I jumped it again. Was that a good decision?" I knew it was the right decision, but I still wanted to hear it from Rob.

"We'll see what the judges think," he said. "After the regionals, I don't even want to try to predict what they're thinking."

Here we were, weeks later, and Rob was still fixated on Tara's losing the regionals. I felt like screaming at him: *Get over it already!*

"You can head back." Rob paused, then added, "And Francie?"

I was still dying for something more. Just one word that said I was better than fine. *Don't do it*—I told myself—*don't hope.* "Yes?"

"Bring up my rain gear, huh?"

"Sure," I mumbled, and turned from Rob, my whole body sinking from his words or lack thereof. Why couldn't he for once just say something, anything, nice to me?

I looked up to see Colby waiting for me. I hadn't even known he was watching my round, and the thought gave me the good kind of shivers.

"You were awesome," he said. "It was a good decision. I saw one of the judges nod when you went through the second time."

A man I assumed must be Colby's father walked up to us

and handed him a coffee. He looked like Colby, same blond hair and brown eyes.

"Francie, this is my dad," he said.

"Nice to meet you," I told him. I tried to keep a straight face, but all I was thinking about was what Colby had said once about how his dad spent all his time sucking fat out of one place and sticking it into another.

"That was a beautiful round," his father said. He reached out and clapped Colby on the back. "I only hope Colby can put in half the trip you just did."

Colby wouldn't meet his eye.

"Well, I did have to do a line over," I pointed out, trying to come to Colby's defense in any small way.

"Still, it was impressive."

Colby and I exchanged a look and he asked, "Didn't you want my help back at the barn?"

"Sure," I said, taking the hint. "That would be great."

But his father shook his head and said, "Don't you think you better be studying these trips?" Only it didn't sound like a question.

"Right," Colby said.

"Well, I'll see you later," I offered, trying to say more with my eyes. "Good luck, okay?"

Colby rolled his eyes. "Yeah, see you later."

It turned out that I didn't see Colby for the whole rest of the day. I was busy tacking up Riley for Tara, so I didn't get to see him ride, but I heard from Katie that he was good. Then his father must have whisked him away, because he was nowhere to be seen.

So that night when Dad was in the shower, I picked up the

phone, pressed zero for the front desk, and asked for Colby Scharmor's room. I knew he was staying at the same hotel, and I couldn't stand not knowing anymore what was going on with us.

"We've got two rooms listed under Joseph Scharmor," the operator said.

"Oh, so you can't tell whose—"

"We've got two rooms," the operator snapped back. "Would you like one of them or not?"

"I'll take the first one." If Colby didn't answer, I figured I'd hang up. The operator connected me, and as the phone rang, I doodled flowers furiously on the hotel notepad. I let it ring three times and was about to hang up when he picked up. "Dad, I don't think I need you telling me when to go to bed."

I hesitated and then said, "Hi . . . It's Francie."

"Francis!" Colby said. "I thought you were my dad. I was going to kill him. What's up?"

Colby sounded happy to hear from me—definitely a good thing.

"My dad's in the shower, so I can't talk for long, but I was wondering if you wanted to meet somewhere for a few minutes?"

"Yeah, where?"

"I don't know. Vending machines?"

We agreed to meet in ten minutes at the third-floor vending machines. When Dad came out of the bathroom, I told him that Katie had called and that she was freaking out about tomorrow and had asked if I could come over for a few minutes.

"I didn't hear the phone ring," Dad said.

"I picked it up right away."

He checked his watch.

"I'll only stay a little while," I promised.

"Fine."

I pulled on jeans and my West Hills jacket over a T-shirt and walked down the puke-green-and-hot-pink-carpeted hallway to the elevator. I wondered why hotels always had such awful interiors—whether there was some logical reasoning behind it that I just didn't know about. Colby, wearing a UCLA sweatshirt and Kings hat, was already at the vending machines with two Cokes. "Did you know Coke is called Coke because when it first came out, it had traces of cocaine in it?" he asked.

"Really?"

"Uh-huh."

He handed me a can, and I popped it open.

"So I was glad you called," he said, looking straight at me.

"I was glad you answered. I wasn't sure if I'd get your room or your dad's. Was he happy with your round?"

Colby shrugged. "He's never happy. He spends his life making people who look fine look better."

I didn't know if I should be asking, but I said, "Is your mom here too?"

Colby shook his head. "They're divorced—the ugly kind where they can't be in the same place without lots of screaming, yelling, and throwing of hard objects."

"Oh," I said, and then I didn't know what else to say.

"My dad comes to the shows, but I live with my mom."

"He's tough on you," I said, and then I wished I hadn't, because it sounded like I pitied him.

"You could say that."

"What about your mom?"

"She's okay," he said.

"I don't even know my mother," I offered.

"Like not at all?"

"I mean, I know who she is. I know her name and her address—swiped from a Christmas card she sent to Rob—but I've never met her."

I filled Colby in on the saga of Dad and Elaine McBride, now Elaine Reeves. I couldn't believe I was talking to someone about my mother. I'd never talked to anyone about her—not even Katie or Becca. But there was something about Colby that made me tell him things I usually didn't talk to people about.

"Do you think you'll ever go meet her? I mean, are you curious?"

"Sometimes I am, but she didn't want me, you know? And she has a new family now." I thought of the Christmas card—the smiling faces that made me sick to my stomach.

"Maybe she thinks about you. I bet she does. She just might not know how to pick up the phone and call."

"If that's true, it's lame," I said. But lately I'd been thinking more about how young my mother had been when she'd had me. Times had changed, but eighteen was still young. She'd been only a year older than I was now. How would I handle it if I got pregnant now?

"Sometimes people are paralyzed by fear," Colby said. "Fear: four little letters, huge impact."

"Your sister's self-help tapes?"

Colby smiled. "How'd you guess?"

"What's up with that?"

"She's all about introspection. It's the divorce. We're both older—it's not like we're young kids anymore—but that doesn't mean it still doesn't suck and mess you up, just to a lesser degree, I guess."

I loved talking to Colby. He really thought about things

like so many other people didn't. Or if they did, they didn't let on.

"More than meeting my mother, I'd like to go to Mexico and meet my grandmother and my aunt," I told him.

"You've never been?"

I shook my head. "It's like my dad wants to keep all that from me. I guess he just wants my life to be here. He doesn't understand how I can't just be American—I'm Mexican too, whether he likes it or not."

"Has he ever thought of remarrying?" Colby asked.

I shook my head. "No way."

As far as I knew, Dad had never even been out on a date. He was always so busy at the farm he barely had time for his gardening, let alone meeting women.

"My mom's getting remarried," Colby said. "And I think I like him better than my dad."

"Jeez." I wasn't sure what else I could, or should, say, but Colby just shrugged. "We don't pick 'em, right?" he said.

He took a sip of his Coke and then asked, "Any good finds lately?"

"It's been a slow week," I said.

He drained the rest of his Coke and shot the can into the nearby trash barrel, a perfect two-pointer.

"Anything ever happen with the test?" he asked.

"Nope."

"That's good."

I downed the rest of my Coke and tossed it too, but my shot fell a few inches short. I headed toward the barrel for the rebound, but Colby reached it first and tossed it in. "Perfect alley-oop."

We were only a foot apart. Before I could get up the nerve

to ask what was going on between us, we started kissing. Down the hall the elevator dinged, but Colby kept kissing me. He'd moved his hand down to my waist. I thought I heard footsteps. "Someone's coming," I whispered.

"So?"

"So, they're going to see us."

"I don't care," Colby said.

"But what if it's my dad?"

I was still half kissing him and half pushing him away when I heard Katie yell, "Thanks a lot, Francie! Thanks a lot!"

Chapter Thirteen

I tossed and turned all night, both because I was nervous about how I'd do in the jumping phase and because I was wondering what I'd say to Katie in the morning. When we got up, it was downright pouring. The one outside final we had, and it decided to rain. But after what had happened the night before with Katie, the rain seemed only fitting.

It was 5 a.m. as I pitched manure from Riley's stall into the wheelbarrow and tried to figure out what I would say to her. Maybe she'd have thought about it overnight and realized she was crazy to be mad at me. After all, it wasn't like she had some claim on Colby. Or maybe the more she'd thought about it, the more upset she'd gotten.

I still hadn't decided what I should say when I ran into her coming into the barn as I was going to the Porta Potti to change into my breeches. She averted her eyes, and it was clear she was just going to keep walking right past me.

"Katie," I said, stopping her. "I'm sorry about what happened last night. . . ."

She squinted at me before saying, "I thought you were my friend."

"I am," I tried. I thought about how she had put her arm around me after we'd left the tack shop, and I felt incredibly guilty for not having told her about Colby in the first place.

"Yeah, right."

"Do you still want to borrow my spurs?" I asked gently.

"What do you think?" she snapped, and stalked off.

The one Porta Potti next to the barn was occupied, and I had to wait in the rain for the longest time. I knocked to try and encourage the person to hurry up, but all I heard back was what sounded like a moan and then some shuffling around. I was about to go find another one when the door finally opened and Tara stumbled out looking green.

Maybe it was because I'd just screwed up everything with my friendship with Katie or because I felt sorry for Tara, but I decided to be nice to her.

"Are you okay?" I asked.

She leaned against the door of the Porta Potti, closed her eyes, and swallowed. "I can't do this, Francie."

"What do you mean?"

She opened her eyes. They were glassy with tears. "I just can't believe him," she choked out. She was close to breaking down in full-out tears, and for once she seemed almost human.

"He's a total jerk," I said. "You just have to forget about him and ride."

"I can't."

"Yes, you can. You know you can." I couldn't believe the words coming out of my mouth. Was I giving Tara a pep talk?

"No, I can't!" Tara yelled. "You don't understand anything! It doesn't really matter how you do. You can go to college if you want. This is my life! This is all I have!"

Our short-lived bonding experience came to an abrupt end as Tara burst into full-fledged tears and then ran off back toward the barn, leaving me with a putrid-smelling Porta Potti.

"Weak, weak, weak!" Rob yelled at Tara.

I was standing on the edge of the schooling area in my rain pants, raincoat, Wellies, and a now-soaked Red Sox hat while Rob readied Tara to go into the ring. The whole show grounds had turned to mud, which meant you'd have to ride even tougher. Yet Tara was flopping in the saddle like a kid on a pony ride. Apparently my attempt at a pep talk had failed.

"Jump the vertical again!" Rob called to her. "And for God's sake, pull it together!"

Tara managed to ride the vertical decently, and Rob said, "That'll have to do. Let's head up to the ring."

At the in gate Rob stood at Riley's neck facing Tara while I wiped off her mud-splattered boots. He spoke in a firm but quiet voice and stared at her without blinking.

"Ride aggressively, Tara. Don't be weak at any jump. It's slick, and who knows what he'll do out there. *You* have to be the one to know. It's up to you now. Get it done."

Tara straightened in the saddle like she was coming back to life and moved forward into the ring. I went to stand on the sidelines. As Tara began her course, I scanned the stands for Katie but didn't see her.

Tara cleared the first few fences perfectly, and I began to think she'd managed to get herself together. She headed toward the bank, and I almost found myself rooting for her to pull it out. Riley jumped up the bank and then off neatly—the crowd becoming quieter with each jump. She nailed the water jump, handled the grob with ease, and cantered to the last line, clearly in position to win the class. She met the last two jumps well, and Rob clapped like crazy. I turned from the ring, suddenly not wanting to see Tara's smug smile.

But just then the crowd gasped. I looked back to see Tara flat out on the ground and Riley standing over her like he didn't know what to do next.

"What happened?" someone next to me said.

"She just slid off," came another voice.

"What do you mean, she just slid off? She fell off?"

"No, she *slid* off. Like she collapsed or something."

Susie ran into the ring first. Rob followed. I hesitated, still in shock. Rob yelled to me to come get Riley and I jogged in. When I reached Riley, the EMT was kneeling by Tara. "Get the ambulance in here," he called over his walkie-talkie.

Tara's parents joined us, her mother frantically calling her name. "What's wrong with her?" she asked the EMT. "Why won't she wake up?"

"Did she ingest anything unusual?" the EMT asked Tara's parents. "Drugs of any kind? Cold medicine, diet pills? We need to know what we're working with here."

Tara's mother's hand flew to her mouth. "She begged me to give her extra so she could lose a few more pounds."

"Extra what? Diet pills?"

"No, just laxatives. Oh my God, my baby."

"She's fine. She just passed out," her father said. "She'll be good enough to ride in the test." He looked to Rob for confirmation.

"You don't get to test when you fall off before you leave the ring," he said, deadpan.

Was this actually happening? Had Tara really just laid down the perfect trip only to fall off before leaving the ring? And was I happy she'd fallen off, or did I almost feel sorry for her? Everything I felt about her was all jumbled up.

As I led Riley out of the ring, Tara's father asked Rob, "So that's it? She's out?"

"Yes!" he snapped. "She fell off! She's out!"

On my way back to the barn with Riley, I passed Katie coming up to the ring on Stretch. She was bundled up in a raincoat and had the hood over her helmet so I could barely see her face. I was pretty sure it was futile, but I figured I would try again anyway.

"Tara just fell off," I said, hoping we might be able to come together over that at least.

"Do you think I care?" she said, and continued on past me.

After putting Riley in his stall, I went back up to the ring to help Camillo with Katie. Tara's mother called from the hospital and talked to Susie. "She's on fluids and should be released in a few hours," Susie reported after fielding the call.

"I'm *so* relieved," Rob said, his voice full of sarcasm. I knew all he cared about was that Tara had ruined his chance at the win.

"Rob," Susie said. "Brad broke up with her yesterday."

"So? Her boyfriend dumps her and she can throw it all away?"

"It wouldn't kill you to have a little compassion," Susie muttered.

I wasn't sure if I was imagining it, but lately things seemed tense between Rob and Susie.

"You ready to jump?" Rob called out to Katie.

The schooling area was a plain old mud pit at this point.

The good thing with all the rain, though, was that Stretch jumped the naturals fine, so Katie should have no problem. The fact that the field was a mess could even benefit her. There'd been so many problems out there that anyone who got around—even Katie—had a shot at a ribbon. I could just imagine how happy that would make her father. It would also mean Rob would get his bonus. A quarter of a million dollars was what Katie had said. All that just for a ribbon at the finals.

Katie picked up a trot, and at first I thought I noticed something funny in Stretch's gait. But then she pressed him into a canter and he looked fine again. I figured it must have been the mud.

Katie schooled all right, and we went up to the in gate. As she rode her opening circle, I still couldn't help but wonder about Stretch. He didn't look quite right. Not completely off or lame but a little uneven behind. Rob noticed it too.

"Susie, he look a little off to you?" he asked. "Right hind?"

"He schooled fine," she said.

Katie picked up a canter.

"Camillo!" Rob called. "You notice anything this morning?"

Katie had cleared the first three jumps fine and was heading to a line near the in gate.

"*Si*, little big in back," Camillo said.

"Swollen hind right or hind left?"

"Right."

Rob spun around to face him. "Damn it, Camillo. You're supposed to tell me these things. Do you know how much that horse is worth?"

Camillo had his eyes on the ground. Susie touched Rob's arm, but he shook her off. In the ring, Katie had jumped the first part of the line and was headed to the second element, a big square oxer. Before I could cross my fingers, Stretch propped like he was going to stop. Because the footing was slick, he careened straight into the oxer. Rails crashed to the ground. Katie spun Stretch in a circle while the jump crew reset the fence. Then she tried the oxer again. He crow-hopped the jump, landing in a heap on the other side, the whites of his eyes gleaming.

"Hold up!" Rob screamed out to her. "Stop!"

Katie brought Stretch to a trot and he was worse than before, much worse.

"Oh God," Susie breathed.

Katie walked Stretch a few steps more and then stopped. Rob jogged into the ring to meet her and Camillo followed.

"Get off," Rob told Katie. "He's hurt."

Katie dropped her reins and dismounted. Rob ran his hand down the right hind leg, then the left, and then the right again. "Take him back to the barn," he told Camillo. "I'll be there with the vet in a minute."

His face pinched in a worried frown, Camillo nodded and took Stretch. Katie followed, but she didn't get very far before her father came stalking up to her.

"What the hell was that about?" he demanded. "If you have a refusal, you keep going. You're not out there to learn to quit! I pay good money for you to be—"

Katie cut him off. "Stretch's hurt, Dad."

By this time Rob had joined them.

"Will the horse be okay for the Medal?" Mr. Whitt asked him.

"I don't know," Rob said. "We're taking him to the vet right now."

"It's Katie's last show," he said, as if this weren't obvious to everyone.

Rob held up his cell phone. "I'm going to start calling to find out what else is available." Rob had plenty of other horses at the farm but none good enough to cart Katie around the Medal Finals. She didn't need just any horse; she needed a seeing-eye horse.

"What are you going to find her in a week that's as good as Stretch?" Mr. Whitt demanded.

"I'll find her something," Rob said. "That's the best I can do."

Back at the stabling area, Camillo held Stretch while the vet palpated his leg. Stretch tried to pull his foot away several times—it hurt that much. Camillo kept rubbing his nose and whispering to him in Spanish. When the vet finally let go of the leg, Stretch dropped his head and sighed.

"It's the suspensory branch," the vet reported. "We'll have to do an ultrasound to know the extent of the damage, but he's done it pretty good."

Rob pressed his eyes closed. A blown suspensory ligament meant Stretch was out for more than just the Medal Finals. He'd be out for months, maybe a whole year. And at fifteen Stretch was no spring chicken. There was a good chance he'd never really come back to top form. I knew Rob didn't care so much about Stretch being out for the Medal Finals for Katie but about Stretch being out next year and possibly forever. That would mean Rob was out a lot of money. I'd heard Dad say Gwenn's parents had already put a deposit down on Stretch for next year and Rob had used it to secure his mother a place in the nursing home.

"He'll be okay, though, won't he?" Katie asked.

"He might come back," Susie said. "You never know."

"Sure," Rob said. "You never know."

*   *   *

Rob schooled me, but after what happened with Tara and then Stretch he was so distracted, it was like he might as well not have been schooling me.

"Good, Francie." Monotone. "Again like that."

"You know where you're going out there?" he asked at the in gate, looking past me.

"*Yup*," I answered. It was a test of the rules. No *yes*, but *yup*, which was usually enough for Rob to lose it. He didn't even flinch.

I peeled off my raincoat, which was soaked through, and handed it to Susie. The rain pelted down on me, yet once I entered the ring, I didn't feel it. This was my chance. I had to put everything behind me—Tara lying slack on the ground, Stretch's scared eyes as he pulled up lame, Katie's hateful look of just a few hours ago, Camillo back at the barn in tears, thinking he'd caused Stretch's injury. The judges liked my decision in the gymnastics, because I ended up twentieth, which put me fourteenth overall, and so far, many of the top fourteen had messed up, including Tara.

I charged into a canter, finding a good distance to the first fence, and cruised on toward the second. When I was riding, I couldn't hear anything. Being on course was like being in another consciousness. And it was magical when my timing was on. I never felt as strong, as capable, as I did then.

The bank was a game for Tobey. Up he hopped and down again. He popped over the water jump and then we tackled the grob, which had caused tons of stops and spills. I cantered downhill and we leapt the two ditches and then cantered back up again.

We were already at the last line. Three more fences, just don't do anything foolish. Then the final jump. I saw the distance and rode it. I didn't usually have time in the air over a fence to enjoy the feeling because I was thinking about what came next. But this time I let myself. Each horse jumps differently. Tobey's jump was athletic—springing up effortlessly. When I first started riding him, he jumped too high. He would lurch up and stay there, hanging in the air before landing with a thud. I worked on his arc, though, evening it out. But he still powered over. There was still that split second in the air when time stopped. It was like when you're on a swing, and you're swinging as high up as the swing can go, and there's that moment at the height of the upward swing where you stop pumping just before you come back down and you're still in the air, and that was what Tobey felt like at the top of his jump—like he might just keep going up.

I exited the ring to Rob's clapping. I deserved more. I deserved at least one whoop. Before, I would have doubted myself, wondering what Rob saw that I didn't feel. But this time I was sure Rob wasn't seeing things right. Everything with Tara and Stretch had clouded his vision, and he couldn't see that I'd just put in the round of my life.

When the announcer listed the riders that should stand by for the award presentation and I was one of them, I searched the field for Rob or even for Susie but couldn't find either of them. I spotted Colby, though, jogging toward me. I hadn't seen him since he rode. His horse threw a shoe after the sixth fence and he had to pull up. "You looked like you were going to put in the perfect trip," I told him.

"So goes it," he said, making me once again marvel at his carefree attitude. "But you, you're getting a ribbon."

Colby pointed to where his father, dressed in an olive green oilskin jacket and matching rain hat, stood under a giant golf umbrella. "I've gotta go. He's driving me back to the farm. Can you come see me when you get back?"

I shook my head. As hard as it would be, until I had a chance to talk things out with Katie, I was staying away from Colby. "I don't think that's such a good idea."

Colby didn't argue. "You rode great," he said, before he turned and headed back to his father.

After the test the announcer called the top eight riders, including me, into the ring and ran down the results in reverse order. Each rider and horse stepped forward and a woman in a rain poncho and high-heeled shoes browned with mud pinned a soaked ribbon on the horse's bridle. Here I was, about to get a ribbon at the USET Finals, yet everything was wrong. It was still raining. I was soaked to the bone and shivering. Rob and Susie were gone. So was Colby. Stretch was hurt and Katie wasn't talking to me. I had wanted to try again to say something to her about what had happened last night, but after Stretch, I thought it was better to leave her alone.

Each time the announcer called out a name, I expected it to be mine, and each time it wasn't, I knew I was one place higher. Finally he announced sixth and it still wasn't me, which meant I was fifth. The best placing without making the test. I walked out and the woman with the muddy shoes pinned the pink ribbon to the side of Tobey's bridle. I heard Dad clapping and no one else. Because of the mud in the ring, we did a victory trot, not a gallop.

I told myself it didn't matter, that nothing that had happened today mattered, because I was still fifth. I was still fifth at the USET. Only, fifth wasn't winning, and if I ever wanted to be more than the girl the tack shop owner assumed was just a groom, I needed to win. If I had been winning, Rob would be at the in gate—rain or no rain.

We packed up everything as quickly as possible, loaded the horses on the trailer, and hit the road home. I was quiet on the drive. Dad was too. I wished I didn't get carsick when I read in the car, because I had to finish a set of short-answer questions on the case study on the Federal Reserve System and monetary policy we'd read for econ. Finally I broke the silence by saying, "What a day, huh?"

"I know about you and Colby," Dad said, still staring through the windshield.

I was about to ask how. But I didn't need to. Tara, who'd seen us together in the tack room. Why had I even bothered to try to be nice to her? Like Katie had said a while back, maybe I *was* too nice to people sometimes.

"I told you it wasn't a good idea to get involved with him and you went ahead and did it anyway," Dad said. "If Rob finds out, this'll look really bad for us." He sounded really mad. I felt like I had done something terrible, and I had to remind myself I hadn't. I'd lied to Dad about going to see Colby and I'd sneaked out, none of which was good, but it wasn't awful. It certainly wasn't as bad as giving Doug the test.

"What's so wrong with it?" I asked. "Maybe Rob won't care."

"I care," Dad said.

"So it's about you, not Rob?"

Dad finally took his eyes off the road long enough to glance over at me. "It's about staying away from him, Francie."

I was silent for a few seconds. Then I said, "I want to go to Mexico. What if Abuela dies and I never get to meet her?" Bringing up Mexico had become my new tactic, and Dad picked up on it immediately.

"You're changing the subject."

"Doesn't she want to meet me—her own granddaughter?"

"Of course she does." Dad sighed and then added, "If I tell you we can go, you'll stay away from Colby?"

I probably would have agreed, but before I could answer, Dad said, "Well, I'm not making that trade. I'm not making any promises."

"Neither am I," I said.

Chapter Fourteen

On Monday morning I could barely keep my eyes open at school. We'd gotten home at eleven from the USET and I'd stayed up until one finishing my assignment for econ. During second period, which I had free, I went into the computer room to print out my assignment. I was planning on going to the library afterward to study, or maybe to even close my eyes for a few minutes, but of course all the printers were being used, so I had to wait.

I sat down at one of the computers and started poking around the Internet. I went to the *Chronicle* Web site to check if the results from the USET had been posted, which they had. There was my name in fifth. Then, before I knew what I was doing, I was typing my mother's name into Google. I clicked Go and inched forward in my seat, waiting anxiously to see what would come up. I wasn't sure why I was doing it now or for that matter why I had never thought to do it before. Only a few entries came up, and they weren't very interesting: some charity event at what must have been her other kids' school and the results for a 10K race she'd run. But somehow just seeing her name out in space was kind of cool—it proved that she actually existed.

I was still staring at the screen when Becca and Tracy came in. "Hey, there," Becca said, leaning over my shoulder. "I've been looking all over for you. I thought you'd be in the library. What are you up to?"

I moved the cursor to close the window. "Just waiting to print out an assignment for econ."

Becca glanced to the printers. I followed her gaze to see that a few were free now. I opened my file and pressed print. Becca leaned against the desk. "So, I was just wondering about the next test . . . if you could help Doug *study* again?"

I looked around, worried who might hear us. "I don't know," I said.

"Doug'll be so upset if you don't," she said, keeping her voice down—thankfully. "What's the big deal?"

The big deal was that I was finally able to walk around school without breaking into a sweat every time I saw Mr. Yannakopoulos or our principal. I didn't want to go back to living in fear. But I wasn't about to tell Becca that.

"He doesn't need it until next week," Becca said.

"I could get in serious trouble and so could Doug, for that matter," I told her.

"How are you going to get in trouble?" Becca asked. "No one will find out."

My paper had finished printing and I got up to collect it.

"Let's go," Tracy said to Becca.

"We're meeting Doug and the twins," Becca explained to me. "We're going out."

Doug had never asked me again about the lunch he'd said would be on him. I realized he only cared about what, or who, was convenient for him at the time.

"We have English in fifteen minutes," I said, looking at the clock. Becca had always been like me—she'd never missed a class.

"I'm skipping," she replied. "Take good notes for me, okay?"

I gave Katie a few days, to see if things would blow over. In those few days I also kept my distance from Colby, and he seemed to understand why without my having to say anything. By the end of the week Katie still wasn't looking at me, let alone talking to me, and I decided I had to do something. It was too strange passing her in the barn and not even saying hello.

On the way back to the barn from bringing a horse in from the pasture, I passed the work site for the new indoor. No one was working or had been working on it all week, and the site looked like a kid's half-finished Lego project. When I spotted Katie in the field next to the barn, grazing Stretch, I figured it'd be my best chance to talk to her alone. I put the horse in its stall, and before I could change my mind, I walked out to her and Stretch. She was wearing a baseball hat and didn't look up as I approached, just kept staring at the ground.

"How's Stretch?" I asked, even though I knew the answer. Camillo had been cold-hosing his leg five times a day, as well as treating it with a laser and magnets. But the swelling hadn't come down much and Stretch was still hobbling around.

Katie didn't answer, making it clear she still wasn't talking to me.

"At least he hasn't lost his appetite," I added. When I still got nothing from her, I said, "Katie, come on. This is ridiculous. We're best friends."

"We *were* best friends. There's a difference."

"So that's it?" I asked. "You're going to let some guy come between us?"

"*You* let him come between us," she corrected. "You knew I liked him. Would it have been that hard to stay away?"

"I didn't plan on it, I swear," I tried. "I didn't think there was any way he would like me." I knew this was lame; I had known Katie was into him and I should have just told her what was happening between us.

"You're the one who knew how I felt," she said.

"And that was why I told Colby I couldn't get involved with him, but then it just happened. I was going to tell you."

"When?" Katie demanded. "When were you planning to tell me?"

"What about all that with Tom at the party?" I asked. "You should have seen you two in the hall, and you even admitted you were on the prowl."

"I can't believe you're bringing that up," she said.

I sighed and tried once more. "I'm sorry. . . . I want us to be friends again."

"Well, *I'm* sorry, but I don't think I can do that," Katie huffed.

Right then all my guilt over not telling Katie faded. Here I was with my tail between my legs and Katie wasn't willing to give an inch. Who said she had some claim to Colby, and why hadn't she realized the feeling wasn't mutual? Why had she just assumed he'd like her and not me?

"Fine," I said. "Have it your way." I turned from her and murmured under my breath, but loud enough so she could hear, "Spoiled brat."

"What?" she called after me.

"You heard me!" I snapped, spinning back to her. "You just can't believe that he might like me instead of you. Well, this is one thing your daddy can't buy for you."

I couldn't believe the words that had just come out of my mouth. I'd said them as Katie's best friend, or rather, ex–best friend, but the minute they were out, all I could think about was how it wasn't right for me, the groom, to be telling the client off. Maybe that was why I'd snapped like I had, though. For all the times I'd watched Dad and the other grooms take too much from people just because they had more money.

I raced back into the barn and was headed to the tack room when I passed Tara and Camillo. They were laughing and Tara was testing Camillo's biceps between two fingers. "You must work out," she cooed.

"No, I don't, really," Camillo said, his skin more apple than peach at that moment. It was obvious that after everything with Brad, Tara was just trying to make herself feel better. There was no way she was really interested in Camillo. But he didn't know that.

I shot Tara a hostile look and she muttered, "What's your problem?"

"Don't mess with him," I said.

"Why don't you mind your own business?"

"That's ironic coming from you."

"What are you talking about?"

"I know you told my dad about Colby and me."

Tara rolled her eyes. "Believe whatever you want," she said. "I don't care."

Believe whatever you want—like there was anything else to believe. I walked off in a huff to the tack room. I sat down on my trunk, fuming, trying to get Katie and now Tara too out of my mind. I was about to stand up and start in on the tack when Susie walked in.

"Did I see you and Katie having a fight out there?" she asked.

"Yeah."

"Wanna tell me what it was about?"

I didn't think twice about telling Susie. I needed someone—preferably a woman—who would understand. Maybe she would be better able to judge who was right—Katie or me. "Colby," I admitted.

"Oh." Susie smiled. "A guy, how . . . normal."

"She was mad because he wasn't interested in her. She thinks she should get everything she wants. But just because her father can buy her the world doesn't mean Colby should like her and not me."

Susie was nodding along with my rant, but then she put a hand on my shoulder. "Did you ever think it might be hard for Katie to be your best friend?" she asked. "She'll never be the rider you are. Ever."

"I guess," I said. "There's also my dad—he doesn't want me to be with Colby because I'm a groom." I wondered if Susie might remember my mother. But Susie was younger than her by a good ten years, so they wouldn't have ridden with Rob at the same time.

"He's just looking out for you. You know how much he loves you. He'd do anything for you."

"I know," I said.

"Listen," Susie said. "You're really having a great year and I know you can win. I see it in you. Don't let everything with Katie or Colby ruin this for you. You've worked too hard for that."

Susie left, and I filled up the tack bucket in the sink with warm water. As I dunked my sponge in, I thought about what Susie had said. Maybe it *was* hard for Katie to be my friend. But it was also hard for me to be *her* friend. What if I had Stretch instead of Tobey? What if Rob treated me like Katie? But Susie was right about a few things—Dad was just looking out for me. And above all else I couldn't let what was happening with Katie or Colby ruin my last two shows. All I had to do was look at Tara and what had happened at the USET to see that it wasn't worth it. I'd worked too hard to give up now.

After dinner I went back to the barn to do night check. Everything with Katie still clouded my mind, and I was glad for the walk and the chance to be around the horses. I loved the barn at night. Quiet—peppered only with the occasional nicker or pawing—blanketed the barn, making it seem like a sanctuary.

All the lights were off except one, but it threw enough light for me to meander down the aisle. I glanced into each stall to make sure every horse was either happily munching hay or peacefully napping.

When I'd checked on everybody, I went to the tack room to grab a few carrots for Tobey. I noticed the light in Rob's office was on and I heard him talking to somebody. "Okay, take me through it," he was saying. "How does it work?"

There was a long silence and I figured he had to be on the phone.

"That does it?" he asked.

Stretch—I figured. Rob was probably talking to some fancy vet about a procedure that might help repair his suspensory.

I went into the tack room and got the carrots out of my trunk and then went back to Tobey's stall. He was lying down. I eased the door open and slowly stepped toward him, crouching lower as I went. I had read somewhere that a horse will let you pat him lying down only if he really trusts you, because since a horse relies on its ability to run away from predators, it's at its most defenseless lying down. Tobey twitched once like he might get up, but I whispered to him and he rested his chin back down on the shavings. He let me kneel next to him and rub his neck. It was strange looking down on him but not being on his back. He seemed more like a great big dog than a horse.

I fed him the carrots and listened to him breathe in the soft quiet of the barn. I could have stayed in his stall forever, but I knew Dad would be wondering where I was or if one of the horses was sick or got cast rolling in its stall and couldn't get up, so I stood up and headed back out into the aisle.

As I walked by Stretch's stall, he popped his head over the door and whinnied. "I don't have any left," I said, showing him my empty hands.

I headed outside. I only made it a few steps outside the barn door when I heard someone say, "Hey." I turned around to see Colby sitting on the bench outside the barn.

"You scared me," I said, catching my breath. "What are you doing here?"

"Hoping to see you."

"What if my dad had been doing night check?"

"Then I guess I would have scared him instead of scaring you. Did I see you talking to Katie earlier?"

"Sort of."

"What does that mean?"

"It means I tried to say I was sorry, but I ended up calling her a spoiled brat, which, by the way, she probably is."

"She'll come around. You just have to give it time."

But I had given it time. And Katie was still mad at me.

Colby stood up and moved toward me. "I've missed you," he said.

I thought back to what Susie had said about my putting riding first. At the beginning of the finals I hadn't thought anything could interfere. Now there was so much else going on: Colby, Katie, Becca and the test. "I can't do this now."

"Because of Katie?"

"No."

"Because of your dad?"

"Because of me. I need to focus. I can't have any distractions—not now."

"So that's what I am?" Colby said. "A distraction?"

"Right now, yes," I answered bluntly. "I can't be going out at midnight, swimming in the pool half naked."

"I didn't know it was so awful," Colby said.

"It wasn't; it's just that . . ." I trailed off, unsure how to explain what I was feeling. All I could think about was that horrible lady at the tack shop—*Can I help you?* What if Dad was right? What if things hadn't changed since he met my mother? Maybe it was too complicated and it would never work out between us. "It just won't work," I said.

"That's lame," Colby said.

We stared at each other for a few more seconds. I wasn't sure what else I was supposed to say. Were we breaking up? We hadn't ever officially been together in the first place. Was I supposed to try the pathetic we'll-still-be-friends line? When Colby didn't say anything either, I opted for just, "See you later."

I was twenty feet from the barn when Colby called after me: "Did you ever think this is just what you need right now?"

Chapter Fifteen

From the stands I saw Katie breathing in and out of a brown paper bag. As if she hadn't already had the bad luck of Stretch getting hurt and having to ride a new horse at the Medal Finals, she'd drawn first in the order. I could tell by her pale face and stiff arms that she wasn't going to be good. The horse Rob had found her, whose regular rider had broken her leg the week before, shipped straight to Harrisburg from Cincinnati. The horse was a nice bay that loped along and didn't seem fazed by much.

No one expected Katie to be good, and so when she got around without a refusal or a completely terrible jump, Rob clapped loudly and even whooped. Her father was in the stands a few rows in front of me and he got up after Katie's round was over.

I watched him walk down the aisle, and I wondered what he would do now that Katie was done riding in the equitation. Katie's younger brother, Brian, played soccer. Maybe that would be next for Mr. Whitt, screaming from the sidelines at the referee or, more likely, at Brian.

Ten minutes later, Katie trudged up the aisle alone. I could only imagine what her father had said to her. I expected her to keep walking right past me without even acknowledging my existence like she had been all week, but to my complete surprise, she sank into the seat next to me.

"I'm so glad it's over, Francie," she said.

"You're talking to me again?" I asked.

Katie sighed. "You were right. It was just after everything with Stretch and then with my dad and all that stuff with you-know-who last summer . . . not to mention that guy at the party and the fact that I almost did something I really would have regretted. Things have just been crazy." She shook her head. "I haven't been myself."

"I should have asked you about Colby first," I offered.

Katie had tears in her eyes. I wondered if she would miss doing the equitation more than she thought she would. I leaned over and hugged her.

When Colby entered the ring a few riders later, my stomach lurched for him. As much as I'd tried to put him completely out of my mind, he'd kept popping back into it. I kept thinking back to what it felt like kissing him. It made it even harder that every time I saw him he didn't look away but just stared back at me like he was challenging me to forget him. And the problem was I couldn't. There was definitely still something there between us.

"What's up with you two anyway?" Katie asked as we watched Colby ride.

"I told him I couldn't handle it right now."

"Why'd you do that?"

"Because I need to concentrate, and anyway, he's going back to California after the Garden—what's the point?"

Katie shook her head. "At least one of us should be going after him."

I smiled, wishing it were that simple for me.

Colby finished his course, and Katie and I applauded loudly. Soon after, Tara rode into the ring on Riley. My stomach plummeted again, this time because I wanted her to mess up.

The crowd quieted. I watched Tara, and after each fence I glanced at Rob, who was leaning over the railing, practically into the ring. He had his coat and tie on for the first time this year. It was what he wore when he thought he was going to win, so he'd look good in the photos. That morning at the in gate before the course walk he'd pointed to his jacket. "I've got the coat on. Better not let me down."

I prayed for Tara to make a mistake, even a small one, but as she rolled along, I realized my thoughts were useless. Ever since the USET she'd been that much tougher. The crowd hushed as she neared the end. When she finished, Rob went nuts, whooping and clapping. He turned from the in gate and hugged Susie. As Tara exited, he held his hands up toward her, still clapping.

A few minutes later, Tara bounded up the stairs, not trying to repress her smile in the slightest.

"Nice ride, Tara," someone a few rows in front of us said to her.

"Yeah, very smooth, Ex-Lax," Katie added.

"Screw you, Katie," Tara said. She continued up the aisle, her head held high, to where her parents waited for her. As her mother hugged her, her father showed her his list of riders. "This one's yours, Tara," he said.

Katie turned to me. "You have to beat her."

"You saw her trip," I said. "It was flawless."

Katie grabbed my shoulders. "Beat Tara. You're the last hope."

Back at the stabling area Colby was pulling off his boots. "You rode well," I said, trying to be civil.

"Thanks," he said. "When do you go?"

"In twenty trips. I'm getting on now."

I pulled my saddle off the rack and headed to Tobey's stall. He had his head over the door like he was saying, "All right, let's do this." I led him into the groom stall. I'd spent a half hour that morning currying and brushing him, so all I needed to do was run a rag over his coat and comb out his tail once more. I was laying the saddle pad on his back when Camillo came running in. He was completely out of breath and he kept glancing back to the tack room.

"What's wrong?" I asked.

"*La Migra,*" he whispered.

If immigration was on the grounds, I didn't see why Camillo was so upset—he was legal.

"*Pero, eres legal,*" I said. "*No tienes de que preocuparte.*"

Camillo bit his lip and then shook his head. "*Mi—mi* green card," he stammered. "*Es falsa.*"

Colby must have heard us, because he came out into the aisle. "What's going on?" he asked.

"Nothing," I said. This wasn't something for the clients to be involved in.

"*¿Mi padre sabe?*" I asked Camillo.

"No," he answered.

"Does your dad know what?" Colby said. So much for his Spanish not being very good.

Just then the announcer's voice rang out: "The one-hundredth in the order is now fifteen trips away."

"Damn," I said. I only had nineteen trips until I went and Tobey wasn't even tacked up yet. Camillo needed to get off the show grounds immediately, but if I took him, I'd miss my spot and be eliminated. I glanced at Colby and decided I had to trust him. "It's INS. They're on the grounds and Camillo's not legal."

"I thought you said Rob didn't hire illegals."

"I just found out he has a fake green card," I told him. "Rob has no idea. And neither does my father."

"So what can I do?" Colby asked.

I headed back to the tack room, opened the junk trunk, and pulled out the keys to the farm truck. I tossed them to Colby. "Can you get him out of here?"

"Sure," he said without even having to think about it.

I told Camillo to go with Colby, that he could trust him. To lie down on the floor of the truck and put a blanket over himself and Colby would drive him out of the show grounds. I figured, and hoped, they wouldn't stop Colby if there was a checkpoint. And I'd cover for Camillo with Rob. I wasn't sure what I was going to come up with, but I'd figure out something. The only thing that mattered was that Camillo didn't end up in a detention center and then get deported.

As Camillo and Colby hustled out, I rushed to tack up Tobey and get up to the ring.

"Where the hell have you been?" Rob asked when I got to the schooling area. "You go in five trips."

"Camillo was throwing up. I think he might have food poisoning," I said. "He went to see the EMT."

We did an abbreviated warm-up and then, just like that, I

was in the ring. The good thing about being so rushed was I didn't have time to get nervous. Before I knew it, I was cantering to the first jump. I found a good distance and continued around the course waiting to speed up or get anxious, but I was right there. Right on target.

The crowd hushed, and when I landed off the last jump, Rob whooped like he'd never whooped for me before.

"Great!" he gushed when I came out of the ring. "Smooth as glass. Beautiful."

My body surged and I couldn't stop smiling. *Beautiful,* that was what Rob had said, *my round was beautiful.*

When the first round was over, I was in third. Karen Bay was in second. Tara held the lead. I couldn't believe I stood third out of 211 riders. But I told myself to believe it. To believe in myself.

I'd never walked the course for the second round before. I'd always watched other riders from the stands, and it felt like I'd just scored tickets to a sold-out concert. Tara headed into the ring with Rob, but I jogged a few steps to catch up with them—I wouldn't follow this time. I flanked Rob on the other side as we continued around the course, which had fewer jumps, but more difficult turns and patterns.

"When this is all over, I want two ribbons today," Rob lectured us. "First and second."

I knew Tara assumed she'd be first and if I was lucky, I'd be second. Rob probably thought so too. But maybe, just maybe, I'd prove them both wrong.

As we walked out of the ring, Tara pointed to a box in the stands above the in gate. "See that up there? That's where they interview you if you win." She paused and then added, "That's where I'll be when this is all over. This is my class."

I wished I had something good to say back, but I couldn't think of anything. I decided I would have to answer with my riding instead. Rob schooled Tara and me together, paying attention to both of us. I couldn't believe it when he told Tara to stay in the schooling area with Susie for a few more minutes and then come up. Finally, he was taking me seriously.

By the time I reached the in gate, I was already supposed to be in the ring, which was good because it meant my nerves couldn't build any more than they already had. A hush fell over the crowd as I entered, and I knew it was because I had become a rider to watch. The announcer's voice boomed out over the ring: "And now on course, Francie Martinez."

Before I urged Tobey into a canter, I thought of Colby and how he'd been so cool about everything with Camillo. For a second it was hard to snap back into reality, to start riding, to start my course. I only hoped he'd gotten him out safely. I forced my mind back to the course, and soon I was focused again. The fact that I was third filled me with confidence, and I rode like I believed in myself. I knew Rob was watching me intently this time, even if Tara was about to go one trip after me.

I rode each jump accurately, no mistakes. Solid. Rob whooped. He whooped a lot. He was giving Tara last-minute instructions as I left the ring, but Susie was there to meet me.

"Good job. Rob said to be ready. You should make the test."

I walked out of the chute that led from the ring. Dad was waiting for me. I patted Tobey, my hand still jittering.

"Go get it!" Rob called to Tara as she walked into the ring.

I must have looked exhausted, because Dad said, "You okay? You need a drink or something? You didn't eat any of the stuff that Camillo did, I hope."

"He's not sick," I said. I wasn't lying to Dad.

"What do you mean?"

I explained about Camillo's fake green card and how Colby had to drive him off the grounds.

"Francie, do you know a person can get arrested just for driving an illegal alien?" Dad said. "You should have gotten me. Colby could be in real trouble."

"They would have stopped you driving out in a second. I had no choice. Colby had to do it or else Camillo would have been caught."

Before Dad could answer, Rob whooped, signaling that Tara was finished and had ridden well. He immediately spun around at warp speed. "Susie, get Juan up here with Francie. Francie? Where's Francie?"

"Right here," I answered.

Tara and I stood next to Rob and waited to find out who would be testing. When the judges took a few minutes to make up their minds, Rob muttered, "What's taking them so long?"

Another minute passed before the announcement. "We would like these four riders to return to the center of the ring for additional testing. . . ."

Me, Liz Matthews, Karen, and Tara. I'd slipped to fourth, but I was still in there.

"You're going to have to go first, Francie," Rob said. "Nail it."

As the four of us headed into the ring, nodding at last-minute instructions, Rob called, "This is your win, Tara."

We lined up in the middle of the arena. The announcer explained the test two times. I tried to put Colby and the possibility that he might be in trouble out of my mind. I pieced together the jumps by looking at the course. It was canter fence four, halt, canter fence seven, which would come up quickly if you didn't halt right away, turn back on fence twelve, trot fence two, and then canter directly to fence three. The distance between fences two and three was four strides. Now we were trotting into the line, so I had to decide, would I do the four strides, which would mean I'd have to move off from the trot jump quickly? Or should I ride the trot jump patiently and wait it out in the line for five strides? This was the type of question Rob usually answered.

I looked at Tara for a hint, but she wouldn't meet my gaze. I checked Rob at the in gate. He could have been signaling, holding up fingers, four or five. But he was too far away to see clearly. So I thought about what he always said: Be solid. The trick of the test was to be solid and let the other person make the mistake.

The announcer called, "Number five-oh-five, when you're ready."

I left the line and picked up my canter. I jumped the first fence fine and halted maybe a few strides later than I'd have liked. I only had about seven strides to the next fence, which would have been a problem if Tobey weren't so good at halt-canter transitions. We departed into the canter and found a good distance to the next jump. We turned back on the next and I brought Tobey down to the trot in the turn before hopping the jump and patiently settling back for the five strides. Not bold, but solid. I landed to Rob's whoops from the in gate.

Tara and I didn't talk or even look at each other as Liz Matthews and Karen Bay rode the test. Tara just kept her eyes straight ahead of her. Liz was good enough, nothing spectacular. Karen Bay's horse fidgeted and tossed its head at the halt. Then it was Tara's turn. All she had to do was be decent and she would win. She walked forward from the line and moved into a canter. She met the first fence perfectly. At the halt some people got nervous and moved off too quickly. But not Tara. She soaked it in, relished that every pair of eyes in the stadium was on her. She departed into a canter again and jumped the second fence, turned back on the third. She dropped Riley back for the trot jump effortlessly, and then there was only one jump, five strides, and she would have the win. I felt my old hatred and resentment rising up in my throat.

But Tara didn't melt back. She legged Riley forward. I couldn't believe it, but it looked like she was going to do the four strides instead of the five. Even though I wanted Tara to mess up more than anything, a fleeting feeling of regret shot through me.

Maybe the four strides would work out. If anybody could make it look good, it was Tara. But it was a long four trotting in, and Tara didn't get up the line in time. Riley tried to leave the ground but thought better of it, hesitated, stabbed one foot back down, and then jumped. Rails clattered to the ground. The crowd groaned.

Tara returned to the line. She was staring straight ahead, her lips pressed together and trembling. Even with the less-than-perfect halt, Karen would win. As much as I liked to see Tara lose, I still couldn't help but feel a little bit sorry for her.

The announcer called out the results. Karen led the victory gallop with Liz second, me third, and Tara slipping to fourth. I should have been thrilled to be third and to have beaten Tara. It was a great ribbon and I had ridden really well. But just knowing how upset Rob would be overtook some of my excitement.

Dawn came into the ring to accept the gleaming brass trainer's trophy, all smiles. I was sure Rob was dying. We filed out of the ring, Tara first, looking like she couldn't wait to get out. I was right behind her as she passed Rob.

"You just put a dagger in my heart," he spat.

If there was any hope of Rob being happy about my ribbon, it disappeared right then. As I walked by him, I kept my eyes focused on Tobey's neck. It didn't matter anyway; Rob had already turned away.

Chapter Sixteen

Even though I was completely exhausted, I couldn't sleep on the drive home. I kept thinking of Colby and how he'd helped with Camillo without even worrying about himself. I had wanted to thank him, but he'd left with his father by the time I got back to the barn from the award presentation. Camillo had said everything went fine—no checkpoint, no one stopping them.

"What's going to happen with Camillo?" I asked Dad as we chugged down the New Jersey Turnpike.

"I don't know."

"Are you going to tell Rob?"

"Probably."

"About Colby driving him?"

Dad shook his head. "If I tell him that, I might lose my job."

"I'm sorry." The last thing I'd wanted was to risk Dad's job.

"Can he get his green card if you sponsor him?"

"It costs a lot of money."

"You can use my college money," I offered.

"Nice try," Dad said.

I stared at the cars that sped by us in the left lanes. Even though it was almost eleven, the highway was still pretty busy. A blue Datsun that looked like it shouldn't be going over sixty rattled by with a man tapping out a tune on the steering wheel. Next was a station wagon with one of those BABY-ON-BOARD stickers. It made me think of my mother in the same way that seeing women at the supermarket pushing a shopping cart with a baby in it always did.

"Why did you name me Francie?" I asked Dad. "Why not something more Mexican?"

"Your mother liked the name Francesca," Dad said. "She thought it sounded like a really smart girl's name."

"But it didn't begin with *E*."

Dad wrinkled up his forehead and glanced at me.

"Elaine, Eliot, Ethan, Emily . . ."

"How do you know about all that?" he asked.

"I saw a Christmas card she sent Rob a few years back."

It was a moment before Dad said, "You know you can call her sometime if you want. I've been meaning to talk to you about it—to see if you wanted to."

"Do you talk to her?"

"No, but I have her number. And her address—you could write her if you felt that would be easier."

"Why would I do either?" I said, although the idea of seeing her, talking to her, even writing her a letter telling her all about who I was and what she had missed out on had occurred to me more and more since I had Googled her. But I didn't want Dad to think I wanted to. I wanted him to know that I didn't need anybody but him. Plus, what if she didn't care about me?

As if he could read my thoughts, Dad said, "You might find you want to someday, and if that time comes, you should know you shouldn't feel bad about it."

"Okay," I said. I thought about bringing up going to Mexico again, but I didn't want to fight and I didn't want to talk more about Colby.

I eventually fell asleep and woke a few hours later to the familiar turns of the roads leading from the highway to West Hills. I yawned and checked the clock: 1:23. The horses on the trailer looked as tired as I felt. I snapped a lead rope on Tobey and led him down the ramp first. He dragged me to his stall, grateful to be home. Dad, Camillo, and Pablo brought in Riley, Ginger, and Finch. Since Katie wasn't going to the Garden, the horse she'd ridden had shipped back to Ohio.

As Camillo and Pablo went to clean out the trailer, Dad and I headed to the feed room. He mixed up the bran mashes while I filled a wheelbarrow with a bale of hay and wheeled it down the aisle. Most of the horses greeted me with a nicker or a toss of the head, but I noticed Stretch didn't have his head over his stall door, which was weird because he was always the most impatient of all the horses. I had thought he might be extra grumpy, since he had to stay home from the Medal Finals. With talented horses like him, you got the feeling they liked to compete.

"Stretch," I called as I moved to his door with the flake in my hand. "We're home. Don't tell me you're not hungry?"

I saw a scrap of paper lying in the aisle outside Stretch's stall. Out of instinct I picked it up and stashed it in my pocket. When I looked over the stall door, I saw Stretch—not lying down resting, but flat out.

I yanked the door open and rushed in. "Stretch?" I stopped when I saw his eyes. They were shockingly open, rolled back so only the whites, no pupils, showed. My breath caught in my throat. "Dad!" I screamed.

Dad got to the stall with Camillo right behind him. I hadn't moved. I was still just standing there. Growing up on the farm, I'd seen almost everything. Swollen legs, bad colics, severe gashes. When one of the horses had gotten loose and tangled up in barbed wire, I was the one who held him while the vet stitched him up. But I'd never seen a dead horse. There was something so wrong about such a big, powerful animal lying there lifeless. It was like seeing a car with no wheels—it just didn't seem right.

"Santa María," Dad whispered as he kneeled by Stretch's head and felt under his throat for a pulse.

When he saw Stretch, Camillo wailed, "No!" and pushed by me to fall at Stretch's side.

I stepped out of the stall, my throat dry and my heart pounding. Leaving Camillo beside Stretch, Dad came out and put his arms around me.

"Is he . . . ," I asked, even though it was obvious he was. I felt dizzy, like the air was too thick to breathe.

"He must have colicked," Dad said.

"Oh my God." It was all I could say. I felt like I had the few times I'd fallen off. One minute you're cantering along and the next you're on the ground and you don't know what hit you. I wasn't even crying—I was too shocked to cry. It really didn't seem real. ___ ___yself? Stretch, who had ...ned for years and never ...ie? Finch, I could see. But Stretch?

"Are you okay?" Dad asked.

"I don't know," I managed.

"You never get used to it," he said.

203

"You've seen others?"

Dad nodded. "You work around horses long enough, you see them die. It's a part of life for them too." He guided me away from the stall. "Don't look again. Remember him the way he was—he was a great horse."

The worst part was that we left him there. There was nothing we could do in the middle of the night. It would take the tractor to pull him out, and the stall wall would probably have to come down to do it. Dad called Rob, and a few minutes later he came tearing into the barn, shirt untucked and hair mussed. "Jesus Christ," he muttered when he saw Stretch.

He came back out of the stall and leaned against the door. He looked up at the ceiling and said, "What a day."

The next morning Dad was up at the first sign of daylight. He and Camillo took the tractor out back while I fed the horses and cleaned extra stalls. It was awful walking by Stretch's stall knowing he was still in there, and I willed myself not to look. Seeing him that one time was enough. Like Dad had said, I should remember him the way he really was: cocky and talented—shaking his head when Katie tried to pat him and tell him he was good. *Katie.* After everything Stretch had done for her, she'd be devastated.

As I left to change and catch the school bus, I heard Dad on the tractor digging a hole and I was glad I didn't have to be there. I was in ... drag Stretch out.

I usually took pages ... school. I saw Becca in English. down at a blank notepad. ... ool. I saw Becca in English. Mrs. Hanson had said.

After class Becca asked me, "Are y ... ng. I looked really spaced out or something."

204

I looked at her then and wondered if I should tell her about Stretch. But a horse dying seemed so far removed from school and Doug and all the things she cared about, so I said, "We just got home really late last night from the show."

"Did you do well?" she asked.

"I was third."

"That's good, right?"

"Yeah, it is," I said. I hadn't really had time to even think about how well I'd done. Everything with Camillo and then Stretch had made being third seem like it happened forever ago.

"I better get to my next class," I told her.

I started to walk away, but Becca stopped me. "Wait." She lowered her voice. "Are you going to give Doug the test or not?"

With what had happened with Stretch, I hadn't really thought about it. But I didn't have to anymore. "No," I said. I wouldn't make the same mistake twice.

I expected Becca to get upset, but all she said was, "Oh." I wanted to tell her that I thought she was way too good for Doug, but I knew she would have to figure it out on her own.

"See you later," I said instead.

When I got back to the farm, I found Camillo stripping Stretch's stall clean of bedding.

"How're you doing?" I asked, even though I could tell the answer from his trembling lips and red eyes.

"To me, he come back. I make Estretch come back," Camillo said.

"Does Katie know yet?" I asked.

"She was crying and crying." Camillo swallowed back his own tears.

"You took the best care of him," I told him. "It wasn't your fault. It must have been from being cooped up—not getting ridden or turned out all of a sudden."

"But he eat all the hay. And in the stall there is manure," Camillo pointed out. "And he drink much water. Almost there is no more left in the bucket."

The fact that he'd been eating and manuring meant his system couldn't have been that blocked up. And usually when horses colicked, they didn't drink enough and became dehydrated, which made the blockage even worse and could cause their system to shut down like Stretch's must have. It didn't make sense that his water bucket was almost empty.

"I no understand," Camillo said again. "How is possible?"

I was still asking myself the same thing. It didn't seem real. I couldn't believe Stretch was dead. I shook my head and went to walk away, but then Camillo said, "I want thank you and you *papá* for what you do. You so very good to me since I come here and I no want to tell I no legal."

"It's okay," I said.

"Is not okay. He give me job and I lie to him."

"He understands," I assured him.

After I left Camillo, I headed straight to Katie's room. A giant rolling bag sat splayed open on her bed and she was stuffing clothes into it.

"Hey," I said.

She turned to me, her eyes swollen and her face splotchy.

"I'm so sorry about Stretch."

"Thanks," she managed. She sat down on the bed next to the rolling bag. "I keep thinking it must be some mistake. If it should have been anybody, it should have been Finch. Stretch never colicked—not once that I can remember."

"I know." I couldn't remember a time he'd colicked either. Not even a small tummy ache.

Katie took a deep breath. "And I know some people are going to say it doesn't matter or even that maybe it's better for him this way since he probably wasn't ever going to be what he once was, but I don't care—even if he could have just gotten sound enough to turn out for the rest of his life. He deserved that at least."

I nodded, but I didn't know what else to say. She'd ridden Stretch for four years. He'd saved her butt countless times, and unlike Rob or her father, he'd never once told her she couldn't ride. Since I couldn't think of anything to say that could possibly make her feel better, I asked, "When are you heading home?"

"As soon as I'm packed."

I leaned up against the door frame. Katie was leaving and probably never coming back to West Hills. "I can't believe that this is how it is—I mean your last day here. I can't even believe it's your last day and then . . ." I trailed off.

"I'll call you when I get home," she said.

"And you're coming to the Garden to watch, right?" I wasn't sure I should even have been talking about the Garden, but I couldn't imagine a show without Katie there, let alone the biggest show of the year. In the past when Katie hadn't made it to the Garden, she'd always come to watch.

"I don't know," she said, glancing away.

I couldn't believe Katie wouldn't come to cheer me on. "You have to. I can't do it without you there."

"We'll see."

The fact that Katie might not come hurt me, but I tried to remind myself how much more she was hurting right now.

She stood up, and when I went to hug her good-bye, she started sobbing. Her tears triggered my own. "I just can't believe he's dead," she said.

Katie pulled away. She grabbed a tissue and turned back to stuffing clothes in her bag. I wiped my eyes with the back of my hand.

"Don't forget to call me," I told her.

I walked out into what was a perfect New England fall day: cool but sunny. A day that seemed too perfect for what had just happened. Colby was sitting on the steps of the gardener's house. He stood up when I came out. "How is she?" he asked.

"Okay, I guess."

"How about you?"

"I don't know," I admitted. "I'm pretty freaked out. I was the one who found him. . . ." Tears pressed at my eyes again. "It was awful."

I let Colby put his arm around me. "Hey, it's all right," he whispered.

I sniffled and wiped my tears away with my sleeve. "Thanks for being so cool about everything with Camillo. . . . I never got to thank you. I could have gotten you in a lot of trouble."

"Nah," Colby said.

"Yes."

He shrugged. "It was fun. I felt like James Bond or something."

I sat down next to him and put my head in my hands. "I wanted everything to be perfect this year, and instead everything's gone wrong."

"Including meeting me," Colby said.

"No, not that. That's the one good thing."

"I thought I was a distraction."

I sighed and lifted my head. "It's just that you don't know how hard I've worked for this or how much I want it. To you the finals is just something. To me it's everything."

"I never said I didn't want you to win or to concentrate on winning. I never wanted to distract you from that."

"What did you mean when you said maybe this was just what I needed now?" I asked.

"I just thought maybe you needed someone to believe in you."

"And that someone should be you?"

"Unless you know someone else who wants the job."

"No," I said, thinking of Rob and how he was never there for me. "It's all yours."

Chapter Seventeen

I wasn't sure if we were riding the next day until I saw Tara in her boots and breeches. Tobey was waiting for me at his stall. He flipped his head and I hugged him a little tighter than usual. Whenever I closed my eyes, I still saw Stretch.

There was no new course set up in the indoor, and it was just Tara, Colby, and me in the lesson. I kept waiting for Katie to walk into the indoor on Stretch and for Rob to bark at her because she was late. Instead Rob was all over Tara from the minute we started. Maybe it was because of the Medal Finals, but it seemed like more than that. She came in the slightest bit deep to an oxer and Rob screamed, "Goddamn it, Tara! You can't make those mistakes! Don't you understand that? You have to be perfect. Perfect!"

When Rob's cell rang midway through the lesson, I wasn't the only one who was relieved. Colby dropped his feet out of his stirrups. Tara loosened her reins and shot us a look. "I'm so sick of him," she huffed.

"He's just upset over Stretch," I said, stating what I thought was the obvious.

Tara scoffed. "He's upset over the money he'll be losing—not over Stretch. But there was no way he was coming back. The vet said he was done."

"Camillo thought he might have come back," I said.

"What does he know?" Tara snapped. "He's just a groom."

I wasn't sure if Tara knew what she was saying, but it still cut me deep inside. I didn't want to believe Dad was right—that we *were* different from the clients. That some things hadn't changed and never would. But every time I thought how he was wrong, the memory of the woman from the tack store rushed back to me. I turned Tobey away and walked to the other side of the ring.

"Nice one," Colby told Tara.

He caught up with me and said, "Just ignore her."

"It's okay," I said, anger burning inside me. "It's true. What do grooms know? They're just Mexicans."

"Why are you saying that?" he asked. "You know you don't believe it."

I was so upset I wouldn't listen, and I turned Tobey away from him. For the first time ever I wished Rob would finish his phone call so we could start our lesson again. It was clear from his voice that he was pissed at whoever he was talking to. "I understand there's a procedure to follow. But my horse is dead and I paid all this money so that if something like this happened, I'd be covered." He paused and then said, "I see, I see. Then how long until the claim is processed?"

When he finally did hang up, he barked, "Let's go!" like he had been waiting for *us*. We finished the lesson with Rob being an equal-opportunity yeller and tearing into each of us at least once. Afterward I holed up in the tack room cleaning the bridles and saddles. For once it was nice to work on raising the dirt and not have to think about anything else for a little while.

Tara interrupted my momentary peace when she came in and started pulling things out of her trunk and stuffing them into a bag. I wasn't going to say a word to her after what she'd said to me in the ring and how she'd tattled on me to Dad about Colby, but when she'd emptied practically the entire contents of her trunk, she spat, "For your information, I'm leaving."

"What do you mean?" I asked.

Tara straightened and snapped, "I'm out of here. Riley's a dog and Rob knows it. I'm going to ride with Dawn. You know Erica Wong's horse? Erica didn't make the Garden. Dawn said the ride's mine if I want it."

Riley wasn't a dog. He wasn't the one who'd downed a whole box of laxatives. He wasn't the one who'd gone for the four instead of the five at the Medal Finals. But Tara didn't want to look in the mirror.

"When did you decide?"

"Made it official just now."

Before I could say anything else, maybe tell Tara what I really thought of her, her mother opened the door and said, "You ready?"

"Yup," Tara said. Then to me: "See ya at the Garden."

At home I finally got around to washing our clothes from the horse show. I always made sure to empty our pockets because working around horses, you never knew what you'd find in them—pieces of carrot or peppermint candies, a handful of sweet feed, a spur or a part of a bridle. From the breeches that I'd worn the day of the Medal Finals, I pulled out a scrap of paper. At first I didn't remember where I'd picked this one up. But then it hit me: I'd found it in the aisle right before I'd seen Stretch. With everything that had happened, I'd forgotten about it. The paper was about the size of a ticket stub and had a jagged edge where it'd been torn from a pad. I turned it over to read: *It's all there.* I read through it again and again. My mind started to race and people's words floated back to me. *There was no way he was coming back. The vet said he was done. I know some people are going to say it doesn't matter or even that maybe it's better for him this way since he probably wasn't ever going to be what he once was. I paid all this money so . . . I'd be covered.*

"Dad?" I called, walking out into the living room.

"What's up?" he said, seeing my concerned face.

I held out the piece of paper. "I found this in the barn the day we came back from the Medal Finals—the day Stretch died."

Dad took the note and read it. He didn't look up right away but kept staring at the paper in his hand.

"I stuck it in my pocket and didn't read it until just now. I overheard Rob on the phone today talking to the insurance company, and then I read this and I just started thinking. . . ." I paused, still trying to make sense of the thoughts that were just taking shape in my head. "How could Stretch have colicked if there was manure in his stall?"

As I asked the question, I remembered how just after Stretch had been injured, I'd heard Rob on the phone with someone asking about a procedure, how it worked.

Dad finally looked up, his gaze troubled.

"Dad?"

He still didn't speak.

"Dad?" I tried again.

He stood up and walked toward the kitchen. Thinking he was just walking away, I said, "Where are you going?"

He stopped at the wall and leaned his forehead against it. He brought a clenched fist up against the wall like what he really wanted to do was smash it straight through the plaster and the sheetrock to the other side. Then he dropped his hand to his side, fist still clenched, and turned back to face me. "When your mother left us, I was going to have to go back to Mexico. But Rob agreed to sponsor me. He helped me get my green card."

I wasn't sure why Dad was telling me all this now. It seemed like it had absolutely nothing to do with Rob and Stretch. "But I thought you got your green card when you married her," I said, meaning my mother.

"We were never married."

I couldn't believe Dad had lied to me for all these years. "Why did you tell me you were married?"

"I thought it would be easier for you."

I knew I'd need to process all this later, but right then I just needed to know about Stretch. "But what does any of this have to do with Rob?" I asked.

Dad cleared his throat. He looked up at the ceiling, and I could tell he was thinking hard about what he was going to say next. "It's complicated."

"What does that mean? Did Stretch . . . did Rob?" I still couldn't say the words because then maybe they'd be true.

"Yes," Dad said.

"Yes, what?"

"Yes, it appears he had him killed."

It was like the floor and ceiling were moving toward each other, closing in on me. Rob. I could see him at the in gate that first time I'd gone to the Garden to watch. I thought of how I always stared at his chin when he yelled at me. I'd taken everything from him because he was Rob—the best. Only now the image I'd had of him was crumbling.

"Did he tell you he was doing it?" I couldn't possibly

imagine Dad had known and let it happen. Dad was the one who slept in the barn when horses were sick so he could get up every hour to check on them.

He shook his head. "Of course not. I didn't know anything for sure . . . not until right now."

"But how *can* you be sure? Maybe I'm wrong, maybe I—" I wanted to find some way for it all to come back together again. For there to have been a big misunderstanding that we could clear up. Because otherwise my whole world was collapsing.

"Stretch's left ear," Dad said. "I noticed it when we were hauling him out. I've heard that's how they do it—clip an electrical cord to the ear and then plug it into an outlet. Electrocution looks just like colic."

I felt like I was about to be sick. I brought my hand to cover my mouth.

Dad said, "It's actually fast, Francie. It was over quickly for him. I've heard of people who do it in a lot worse ways."

"And that's supposed to make it better?" I snapped. It felt like all the blood inside my body was rushing to my head. I pictured Stretch munching hay in his stall and someone walking in, clipping a cord to his ear. He was such a trusting horse, he probably wouldn't have even raised his head. Then I saw him falling to the ground, his knees buckling, his body convulsing.

"How could Rob have done this?"

"He's been hit hard lately—he took out a second mortgage to put up the indoor, he's putting his mother in a nursing home. He had to return the deposit on Stretch for next year. Financially he's hurting."

That was why the construction on the indoor had stopped. But it didn't matter—money was no reason to do such a horrible thing.

"Are you going to tell the police? Can he go to jail for this?"

Dad shook his head sadly. "I would be nowhere without Rob. I wouldn't have my green card. You'd probably be in foster care somewhere. We wouldn't have our house, our truck, our life. It may not seem like much to you now, but where I come from, it's everything."

"What are you saying?"

"I'm saying we can't turn him in. I owe Rob everything."

I heard Dad's words, but their meaning was twisted, like a word scramble that I couldn't rebuild. How could we just let Rob get away with it? He'd murdered Stretch, not to mention defrauded the insurance company. "So we're not going to do anything?" I asked.

"What's done is done. The horse is dead. There's no bringing him back."

"I'm just supposed to pretend nothing happened?"

"We'll always remember Stretch, but Rob did what he felt he had to do. There are big financial stakes in this sport—you know that."

"That's not a good enough reason to kill a horse," I said. Tears had started to run down my face.

"Come here," Dad said, moving toward me.

"No!" I yelled, and turned away. I ran to my room and slammed the door, not sure who I hated more right then—Rob for killing Stretch or Dad for letting him get away with it.

I didn't come out for the next three days. I didn't go to school or the barn. Dad didn't argue with me at first. He told everyone I had the flu. Becca called to see if I needed any of my assignments, but I told Dad to tell her I couldn't come to the phone. Mostly I just stared at the ceiling. For my whole life I probably hadn't gone fifteen minutes without thinking of riding, the finals, Rob, or the Olympics. Now all I could think was that I never wanted to ride again. I barely ate anything and didn't sleep much either. I couldn't stand the idea of seeing Rob, not after what I knew.

On the third day of my self-imposed isolation, Dad came home from the barn and knocked on my door. "Come in," I mumbled.

He sat down on the farthest corner of my bed and I drew my knees up to my chest. He smelled musty, like horses and the barn—a smell I hadn't realized I'd missed until right then.

"Rob keeps asking about you."

"I don't care."

"Francie—" Dad tried.

I turned from him, tears slipping down my face. I had broken rule number three so many times in the last few days. "He killed Stretch," I said. "He was going to be okay and he just killed him for the money. And you don't even care."

"Don't you think it's eating me up too?" Dad asked. "I loved that horse. I love all the horses. Next to you they're my babies—you know that. But we can't do anything. Sometimes this is what it means to work for someone else."

"Why can't we leave? You can get another job somewhere else."

"And give up our house? Our life here? How many other trainers are going to hire a Mexican as their barn manager? Rob's a good boss. He treats us well."

"How can you say that? He's a murderer. A cold-blooded killer who cares more about making money than the horses that give their heart and soul for him." I had always agreed with Dad about practically everything when it came to the horses, but I couldn't understand how he could let Rob get away with killing Stretch.

"Maybe he made a mistake," Dad tried. "Maybe he regrets it." When I looked away, Dad added, "So what, are you ever going to come out again or are you going to stay in your room for the next fifty years of your life? What about the Garden?"

"What about it?" I said. The Garden had been everything to me, but now it seemed irrelevant.

Dad looked me in the eye. "Don't punish yourself for something someone else did."

Later that night I was looking through my collection of odd things wondering how many secrets were out there still waiting to be discovered, how many people got away with things they shouldn't have, when I heard a knock on the front door. I prayed it wasn't Rob. I was relieved when I heard Colby's voice. "Hello, Mr. Martinez. I was wondering if I could see Francie for a few minutes?"

I expected Dad to turn Colby away, but he came into my room and said, "Colby's here to see you."

I got up and went into the kitchen, where Colby stood in his scrubs and UCLA sweatshirt. "Hi there," he said gently.

"I'll leave you two alone," Dad said, retreating into the TV room. I led Colby outside, to get some fresh air and because I didn't want Dad to hear us. My hair had come loose from its ponytail and I smoothed it back behind my ears. I hadn't brushed it in days. I knew I looked terrible, but I didn't care. All the things I'd cared about didn't matter anymore.

"How're you feeling? You don't look as sick as I thought

you would," Colby said. "I thought you'd have to be deathly ill for it to keep you from riding, with the Garden only a week away."

"I'm not going to the Garden," I said.

"What are you talking about?"

I started crying again. I wiped the tears away with the back of my hand but more raced to replace them. "What's wrong?" he asked. "You're not sick, are you?"

I shook my head but couldn't manage words. I needed to tell someone, to talk to someone other than Dad. Colby had become the one person I could talk to, and he'd been so great about Camillo. I wasn't sure, but I thought I could trust him.

"It's about Stretch," I choked out.

I led him farther away from the house and told him everything. When I got to the part about how Rob did it, Colby shook his head. Then I explained about the green card and how Dad said we couldn't turn Rob in. "I can't believe I'm even telling you," I said. "If my dad knew."

"I won't tell anyone if you don't want me to."

"I don't know what I want," I said. "I can't believe we're just going to let him get away with it."

"Sounds like you don't have much choice."

I looked down at my hands. I hadn't held the reins in days and missed the feel of leather between my fingers. I missed Tobey, and I missed the feeling of working together with such a powerful animal.

"You can't let this stop you from going to the Garden," Colby said.

"You were the one who always acted like the finals didn't matter," I argued.

"But they matter to you," Colby said. "You can't let Rob take that away from you."

"That's what my dad said."

Colby smiled, but it was still a sad smile. "I knew I liked your father."

Chapter Eighteen

Dad insisted on turning off the radio. Driving the trailer into the heart of New York City was no joke. It was the one time of year trailers, small two-horse ones and bigger rigs carrying six or more horses, snaked into the city and lined up on Seventh Avenue. Because the Garden was a sports complex in the middle of New York City, there wasn't much room for stabling, like at the other horse shows. In fact, there was only space for about one hundred and fifty horses crammed into the underbelly of the stadium. Other divisions competed all week, so they didn't allow the equitation horses in until eight o'clock the night before the Maclay.

We parked outside and unloaded the equipment first. We only brought in the essentials because we'd be there less than twenty-four hours. Once we'd set up the stalls, we unloaded Tobey and Ginger. Tobey backed off the trailer quickly onto the street and pranced out with his head high, snorting. His shoes clattered on the pavement and he jumped when a nearby cab honked. I led him on the sidewalk and down the big ramp that was usually used for TV equipment and food supplies.

Inside the narrow passageway that led to the stabling area, low ceilings with exposed vents and pipes loomed above us, threatening to bump Tobey if he raised his head too high. I turned him loose in his stall and tossed him a flake of hay. He checked to make sure he was safe and then took a bite.

We got the horses settled and organized our stuff. Then Colby and I went to the horse show office to pick up the order of go. Colby's father had flown into Boston, rented a car, and driven him to the show. He was now over at the hotel checking in. Only one hundred riders showed in the Maclay, but looking at the order of go, you knew it was the best of the best. There was never a gap where you had five not-so-good riders or someone you'd never heard of. I'd heard of all the riders, and each one was excellent. I scanned the list for my name and located it right next to Tara's. If I hadn't known a computer spat out the list, I would have thought that someone had planned it as a bad joke. Tara went thirty-seventh. I went thirty-eighth.

"Look," I said, pointing it out to Colby.

"That doesn't matter anymore," he said.

When we got back to the stalls, Dad had just fed the horses. We locked the trunks and the three of us headed across the street to the hotel.

"What are you doing for dinner?" Colby asked.

"We'll probably just grab a bite somewhere fast since it's so late," I said, looking to Dad for confirmation. It was already nine o'clock and we had to get up at four.

"You can join us if you want," Dad offered.

"My dad's probably got someplace already picked out," Colby said. "But I'll see you tomorrow. Get a good night's sleep."

"You too," I said.

After Dad and I had both showered, he insisted on going to the restaurant in the Garden where all the riders usually ate.

"It's expensive," I said. "Let's just get pizza or something."

Dad threw an arm around me. "No way. This is your last time doing the Maclay Finals."

We sat down at a table for two next to other riders, trainers, and parents. I ordered pasta primavera, and Dad ordered grilled salmon. As the waiter brought our food, I realized just how hungry I was. But while I devoured my pasta, Dad didn't seem hungry.

"I'm sorry if you're still mad at me," he said, glancing up from the salmon he'd hardly touched.

Over the past week I'd come to understand his decision about Rob, even if I didn't really agree with it. Talking to Colby some more about it had helped. And thinking more about what I would have done in Dad's place. It was easy to sit back and say I would have done this or that, but the truth was, I hadn't even been able to tell Doug and Becca no about the test to begin with. Dad had a lot more to lose with Rob than I had had with Doug and Becca. Dad had always tried to keep the hard part of his life from me, but now I saw how life was still hard for him—how at times he had to compromise to get what he wanted for us. "I'm not mad at you anymore—not really," I said.

"You know what kind of person I am, don't you?" he asked. "Because that's important to me."

"Yes," I told him.

Dad reached out and covered my hand with his. "Good."

After dinner we walked back to the hotel. In the lobby I asked Dad if it would be okay if I went to see Colby. "Just for a few minutes," I assured him, since it was almost ten now.

"Oh, a hot date, huh?" Dad teased.

He went upstairs while I asked the woman at the front desk for Colby's room number. She looked annoyed and said she couldn't give it out to a total stranger.

"But I'm a friend of his," I tried.

"Those are the rules," she huffed.

"Fine, then can you call him for me and I'll ask *him* for his room number?" I wondered whether it was really hotel policy or whether it was hotel policy for *me*. I hated how suspicious I was becoming.

The woman picked up the phone, punched a few numbers, and handed it to me. "I want to come up and say hi, but they won't give me your room number," I told Colby when he picked up. "They think you're famous and that I'm a groupie or something."

Colby laughed. "I *am* famous, didn't you know that? Room 303. Come on up."

I triumphantly handed the woman back the phone and took the elevator to the third floor. Colby was waiting with the door open. "How long was the Hundred Years' War?" he asked.

"A hundred years?" I ventured, realizing that after the Garden I would miss what I had come to think of as Colby-isms. Of course, I would miss Colby too.

"One hundred and sixteen. I've got another one for you. What animal are the Canary Islands named after?"

"I give up," I said.

"Dogs."

There were two queen beds in the room, one filled with Colby's clothes. Colby sat down on the other. I plopped down next to him. "You nervous?" he asked.

"Not really," I said. "Isn't that weird?"

"No, it just means you're in the zone."

"Ah, the Zen thing again."

Colby reached out and pulled at my ponytail. "How come you never wear your hair down?"

"Because I just don't. It's a pain."

"You should. I bet it'd look really pretty."

He inched closer and kissed me. After a few minutes he lay back on the bed and pulled me onto his chest. We kept kissing and Colby moved his hand up the back of my shirt. It drifted down on the outside of my jeans.

"What are we doing?" I asked, pulling away.

"Getting busy—or at least that's what I think those crazy kids are calling it these days," he joked.

"No, I mean you're going back to California tomorrow and I'll probably never see you again. I never even asked if you have a girlfriend."

"I do."

I bolted upright. Colby reached out and grabbed my arm. "Aren't you my girlfriend?"

"You jerk," I said, looking away. But I couldn't be mad at him, especially since he'd just said I was his girlfriend.

"Well, aren't you?" he asked.

"I guess for today, yeah."

Colby pulled me back so I was lying next to him again. "Don't think so much about tomorrow. We'll figure it out. Maybe I can come visit you over Christmas, or maybe you can come to L.A."

"Yeah, maybe," I said. I didn't think either was likely, but for once I wasn't going to worry. I rolled back toward Colby, kissed him again, and said, "By the way, I think getting busy implies having sex."

Colby raised his eyebrows, a hopeful look on his face.

"The power of no," I said, smiling. "Two little letters: big impact."

Fall always seemed to turn to winter right at the Garden, and it was dark and cold out as Dad and I scampered across the street to the stadium at four the next morning. My West Hills jacket wasn't warm enough, and Dad noticed me shivering.

"How about putting on my jacket?" he offered. "It's much warmer than that one."

I shrugged out of my jacket and traded it with Dad. As I handed it to Dad, I knew I never wanted to wear it again. I still couldn't look at Rob without thinking of Stretch. The first time I'd seen him when I went back to the barn had been the hardest. It had been nearly impossible not to tell him I knew, not to tell him what I thought of him now. I had kept my mouth shut, but I had a feeling he must have known something had changed with me.

At six, the course was posted. I saw Rob, Susie, and Colby standing at the in gate. I couldn't believe it. No Tara, yet there was Rob in his coat and tie. After everything that had happened, he had to pick *now* to start believing in me.

The course was difficult. The hardest part was a bending line curving around at the end of the arena, a vertical, then three strides to an oxer, and then either a forward six strides, or a steady seven strides to another vertical. The three was tight, so if you planned on doing the six strides, you had to make sure to get it done early or else you would leave too long or, even worse, end up chipping in seven strides. There was also a narrow, orange box wall with no jump standards that a lot of horses would probably spook at. Colby and I watched the first ten riders. A few of the riders made miscalculations in the bending line, and a bunch of the horses spooked at the wall, sticking off the ground or even stopping. I kept checking the stands and expecting to see Katie, but she wasn't there. I'd told her on the phone how much I wanted her to be there, but she still wasn't sure she could handle coming after what had happened with Stretch. I couldn't really be mad at her for that, so I gave up trying to find her in the stands. Soon enough it came time for me to get on, but Colby caught me and said, "Wait, I haven't given you my pep talk yet."

"You have one ready?"

"Been working all night on it."

"Okay," I said, waiting.

"Here goes," he said. "Kick butt!"

Colby was right. It didn't matter anymore that Tara went right before me. In the schooling ring, Rob's eyes were on me and only me. The crazy thing was I didn't even care. I didn't look at Tara either. The only time I glanced over was to make sure we weren't about to crash into each other. It was a legitimate concern because the schooling ring was tiny, about the size of a backyard pool. There was only room for two jumps, and a pillar stood right in the middle of the ring. It was hard to even get a true canter, and once you did, it was only a few strides to the jump and then a few more strides to the wall on the other side.

Tara was already in the ring when I approached the in gate. Dad wiped my boots and then he painted Tobey's hooves with oil so they gleamed.

From the in gate I could make out some of Tara's round. What I saw looked outstanding. Her horse was huge, and she made the flowing six strides in the second part of the broken line look easy. The horse didn't spook at the orange wall, which had killed a lot of top riders' hopes, including Karen Bay's. As Tara finished up, I began to think maybe she looked even better on Erica Wong's horse than she did on Riley. She finished to loud applause and cheering, but it seemed quieter without Rob's whoops.

"Go get 'em," Rob called to me as I entered. "Nail it."

I pressed Tobey forward into the ring, barely hearing Rob's words. Tara passed me on her way out. "Good luck," she said, not meaning it in the slightest.

I could see the whole ring now. With the lights on full blast it glowed. A decent crowd filled the stands, and I had to remind myself to breathe. I looked over at the orange box wall. I had no idea how Tobey would react to it. Even horses that were usually bold had been spooking at it.

I walked for a second longer than usual and listened to the announcer call out my name. *And now on course, Francie Martinez.* The crowd quieted. I gulped a breath and waited for nerves to hit me, but they didn't come. For the first time ever I wasn't riding for Rob. I wasn't looking to please him, and I wasn't worried I'd disappoint him. I was riding for me. It took realizing Rob wasn't who I thought he was for me to truly believe in myself.

I picked up the canter and headed to the first jump. At the USET, I floated. At the Medal, I glided. Now I was cantering and I knew I could do it. I rode the first four fences well and it was like everything was in slow motion, just how I always wished it would be. I wasn't rushing to finish up or worrying whether I was good enough—I knew I was. I felt exactly the way I did in my riding dream—all confidence.

I approached the line with the three jumps. I rode the first part and then melted back in seven strides the way Rob and I had planned. It might not have been as bold as Tara's ride, but it was the safer option. Then around the corner over a vertical, roll back turn to a triple bar. We stayed patient, taking a conservative distance to the vertical and then loosening up and flowing to the triple bar. Next came the orange box wall. I pressed my legs against Tobey's sides harder than usual and stayed behind him even more with my upper body. Whatever distance I saw, I couldn't risk leaning. I had to be there for him in case he wavered. Thankfully, I saw a good distance, not too long and not too tight. He peeked slightly, looking down, but I was there to encourage him. And then it was just one more fence, a long approach to an oxer. It was the one part on the course where Rob told me to carry a little more pace. The rest of the course was controlled, but the last jump was my place to show the judges I was comfortable riding forward. I let Tobey's stride out and headed toward the oxer. The perfect distance was right there when I turned the corner. Maybe the distance to all the jumps had always been there before, but I was just worrying too hard that I wouldn't see it. I rode the last jump, and Rob and Susie whooped practically before I landed.

Rob was still clapping as I left the ring. "Perfect," he said. "That's my girl."

They were the words I'd waited years to hear from him, but now they didn't mean a thing.

After the flat phase I was in fifth, with Steve Farmington in fourth, Kristy Blythe in third, Liz Matthews in second, and Tara on top. The second round looked straightforward. No tricks, but places to make yourself noticed: a halt and a hand gallop. After the second round, the judges would probably test four of us. I needed to move up a spot to guarantee I'd make the test.

Rob went over the course with me, but I hardly listened. I didn't need him. I knew what I had to do. I had to go against everything he had always taught me. I couldn't just go for the safe ride. If I wanted a shot at the test, I had to go for brilliant.

I cantered into the ring, and I felt hungry to be at the first jump. I met it well and continued on to the second and the third. I eased Tobey back to the halt and he stood stone still. I waited there with my head held high and savored the moment. I had that poise, that presence that I thought only a rider like Tara could have. Then, at the hand gallop, I went for it. I really and truly galloped. If I made a mistake trying to go for it, so be it. But I wouldn't lose my chance at winning because I wasn't willing to risk it all.

I legged Tobey to a strong gallop. Fast and powerful, yet in control of his stride. I galloped the jump and landed to Rob's whoops. After I came out of the ring, I practically collapsed on Tobey's neck, hugging and patting him. I couldn't stop smiling. I had done it. Whether I made the test or not, I had put in the round of my life.

"Nailed it," Colby said, meeting me at the in gate.

Katie was next to him. "That was awesome!"

"I didn't know you were here," I said, still breathless.

"I wasn't. I was sitting at home thinking of you until I finally jumped in a cab. I got here just in time to see you kick some serious butt."

It was true. I was good, very good. But so were Tara, Kristy, and Liz after me. Steve had a rough lead change, so he was out. It was down to the four of us. Maybe the judges had seen enough and didn't need to do any further testing, but maybe they'd bring us back.

I waited with Colby and Katie until finally the announcer's voice came over the ring. "The judges have requested that number 307 and number 238 please return to the ring for further testing."

Tara and me.

My first reaction: *Yes! I'm in it*. My second: *It's Tara and me*.

Chapter Nineteen

"Listen up," Rob said before I returned to the ring. He leaned close and lowered his voice. "They're going to make you switch horses—I just know it. If they do, tighten up the curb chain on Tobey's pelham before Tara gets on."

I almost said, "But Tobey hates the curb chain tight." Then I realized that was the whole point. He was telling me to cheat.

When the announcer called out, "Number 238, please return to the ring," it jarred me back into reality. I noticed I was still staring at Rob.

Speaking loudly again, he said, "You can win this. Nail it."

Still slightly numb, I entered the ring. Tara was already lined up awaiting the announcement of the judges' requests.

I prayed for the test to be anything but switching horses. A hard test with a counter-canter, a trot jump, even a verbal question. But not switching horses. The stadium was dead quiet. Everyone was waiting to see what we would be asked to do. Then the announcer's voice reverberated over the PA:

"The judges have requested that the riders switch horses and ride the test again. Riders, please prepare to ride. Number 307 will ride first."

Without a word, Tara and I dismounted. I started to undo my girth to slide my saddle from Tobey's back. It was the only thing we'd switch. When it came to catch-riding, Tara had so much more experience than me, which was why Rob had told me to tighten Tobey's curb chain. If I did, Tobey would definitely flip his head at the halt, maybe at other places on course. It wouldn't guarantee me the win. I would still have to ride well. I couldn't make any big mistakes. But it would up my chances enormously.

I tried to steady my breathing and glanced over at Tara. She was undoing her girth and was about to slide the saddle off. All I had to do was quickly tighten the curb chain a few links. It would be easy enough to do. We were far enough away from the spectators and judges that they wouldn't be able to see. All I could think about was Rob, standing at the in gate in his coat and tie. I'd thought he finally believed I could win, but he didn't. He didn't believe I could do it on my own. He thought the only way I could beat Tara was by cheating.

I looked at the curb chain. I had only a few seconds left before it would be too late. But I didn't need any more time to know that I wouldn't do it. I wanted to win and I would go for the win, but I would only do it the right way.

Still without speaking, Tara and I switched horses and mounted up. I wondered if other riders in this situation exchanged hints about each other's horses, explaining how much leg or hand they needed. Tara's horse stood much taller than Tobey, probably 16.3 hands to Tobey's 16.1, which meant I'd look very small on him. I hadn't watched him as much as many of the other horses because until today he'd never had a very promising rider, but from the little I'd seen, he looked uncomplicated. We had to mount from the ground. Since I was short and the horse was so tall, I had to lengthen my stirrup to get my foot into it and hoist myself up. Tara didn't. But I wouldn't let it bother me. Not after I'd come this far.

After I adjusted my stirrup back, I looked at Tobey and Tara and wished she didn't look so good on him. I thought of all the work I'd put into him and how Rob had said to me way back when: *Maybe you can figure him out.* I had done just that, and now Tara might be the one to benefit from it. It didn't seem quite fair, but still, I didn't regret disobeying Rob for a second.

"Number 307, Tara Barnes, will ride first," the announcer called.

Silence settled over the ring.

As Tara shortened her reins, she turned to me. "This win's mine," she said, quiet enough for only me to hear.

"Well, good luck," I came back. "Because I'm gonna nail it."

I watched as she urged Tobey into a canter. Her first few fences were perfect. She halted well, held her head high, and then blasted off into the hand gallop. She finished to loud applause and returned to stand next to me.

I stepped forward. All I could think as I began my course was, *I'm gonna win.* I wanted to prove Rob wrong so badly— to show him once and for all how he had underestimated me and how well I could ride. I squeezed the horse's sides with my calves and registered that he moved off slowly. Tobey was sensitive and listened to every aid I gave him without having to tell him more than once. I asked for the canter harder than I would with Tobey, and suddenly I was cantering on a completely different horse. This horse's canter felt like riding in a Cadillac, long and smooth, where Tobey felt like a sport-utility vehicle, condensed and springy. Before I had much time to think about it, I was at the first jump. The horse jumped flat and even, like I'd just cantered over a pole on the ground.

I landed and turned, jumped the next fence. I continued around without error. I halted—took my moment—and then cantered off again. I jumped the next fence, and then came the hand gallop. I pushed the horse forward, found the distance, and returned to line next to Tara. I had done it. I had ridden just as well as Tara.

Usually watching a class, I had a feeling for who would win, but Tara and I were dead even. I knew it could go either way. They might ask us to perform an additional test, one more chance to see who would come out on top, or maybe they had already decided. We waited in tense silence for a few moments before the announcer's voice boomed out over the PA system. "The judges have let us know there will be no further testing. Please stand by for the award presentation."

While the eight riders who had placed below us, including Colby, joined us in the ring on their mounts, Tara and I switched horses again. It felt good to be back on Tobey, like falling into your own bed after a week away from home.

The ring crew rolled out the red carpet and laid the ribbons on a table. As the announcer started the countdown in reverse order, I began to feel that it was all a dream—that I hadn't really just gone head to head with Tara for the win.

I stood next to Tara and watched the other riders receive their ribbons. Colby finished sixth—a great ribbon. Steve was fifth, Kristy fourth, Liz third.

It was down to first and second, me and Tara. I held my

breath. My whole body was trembling. The announcer's voice cut the silence to award second place. "And our ASPCA Maclay Reserve Champion . . . is . . . Miss Francie Martinez."

My stomach dropped and tears pressed at my eyes. I glanced at Tara. She had started crying, but her tears were happy. "I can't believe it," she breathed. "I can't believe it."

That was it. It was over. There were no more finals, no more chances. Tara had won. I had lost. Rob had been right—I couldn't beat Tara on my own.

"I needed this, Francie," Tara said. "You don't know how much I needed this win."

Still shaking, I walked Tobey forward and halted in front of a man in a crisp navy suit who pinned the red ribbon on Tobey's bridle. Tobey turned his head to the side and glanced back at me. And right then, instead of crying, I started to smile. In that moment, as Tobey looked back at me, I realized I didn't *need* to win. Not like Tara thought she did. Not like Rob thought he did. Maybe Tara had won because she was a better rider, or maybe it had just been her day. But I had ridden my heart out and done things the right way. Whether I went to college or turned professional right away, I had learned to believe in myself, and I had also learned that some things were more important than the blue ribbon.

I reached down to hug Tobey. More than anything else, I was so proud of all that we had achieved together. No one had ever thought we'd get this far. As I let go and walked him back to line, the announcer's voice raised a decibel. Goose bumps rose up on my arms.

"And winning the ASPCA Maclay Finals . . . Miss Tara Barnes."

Samantha Potter, last year's champion, was there to present this year's award. She looked so different out of her riding clothes. She wore a dark pantsuit, and her blond hair brushed her shoulders. I hadn't seen her since this time last year, and I remembered she was a freshman at Vassar now.

Tara led the victory gallop with me behind her. For once I didn't mind being second to her. I looked at the beautiful red ribbon fluttering on Tobey's bridle as I cantered and felt I had achieved all that I wanted. As I passed the in gate, I saw Katie and Dad leaning into the ring cheering wildly.

When I came out of the ring, Rob was waiting for me. He looked angrier than I'd ever seen him look before and that was saying a lot. But it didn't affect me like it usually did. For once I wasn't scared of what he would say to me.

"What did I tell you to do?" he growled at me. "How could you let me down like that?"

I looked him straight in the eye. I didn't care about rule number six anymore, *Never talk back*. And I didn't waver when I said, "No, Rob, how could *you* let *me* down like that?" and walked away.

Epilogue

It was finals time again, and I took the train from Skidmore, where I was at college, into New York to go to the Garden and watch the Maclay. I waited at the Krispy Kreme at Penn Station, checking my watch and looking for Katie, who was ten minutes late. She finally showed up, in jeans and a black long-sleeved shirt, looking skinnier than I'd ever seen her before.

"I thought you gave up Weight Watchers," I said as I hugged her hello.

"I did."

"You look amazing."

Katie did a little twirl and grinned. "I guess that's what love'll do." Katie was at NYU now and was still planning to go to the Fashion Institute of Technology after graduation. She had met Phil in her freshman English class, and according to her it was love at first sight. "Sorry I was late," she said. "You look great too—all dressed up."

I had put on a skirt that fell just past my knees and a new sweater I'd bought on a mini–shopping excursion with some of my friends from school. I had a part-time job at the campus bookstore. It wasn't as tiring as working in the barn had been, but it wasn't as fun either. Still, it helped me pay for my books, and sometimes I had a little left over. Katie and I walked through the swarms of people coming and going to different destinations up into the Garden. Dad had left passes for us at the back entrance, and we walked down the passageway to the stalls and stadium. Riders in breeches and boots passed us, some we knew and lots of new faces too, and it felt strange to be dressed in civilian clothes.

Katie said, "This is kind of weird, isn't it?"

"Yeah," I agreed, glad that Katie was there to share it with me.

We went to the stalls first and found Dad. "There's my college girl," he said, hugging me tight. Camillo and Pablo were there too, and they asked me all about school, even though I knew Dad reported to them every week after he talked to me.

"Have you seen Tobey?" I asked him. I had been looking forward to seeing him ever since I got on the train. After I did so well with him, Rob had sold him. He knew he was hard to ride and figured he should get what money he could for him, which was typical Rob. The day before he left the farm for his new barn, I took him for a last hack around the fields, trying to imprint in my brain just how he felt at the walk, trot, and canter. Then I took him for some grass, and finally I spent over an hour with him in his stall, trying to say good-bye. I waited for it to feel right, for something to hit me so I could kiss him and leave. I decided that saying good-bye to Tobey and that part of my life would never feel right. Even if I waited forever, the moment would never come. I just had to do it—kiss him, wrap my arms around him, bury my face in his neck—and walk out without looking back.

"Not yet," Dad said. The class was just about to start, and I asked him if he needed any help. He gave me a look and said, "And what? Get you all dirty? No way. Go watch. Enjoy being a spectator for once."

As Katie and I headed up to the stands, I wasn't sure I *could* enjoy being a spectator. After what had happened with Rob, I decided to go to college. In lots of ways it had been nice to concentrate on school over the last few months and have a regular life. I lived in a suite with three other girls, and we had all become good friends. We stayed up too late watching TV and movies, talked about boys—all the things I'd skipped in high school. But then I started to miss the part of me that was connected to the finals. I hadn't given up my dream of the Olympics; I'd only put it on hold. I'd been riding for the school team, and in the summer I was planning on working for Susie, who'd started her own stable in New York after she left Rob and West Hills a few months after the Garden. I wasn't sure what I was going to do when I graduated—but that was a long way off. I had a feeling I'd be back in the horse world again, but if not, like Dad said, I'd have a solid education to fall back on.

Katie and I sank down into seats near the in gate and watched the first few rounds. "Does this feel surreal or is it just me?" I asked her, thinking about how strange it was not to have to go get on or to focus on how to ride the course.

"Totally surreal."

Gwenn entered the ring on Finch, and I saw Rob for the first time since I'd left for school. I still wished that Rob had been caught. That the insurance company had suspected something fishy and investigated, or that Dad had finally said we should tell, or that Rob had turned himself in out of a guilty conscience. But that wasn't what happened. Nothing happened. Rob got away with killing Stretch. No one but Colby, Dad, and I would ever know. Maybe Susie found out too. Maybe that was why she left Rob. Rob finished building the new indoor, put his mother in a fancy nursing home, hired a new assistant trainer when Susie left, and went on with life. I still thought about Stretch now and then, and Katie and I talked about him sometimes. I guess the only way I made myself feel okay was in knowing that no matter what, I'd always put my horses first and my ambitions second.

Gwenn turned in a decent trip and Rob whooped a few times.

"She's gotten better," Katie said.

"Yeah."

"So, how's Colby? Talked to him lately?"

Thanks to free minutes on Colby's cell phone, we talked a lot, and we e-mailed and instant-messaged the rest of the time. He was at the University of Colorado at Boulder and, to his disbelief as much as mine, he was pretty sure he was going to be pre-med. No specializing in boob jobs, though, he promised. We weren't officially going out—we'd agreed that it didn't make sense, since we lived two thousand miles apart. But so far neither of us had met anyone else.

"He's good," I said. "I'm thinking of trying to stop and see him on the way to Mexico over Christmas break."

"So you're really going?" Katie said.

"Yup, my dad finally broke down and agreed."

"Look." Katie pointed a few rows over. "Tara."

Tara had come today to award this year's winner the blue

ribbon. She had taken a job with a grand prix rider down south. She and her mother had scraped together enough money to buy a young horse that she hoped would be her future Olympic mount. Maybe someday we'd be riding against each other again, but for now I was all right with being a step behind her.

"She looks good," Katie said. She did look good—she had gained a little bit of weight and had cut her hair—but I was surprised Katie would say something nice about her.

"There's something I never told you," Katie said, in a serious tone.

"What?"

"It's so long ago now, but you know how I've really gotten myself together this year and I can talk about things now, like what happened with Mike. . . ."

Katie had traded the sports shrink for a regular shrink and now, among other things, she could actually say Mike's name.

"Tara didn't tell your dad about you and Colby. . . ." Katie hesitated. "I did. I was so mad at you over Colby, but that's no excuse. It was an awful thing to do. I'm sorry."

Even though it was so long ago, I was still shocked. I'd been so sure it was Tara. It had never even occurred to me that it could have been Katie. If I had found out at the time, I would have been angry, but it was all behind us now. I glanced over at Tara. "So it wasn't Tara, huh?"

"No," Katie confirmed. "It was me."

Katie and I talked more about school and classes until Tobey came into the ring. Then we fell silent. At first it was tough watching someone else ride Tobey. I tried to remember what he felt like in the air over a jump, but it was hard to recall. His new rider was small and looked tentative. She turned in a decent round until the fourth-to-last fence, when she pulled too much and chipped in. Tobey seemed unfazed by her mistake, though, and kept going like nothing had happened. He seemed to understand that she was starting from the very beginning and it was his job to help her. Maybe over the next few years she'd get there, get to where she was competitive. And maybe she'd even end up believing in herself like me.

Author's Note

The ASPCA Maclay Finals began in 1933 and for over sixty years were held in conjunction with the National Horse Show at Madison Square Garden in New York City. In 2002 the National Horse Show left the Garden, and in recent years the Maclay has been held at the Show Piers on the Hudson in New York City. In writing *The Perfect Distance*, I called on some of my own memories of watching and riding in the equitation, and so it seemed only fitting to set the Maclay at the venue where I came to know and love the event—the Garden. Today there are more equitation finals for junior riders to compete in. Still, the USET, Medal, and Maclay remain the most difficult and prestigious, and winners of these finals often go on to illustrious careers in the grand prix ranks.

I'd like to thank the people who have been an integral part of my riding career and the writing of this book. First and foremost, I'd like to thank my parents, who had no idea what a few Saturday-morning riding lessons would lead to. They were my greatest fans and spent countless early mornings and late nights driving the trailer, polishing boots, and making bran mashes. Sharing my riding with them has been incredibly special. I'd also like to thank my grandparents for their constant support, from my first pony on up to my own forays in the finals; my husband, Matt, for knowing I was horse-crazy and marrying me anyway; Jenny Belknap, who shares my love of horses and writing and always believed in this book; Bill Holinger, under whose direction I began writing this book; Liz Benney, who has been a great riding mentor and also a great friend; trainer Timmy Kees for his expert read; Nancy Hinkel, my amazing editor, for helping me take the manuscript to an entirely new level; Jeff Dwyer and Elizabeth O'Grady; Lara Zeises; Melissa Nelson; Artie Bennett and his copyediting team; Allison Amend; Shanta Small; and the entire group at Knopf. And, finally, I wouldn't be anywhere without the wonderful horses I've been fortunate enough to ride and love.

ALSO BY
Kim Ablon Whitney

Sixteen-year-old Bridget and her family are Travelers; they spend their lives on the road, moving from place to place in trailers, making a living through con jobs and petty thievery. The trade is risky, to be sure, but it's not the fear of getting caught that keeps Bridget up at night. No, what worries her is the possibility of *never* getting caught, of nothing ever changing, the prospect of an entire life filled only with trailer parks and everyday scams. Her parents and friends may not understand it, but Bridget actually *likes* going to school. She longs for a real education, a regular job.

Bridget's options, though, seem to be shrinking by the day—her parents have already promised her in marriage. With the wedding date set much sooner than expected, Bridget is forced to decide between her family and her heart, between the life she knows and the one she's always dreamed of.

★ "This is a wholly absorbing read that raises provocative questions about culture, as well as character, that teens will want to discuss." —*Booklist*, Starred